Death by Tiara

Center Point
Large Print

Also by Laura Levine and available from
Center Point Large Print:

The Jaine Austen Mysteries
Death of a Neighborhood Witch
Killing Cupid

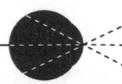

**This Large Print Book carries the
Seal of Approval of N.A.V.H.**

Death by Tiara

A Jaine Austen Mystery

LAURA LEVINE

CENTER POINT LARGE PRINT
THORNDIKE, MAINE

This Center Point Large Print edition
is published in the year 2016 by arrangement with
Kensington Publishing Corp.

The text of this Large Print edition is unabridged.
In other aspects, this book may vary
from the original edition.
Printed in the United States of America
on permanent paper.
Set in 16-point Times New Roman type.

ISBN: 978-1-68324-075-4

Library of Congress Cataloging-in-Publication Data

Names: Levine, Laura, 1943– author.
Title: Death by tiara : a Jaine Austen mystery / Laura Levine.
Description: Center Point Large Print edition. | Thorndike, Maine :
Center Point Large Print, 2016.
Identifiers: LCCN 2016021977 | ISBN 9781683240754
    (hardcover : alk. paper)
Subjects: LCSH: Austen, Jaine (Fictitious character)—Fiction. | Women
authors—Fiction. | Beauty contests—Fiction. | Teenage girls—Fiction. |
Murder—Investigation—Fiction. | Los Angeles (Calif.)—Fiction. | Large
type books. | GSAFD: Mystery fiction.
Classification: LCC PS3612.E924 D434 2016 | DDC 813/.6—dc23
LC record available at https://lccn.loc.gov/2016021977

DEDICATION

In loving memory of
Mark Lacter
1954-2013

ACKNOWLEDGMENTS

As always, a big thank you to my editor extraordinaire, John Scognamiglio, for his unwavering faith in Jaine—and for coming up with the idea of sending Jaine to a beauty pageant. (I tried to get him to write the whole book, but for some crazy reason, he expected me to do it.)

Thanks also to my ever-empathetic agent, Evan Marshall, for his ongoing guidance and support.

Thanks to Hiro Kimura, who so brilliantly brings Prozac to life on my book covers. To Lou Malcangi for another eye-catching dust jacket design. And to the rest of the gang at Kensington who keep Jaine and Prozac coming back for murder and minced mackerel guts each year.

Special thanks to Frank Mula, man of a thousand jokes. And to Mara and Lisa Lideks, authors of the very funny Forrest Sisters mysteries.

Extra hugs to Joanne Fluke, who takes time out from writing her own bestselling Hannah Swensen mysteries to grace me with her insights and friendship—not to mention a cover blurb to die for.

Thanks to John Fluke, product placement guru. To Mark Baker, my Ultimate Frisbee technical advisor. And to Jamie Wallace (aka Sidney's mom), the genial webmeister at LauraLevine Mysteries.com.

A loving thanks to my friends and family. And a special shout out to all my readers and Facebook friends who've taken the time to write me and/or show up at my book signings. You guys are the greatest!

And finally, a note of remembrance about my late husband, Mark Lacter, an award-winning journalist in his own right, who supported me every step of the way on my journey with Jaine and Prozac, who held my hand through good times and bad, and who didn't mind (well, not much, anyway) when I interrupted his football games to ask him if he liked my jokes.

I miss him every day.

Death by Tiara

Prologue

It's ironic, really, when I think of how optimistic I was when this whole mess began—how rosy everything seemed, how rife with possibilities.

I lay in bed that sun-kissed morning, listening to the sweet sounds of the birds chirping, the bees buzzing, and Mrs. Hurlbutt hollering at Mr. Hurlbutt across the street to move his fanny and take out the trash.

I was convinced that I was about to start a whole new chapter in my life. After years of toiling away as a freelance writer, churning out ads for Toiletmasters Plumbers, Fiedler on the Roof Roofers, and Tip Top Dry Cleaners, I was about to become a professional songwriter!

Just a few days earlier I'd answered an ad on Craigslist from someone *Seeking Songwriter to Write Lyrics for an Industry Star.*

This was the gig for me! What fun it would be to write lyrics for a famous singer.

Maybe I'd get to travel the world, staying in fancy hotels and showing up at the Grammys in a limo and slinky dress. Maybe this songwriting gig would lead to a career on Broadway, where I'd show up for the Tonys with an even bigger limo and slinkier dress. (And maybe I'd lose enough weight to actually fit into one of those slinky dresses.)

True, the only lyrics I'd written up to that point in my life had been a little ditty for the Toiletmasters Christmas party. Which went something like this:

When your toilet's on the blink
And you've clogged your kitchen sink
When hairs stuff up your shower drain
And when you bust a water main
When life is filled with plumbing disasters
Just call the guys at Toiletmasters!
We'll snake your pipes and have you
  humming
And when we're through, we'll do some
  plumbing!

Okay, so I'm no Cole Porter. But the guys at the Toiletmasters Christmas party seemed to like it a lot. And so did Heather Van Sant, the gal who placed the ad on Craigslist. Not a half hour after I sent her my lyrics I got an email from her, saying she was eager to meet me and introduce me to her client.

Yes, I was in a great mood as I stretched out in my bed, my cloud of bliss punctured only by my cat, Prozac, who sat on my chest clawing me for her breakfast.

Ever at her command, I hopped out of bed and headed for the kitchen. Soon I was sloshing Minced Mackerel Guts in Prozac's bowl and nuking myself a cinnamon raisin bagel. With a dab of butter. And the teensiest bit of strawberry jam. (Okay, it wasn't so teensy.)

After a quick shower, I dressed with care, donning my best elastic-waist jeans along with a white silk blouse and faux suede jacket. I finished off my ensemble with a brand new pair of knee-high boots, hoping to impress the music industry mogul I'd be meeting with.

I twirled around in front of the sofa, where Prozac was giving herself her morning gynecological exam.

"So, Pro? How do I look?"

She gazed up from her privates and eyed my boots with interest.

Oh, goodie. A new chew toy.

Making a mental note to keep the boots on the very top shelf of my closet, I grabbed my car keys and headed for the door.

This was a red letter day, all right. I could feel it in my bones. I was walking out the door as a freelance writer, but I'd be coming back as a star!

Which just goes to show how little my bones know.

As things turned out, I'd be coming back as a murder suspect.

Stick around, and I'll tell you how it all went down.

Chapter 1

I should have known something was amiss when I checked the address Heather had given me and saw she lived in Orange County.

Now there's nothing wrong with Orange County if you happen to like oranges and Disneyland and shopping plazas the size of third-world countries. But it's not exactly Nashville.

Why would a music industry star be living so far from the action, I wondered, as I made my way south along the 405 freeway. And I had plenty of time to wonder. After slogging along in traffic for almost an hour, I finally arrived at the town I shall call, for purposes of this narration, Alta Loco—a quaint conglomeration of gated communities and tanning salons nestled among the freeway off-ramps.

Driving past a succession of residential enclaves, each with a name more aristocratic than the next—Coventry Hills, Pembroke Gardens, Buckingham Villas—I finally arrived at the gated entry of Alta Estates, where a grizzled guard sat in a booth, reading *USA Today.*

Squinting down at my ancient Corolla, he growled:

"Deliveries through the back entrance."

"I'm not making a delivery," I huffed. "I'm here

to see one of your residents, Heather Van Sant."

Eyeing me like I was a cockroach on a BLT, he picked up a phone and dialed. Soon I heard him saying, "Good morning, Ms. Van Sant. You expecting some gal in a crappy Corolla?"

Okay, so what he really asked was, "Are you expecting a guest?" But I knew what he was thinking. And I didn't like it one bit.

Having received permission to let me in, he grudgingly opened the gates and gave me directions to Heather's house.

Once inside Alta Estates, I drove past one cookie-cutter McMansion after another, all painted in various shades of beige, dotted with balconies and palm trees and gurgling fountains out front.

I found Heather's house and parked my Corolla, the only car on the street except for a gardener's truck. After fluffing my curls in my rearview mirror and checking to make sure there was no lipstick on my teeth, I made my way up a path past the requisite gurgling fountain to Heather's front door.

The doorbell set off a series of musical chimes, and seconds later I heard the sounds of clacking heels. The door swung open to reveal a statuesque beauty in tight capris and even tighter tank top. Raven hair extensions tumbled down past her shoulders, and surgically enhanced breasts stood at attention in her push-up bra.

Her face, with its pinched nose and pouty lips, had the slightly sandblasted look of someone who'd spent many a happy hour at her dermatologist's.

"You must be Jaine," she said, taking in my on-sale-at-Nordstrom outfit. I only hoped she couldn't see through my blazer and silk shirt to the elastic clinging to my waist.

"I'm Heather Van Sant," she said, holding out a ninety-dollar manicure for me to shake. "C'mon in."

I followed her along gleaming hardwood floors into a hangar-sized living room furnished all in white. The only pops of color were some hot pink throw pillows and a huge portrait hanging over the fireplace—of a younger Heather, wearing a tiara.

"That's me," she said, following my gaze, "when I was crowned Queen of the Gilroy Garlic Festival." Her eyes misted over at the memory. "That was the happiest day of my life," she sighed.

Then, snapping out of her reverie, she said, "Have a seat, won't you?"

I headed for an enormous white sectional and was just about to sit down on what I thought was a furry white throw pillow when suddenly the pillow let out a ferocious yap. Yikes. The little thing was a dog!

Sure enough, it suddenly sat up, barking furiously.

"Oh, hush, Elvis," Heather said, scooping him up in her arms. "Be nice to Ms. Austen.

"I think he likes you!" Heather beamed, oblivious to the death glare her doggie was shooting my way.

Making sure there were no other living critters nesting there, I lowered my fanny onto the sectional.

"Snack?" Heather pointed to a platter of supremely unappetizing celery and carrot sticks on her coffee table. With nary a dollop of dip in sight. How utterly depressing.

"No, thanks. I'm fine."

"I absolutely loved your plumber's song," Heather gushed, plucking a carrot stick, "and I just know you're going to write something fantabulous for Taylor."

Taylor? Good heavens! Was it possible that Taylor Swift had moved to Orange County with a former garlic festival queen and a dog named Elvis?

"Taylor, sweetheart!" Heather trilled. "Come downstairs and meet Ms. Austen!

"You're going to adore Taylor." Heather beamed at me. "She just oozes talent. Doesn't she, snookums?"

This last question was directed at Elvis, who replied with a mighty yawn.

"You're just oozing talent, too, aren't you, darling Elvis? Let's do a trick for Ms. Austen and show her how talented you are."

She plopped him on the floor and commanded, "Sit, Elvis! Sit! Sit!"

But the little devil just shot her a defiant glare and proceeded to take a poop.

"Oh, well," Heather said, staring ruefully at the tiny mess. "He was just one letter off."

With a weary sigh, she got up and headed for her kitchen. Seconds later she was back with paper towels to clean up the mess. When she'd disposed of Elvis's little present and there was still no sign of Taylor, Heather's brow furrowed in annoyance.

"Taylor!" she screeched at full throttle. "Get down here this minute!"

The screeching seemed to do the trick.

Soon a tiny slip of a teenaged girl came slouching into the room, clad in baggy sweats and carrying a book. Her dark hair was caught up in a messy ponytail, and a pair of round tortoiseshell glasses were perched on her nose.

Her feet slapped in flip-flops as she walked across the hardwood floor.

This was the "industry star" I was supposed to be writing for?

As if reading my mind, Heather piped up, "Taylor hasn't exactly been discovered yet, but she will be. Just as soon as she wins the Miss Teen Queen America pageant."

"Miss Teen Queen America?"

"It's a national competition for teens across the country. As I've been trying to explain to Taylor, beauty pageants are a gateway to a fabulous career as a model or show business performer. Or, as in my case, a very financially rewarding marriage."

She glanced down with pride at a diamond on her finger the size of a grapefruit.

Taylor plopped down into an armchair and opened her book. Which I now saw was Hermann Hesse's *Siddhartha*. Most unusual fare for an Orange County teenager.

"Mom," she groaned, "how many times do I have to tell you, I don't want to be in this stupid contest?"

"Of course you do, sweetheart. You just don't realize it. Some day when you're singing to a sold-out audience at Caesars Palace, you'll thank me. And in the meanwhile," she added, eyeing *Siddhartha* with disgust, "will you please stop reading that silly book?

"She's always got her nose in a book," she confided to me with motherly dismay. "If she insists on ruining her eyes, I don't understand why she can't read something useful like *Vogue*."

Taylor slammed the book shut and glanced over at the plate of celery sticks.

"Veggies again? Can't I ever have something decent to eat around here?"

"Not if you want to be a size zero for the contest."

"I don't care about being a size zero. You're the one who wants me to be skinny."

"Anyhow," Heather said, ignoring Taylor and turning to me, "Taylor's going to compete in the local division of the Miss Teen Queen America pageant this weekend, and I need you to write her some snappy lyrics."

"This weekend?" I said. "That doesn't give me much time."

"Yes, I know it's awfully short notice. But at the last minute I decided to go with original lyrics to make Taylor stand out from the crowd. She's already got the most magnificent gowns. . . . Wait! I'll go get them!"

As Heather rushed off to get Taylor's pageant outfits, Taylor turned to me with a hopeful smile.

"I don't suppose you've got anything to eat?" she asked. "I'm dying for something sweet and sugary with no nutritional value whatsoever."

"One of my favorite food groups," I assured her.

I fished around in my purse and pulled out a package of M&M's I'd brought to keep me company on the drive down to Alta Loco.

"Help yourself," I said, handing them over. "I ate most of the red ones."

"You're an angel," she said, grabbing a handful. "My mom's driving me crazy with this silly contest. I'll never win the darn thing."

I wasn't so sure about that. Behind those tortoise-shell glasses was a most appealing doll-like face.

"And besides, I don't want to be a beauty queen. I want to be a writer like you."

"Like me?" I beamed with pride.

"Well, not exactly like you. I don't want to wind up writing jingles for plumbers' Christmas parties. But I still think it's cool that you're a writer."

Just then we heard Heather's footsteps. Taylor quickly stashed the M&M's in her pants pocket as Heather returned with two gowns.

"What do you think?" she asked, holding out one of them, a bedazzling ice-blue beaded number. "Vera Wang. Fifteen hundred dollars."

Holy moly! Fifteen hundred dollars for a dress for a teenager to wear to a contest she didn't even want to enter? And people say I'm crazy for spending money on the Fudge of the Month Club.

"It's beautiful," I managed to sputter.

"And look at this one." She held up a neon Carmen Miranda extravaganza, complete with spiraling headdress made of plastic fruit.

(Class assignment: For those of you too young to remember Carmen Miranda, go watch one of her movies. Right now. No excuses. Pop quiz to follow at a future date.)

"Taylor's going to wear it for the talent competition," Heather said, ruffling the dress's tiered flounces. "Fantabulous, huh?"

I managed a faint nod.

"So what do you think, Jaine? You think you can write lyrics that will make my little princess sparkle?"

Me, write for a beauty pageant? Absolutely not.

No way was I going to participate in an institution that objectified young girls by making them parade around in swimsuits, twirling batons and spouting about world peace. I have my standards, you know.

"I'll pay you five hundred dollars."

On the other hand, who was I to say no to world peace?

Chapter 2

Back in my car, I checked my phone messages and was thrilled to find one from my boyfriend.

Yes, you read that right.

I, Jaine Austen—a woman whose spiciest romance in the last several years had been with Chef Boyardee—was actually dating someone! An adorable homicide detective named Scott Willis, with huge brown eyes and a most appealing Adam's apple. I'd met him several months ago while tracking down a killer (a stirring saga you can read all about in *Killing Cupid*, now available in paperback and on all the usual e-gizmos).

I knew he was my kind of guy when, on our first date, at a movie revival of *Rear Window*, he ordered extra butter for our popcorn. Afterward, we spent hours at a coffee shop yakking about our favorite Hitchcock movies. (His: *Strangers on a Train*. Mine: *Shadow of a Doubt*.)

What a treat it was to be on a date with a guy who (unlike my ex-husband, The Blob) didn't grab handfuls of sugar packets to take home and decant into his sugar bowl.

All in all, it had been a most gratifying encounter (especially the sizzling good-night kiss at the end). I thought for sure I'd hear from him again. But alas, I heard nothing. Nada. I was back in dating limbo.

I'd chalked the whole thing up to my bad dating karma when a few weeks ago, out of the blue, Scott called, apologizing profusely for his disappearing act. He said he'd had a reconciliation with an old girlfriend, but it hadn't worked out. This time, he was certain, the relationship was over for good, and he begged me to give him another chance.

I figured anyone who could recite all of Alfred Hitchcock's movies in chronological order deserved a second chance, so I said yes, and we've been dating ever since.

And by "dating," I mean we'd seen each other exactly four times. But in my world, that constitutes a whirlwind romance.

Now, in my car outside Heather's house, I listened to his message eagerly.

Jaine, I hope you're free Friday night for dinner with my parents. Let me know, okay?

Omigosh, he wanted me to meet his parents! Did that mean what I thought it meant? Was Scott getting serious about me?

I spent the whole drive home in a daze. I should have been thinking about lyrics for Taylor's song, but nary a syllable came to mind. No, all I could think about for the next thirty-seven miles was what it would be like to be married to Scott Willis and his heavenly Adam's apple.

• • •

The minute I walked in the door, Prozac glared up at me from where she was hard at work shredding a sofa cushion.

Where the heck have you been? Do you realize it's been a whole three hours and twelve minutes since my last snack?

She raced to my side and was about to launch into her patented Feed Me dance, weaving in and around my ankles with frenzied abandon, when suddenly she stopped and sniffed, her eyes narrowing into suspicious slits.

Wait a minute. I smell dog! You've been cheating on me!

Oh, dear. Clearly I'd picked up some of Elvis's dog hairs from Heather's sectional.

"I swear, Pro. Nothing happened. He didn't even like me."

An imperious swish of her tail.

As if. I bet you were cooing and cuddling and giving him belly rubs. To think of all the years we've been together, all the hair balls I've coughed up for you, all the dead spiders I've left in your cereal bowl. And this is how you repay me? I'm filing for divorce! Just as soon as I finish my snack—hey, speaking of my snack, where the heck is it?

And just like that, she was weaving in and out around my ankles, doing her Feed Me dance.

What can I say? Her mind tends to wander.

I'd just tossed her some Hearty Halibut Guts when there was a knock on my door.

I opened it to find my neighbor, Lance Venable, a stylish dude with a headful of tight blond curls and, at the moment, a huge carton in his arms.

Lance and I share a duplex in the slums of Beverly Hills, at the very edge of the 90212 zip code, light years from the mega-mansions north of Sunset.

"The UPS guy brought this while you were gone," he said, setting the carton down on the floor.

"It must be my new DVD armoire."

Tired of having my bedroom dresser littered with DVDs, I'd found a beautiful miniature armoire online and was looking forward to storing my treasured discs in faux antique splendor.

"What a stunner!" Lance gushed.

"How do you know? You haven't even seen it yet."

"Not the armoire. The UPS guy." His eyes lit up as they always do at the prospect of a love connection. "He's new on the route. You should've seen him in his UPS shorts. Calf muscles to die for!"

Something told me Lance would be ordering lots of packages in the weeks to come.

"So how'd it go with the famous music industry star?" Lance said, plopping down on my sofa.

I'd told him about my upcoming interview,

back when I thought I'd actually be meeting someone in the music industry.

"And who was it, anyway?" he asked eagerly. "Lady Gaga? Madonna? Cher?" By now, his tight blond curls were practically quivering with excitement. "Did you get me an autograph? Free concert tickets? A photo suitable for framing?"

"Forget it, Lance. There was no music industry star. Some Real Housewife of Orange County wants me to write novelty lyrics for her daughter to sing in a teenage beauty pageant."

"Drat," Lance pouted. "I was counting on those concert tickets to get a date with the UPS guy."

"Sorry to bust your bubble," I said, sitting down next to him on the sofa. "But on the plus side," I added, "I did get a call from Scott."

"The hottie detective?"

Lance had met Scott during the *Killing Cupid* affair, and was thrilled that we were seeing each other. Or, as he'd put it, "At last! You're having a meaningful relationship with someone of your own species!"

"He wants me to meet his parents."

"He does?" Lance sat up, excited. "This is major. The gateway to the wedding altar. The guy's practically proposing!"

"Lance, don't be absurd. Just because he invited me to dinner with his parents doesn't mean he wants to marry me."

"But it means he's getting serious."

Secretly, I couldn't help but agree.

"Omigosh!" Lance jumped up and grabbed my arm. "We've got to go shopping. I can't possibly let you wear anything you already own."

For some insane reason, Lance is convinced I have no fashion sense. He says moths come to my closet to commit suicide. Which is perfectly absurd, as anyone who's ever seen my vintage collection of *Cuckoo for Cocoa Puffs* T-shirts will be the first to tell you.

"Lucky for you, today's my day off," Lance cried. "Now grab your wallet, hon. It's about to get a major workout."

I've never actually hiked up the Himalayas, but I'm betting it's a cakewalk compared to hitting the malls with Lance.

With Lance, shopping is an endurance contest, *The Amazing Race* with accessories.

One of his major principles in life is Never Buy the First Thing You See, Even If It's Exactly What You're Looking For. Lance's theory is that something better may be right around the corner. And by right around the corner, I mean every mall and boutique within a five-mile radius.

And of course, that's exactly what happened when he took me shopping for something to wear to meet Scott's parents.

We saw a perfectly adorable Eileen Fisher outfit on our first stop at Nordstrom—slate-gray silk slacks with a matching V-necked kimono sleeved top. I was a little nervous about the kimono sleeves, thinking they were a tad too dramatic, but Lance insisted they were exactly what I needed.

"Kimono sleeves will add just the right note of glamor to your drab little life," he insisted.

"Who're you calling drab?" I said, brushing lint off an old sourball I'd just fished out from the bottom of my purse.

The outfit was on sale, fifty percent off, and fit me perfectly. But when I took out my credit card to buy it, Lance shook his head in horror, insisting we might find something even nicer elsewhere.

He then proceeded to lead me on an expedition much like the one last made by Lewis and Clark. I can't tell you how many stores we trekked through: Neiman Marcus (where Lance works as a shoe salesman), Saks, Bloomies, Macy's, Fred Segal, and Kate Spade. With nary a single stop at a food court! Talk about cruel and unusual punishment. And at the end of our trek? Lance conceded that the first outfit we saw was the best after all.

Honestly, I deserve combat pay for putting up with that man.

I staggered back to my apartment, kicking off my shoes the minute I walked in the door.

"Oh, Pro," I wailed. "I've just spent four hours in shopping hell."

She gazed up at me lazily from where she was napping on my computer keyboard.

Did you bring back snacks?

Okay, so empathy's not one of her strong points.

"What do you think?" I asked, holding out my new outfit for inspection.

She shot me a frosty glare.

Very nice. I hope your new dog friend likes it.

I made a mental note to throw everything I was wearing in the laundry to get rid of all traces of Elvis. And I was just about to do so when I noticed the carton on my living room floor, the one with my new DVD armoire.

In the agony of my shopping expedition with Lance, I'd forgotten all about it.

Soon I was ripping it open and lifting out my faux Chippendale armoire, admiring its sleek cherrywood finish. It was every bit as lovely as it had looked online, with plenty of shelves for my DVD collection. I was certain Alfred H. would be quite happy there.

I spent the next twenty minutes setting it up in my bedroom next to my TV, feeling quite Martha Stewart-ish as I arranged my DVDs in alphabetical order.

Satisfied with a job well done, I started to run the water for a bath, tossing in a handful of strawberry-scented bath beads. Then, after a quick trip to the kitchen to pour myself a much-needed glass of chardonnay, I stripped off my Elvistainted clothes and tossed them into the hamper.

It was with a huge sigh of relief that I eased my shopworn muscles into the tub, inhaling the rich aroma of my strawberry-scented bubbles—not to mention a wee bit o' chardonnay.

Lying there, relaxing in the heat of the sudsy water, I thought about my upcoming dinner date with Scott's parents. Was it possible Scott was really serious about me? Might he even be about to pop the question? Not that I was ready to get married. Not for a long time. Not until next Thursday, anyway.

Taking another glug of chardonnay, I wondered what Scott's parents would be like. What with Scott being a police detective, I figured he came from a down-to-earth middle class family, the kind of people who lived in a cute ranch home with an old-fashioned kitchen banquette and wood paneling in the den. In my mind, his dad was a tall, skinny guy with a hint of a paunch, his mom short and apple-cheeked, fussing over a pot roast in the oven.

I saw myself sitting at their dining room table, laughing at their stories about the funny things Scott did when he was a kid, modestly telling them about my life as a freelance copywriter.

"You wrote *Just a Shade Better* for Ackerman's Awnings?" Scott's mom would exclaim, eyes wide with admiration as she passed me the mashed potatoes.

(Of which I'd be certain to take only one helping.)

After dinner, Scott would get down on one knee in the wood paneled den, his Adam's apple bobbing most appealingly as he proposed to me the old-fashioned way.

And before I knew it, we'd be off on our honeymoon in the Bahamas, drinking mai tais in the infinity pool, after which we'd return to an ivy-covered cottage in Hermosa Beach to raise a family of little Willises. It wasn't until the birth of our third child, a dimpled cutie named Sebastian, that I finally called a halt to my daydream and dredged myself out of the tub.

Slipping into my robe, I drifted into my bedroom still high on cloud nine.

I quickly came thudding back to earth, however, when I glanced over at my new DVD armoire and saw a deep gouge along its sleek cherrywood finish.

And I knew exactly where it came from— Prozac's mischievous little claws, which she was now licking industriously.

"Prozac!" I shrieked. "What on earth do you think you're doing?"

She looked up at me with big green eyes.

Playing with my new scratching post.

Darn that cat. She was getting back at me for Elvis.

YOU'VE GOT MAIL

To: Jausten
From: Shoptillyoudrop
Subject: Exciting news!

Exciting news, sweetheart! The Tampa Vistas Library is having a fashion show luncheon to raise money for the library, and guess who they've asked to be a model? Me! Your five-foot-three-inch, size-fourteen mom. Isn't that positively thrilling?

And clever Lydia Pinkus, president of the Tampa Vistas Homeowners Association, has worked out a deal with Pink Flamingo, one of the most exclusive clothing boutiques in town, to loan us clothing for the show.

Normally, I wouldn't even dream of buying a dress at Pink Flamingo. The Home Shopping Club is good enough for me. Why spend a fortune on designer clothes, I always say, when you can get a perfectly lovely outfit for a fraction of the price delivered straight to your door?

Nevertheless, I must confess it'll be fun to be a model, strutting my stuff at the Tampa Vistas clubhouse. We're having the luncheon outdoors at the pool. Doesn't that sound divine? Lydia's arranging everything. She's such a capable woman—

Good heavens. There's the most godawful racket going on outside.

Must run and see what's happening—
XOXO,
Mom

To: Jausten
From: Shoptillyoudrop
Subject: OMG!

Omigod! I just looked out the window and there was Daddy, waving at me from a beat up old golf cart, a hideous red plaid golf cap on his head, honking a horn that plays *La Cucaracha*!

I'd better get out there before the neighbors start complaining.
XOXO,
Mom

To: Jausten
From: Shoptillyoudrop
Subject: Nellybelle

Of all the idiotic things your daddy has ever bought, this darn golf cart takes the cake. Apparently he answered an ad in the Tampa

Vistas *Tattler* and bought it for $200. Which is about $199 more than it's worth. He absolutely insisted I go for a ride in the damnable contraption, which he's calling Nellybelle.

I told him it looked like it was ready for the junk heap, but he swore it was in tip-top condition, and made such a fuss about taking me for a ride that I foolishly got in.

What a mistake that was!

We hadn't made it to the end of the block when the old junk heap conked out. And guess who had to help Daddy push it back home?

Time for a hot bath and an emergency piece of fudge.

Love and XXX from
Your aching,
Mom

To: Jausten
From: DaddyO
Subject: New Member of the Family

Fantastic news, Lambchop! There's a new member of the Austen family—Nellybelle, my new golf cart. Well, actually it's a used golf cart that I picked up for only $200. Just what I need to tool around Tampa Vistas. Think of all the money I'll save on gas! Took your mom out for an inaugural spin this afternoon. A wonderful adventure, until Nellybelle stalled at the end of the block. But not to worry. Your mom and I pushed her back home, and now she's resting comfortably in the garage. I'll have her up and running in no time!

Love 'n' snuggles from

Mr. Fixit, aka Daddy

P.S. Forgot to tell you: The guy who sold me Nellybelle threw in a free golf hat, and a horn that plays *La Cucaracha*. Neat, huh? Would you believe his wife made him get rid of all those treasures? Lucky for me, your mom is so understanding.

To: Jausten
From: Shoptillyoudrop
Subject: Feeling Much Better

Feeling much better now, after my hot bath and piece of fudge. (Okay, three pieces.)

Daddy's insisting on fixing Nellybelle himself. Which means, of course, it'll never get fixed, and I'll never have to hear that damn *La Cucaracha* horn ever again.

Life is good.

XXX

Mom

P.S. Okay, it was four pieces of fudge.

Chapter 3

When I woke up the next morning, Prozac was not in her usual position astride my chest, clawing me awake for her breakfast. No, her claws were otherwise engaged, making fresh gouges on my DVD armoire.

"Prozac!" I cried, leaping out of bed.

She gazed at her handiwork with pride.

Who says cats can't draw?

I quickly snatched her up in my arms and hauled her to the kitchen, where I distracted her with a bowl of Hearty Halibut Guts.

Then, with heavy heart, I examined the damage she'd wrought on the armoire. Fortunately she'd only attacked the side panel. Maybe I'd be able to cover the scratches with some wood stain. In the meantime, I had to keep the armoire safe from further harm. So I covered it with the carton it came in, weighing the carton down with two telephone books.

It would have to do until I could think of some other way to keep Prozac away from my treasured purchase.

Carefully closing the bedroom door, I headed back out to the kitchen to nuke myself some coffee and a cinnamon raisin bagel.

Then I settled down at the dining room table,

otherwise known as my office, to check my emails. I was foolish enough to open the ones from my parents, something bitter experience has taught me never to do on an empty stomach.

My parents are perfectly lovely people, but disaster magnets of the highest order. Daddy's the main culprit. The man attracts trouble like white cashmere attracts red wine. Of course, Mom is not without her quirks, having made Daddy move three thousand miles across country to be near the Home Shopping Club, under the mistaken notion she'd get her packages faster that way. Nevertheless, she's been a saint to put up with Daddy's antics all these years. I just hoped she was right about Nellybelle and that the golf cart would soon disappear into the slag heap of Daddy's unfinished projects out in their garage.

But I couldn't worry about my parents. Not now. Not when I had Taylor's lyrics to write. I'd agreed to do a rush job and promised Heather I'd send them to her by the end of the day. Which meant I had less than eight hours to write song lyrics for a teen queen wannabe posing as a Latin spitfire in a fruit headdress.

Why, oh, why had I wasted all that time shopping with Lance yesterday?

So the very minute I finished my cinnamon raisin bagel I buckled down and started writing.

Okay, so the minute I finished my cinnamon raisin bagel, I nuked myself another one. But right after that, I got down to work. I did not get very far, however, staring at the blank screen, wondering what the heck I'd gotten myself into.

The whole thing turned out to be a lot harder than I anticipated.

I don't suppose you've ever given it any serious thought, but many of the words that rhyme with "queen" are a tad uninspired. Like "mean," "bean," and "latrine," to name just a few.

Finally, after countless trips to the refrigerator for inspiration, I came up with the following ditty:

TAYLOR FOR TEEN QUEEN

My name is Taylor
And I'm here to say
I want to be teen queen
In the very worst way
I've got grace, I've got charm, I've got
    poise to spare
Not only that, I've got super shiny hair!
I look good in a swimsuit without sucking
    my gut
And if I say so myself I've got a mighty
    cute butt
I can sing, I can dance, I can play the
    kazoo
But my real ambition is to represent you
So vote for Taylor and I'll never cease

To whiten my teeth and work for world
    peace!
CHORUS
Aye aye aye aye
Taylor's so sweet
Aye aye aye aye
She can't be beat
Aye aye aye aye
Goodwill she'll preach
Aye aye aye aye
Taylor's a peach!
(TAKES A PEACH FROM HER
HEADDRESS AND THROWS IT TO
THE JUDGES WITH A PERKY SMILE)

Something told me I could forget about my career as a future Grammy winner. But it was the best I could do. So I took a deep breath and emailed the lyrics to Heather.

I only hoped she liked them. And what if she didn't? Would she still pay me the five hundred bucks she'd promised? I kicked myself for not ironing out the details of the deal. Oh, well. There was nothing I could do about it now.

Worn out from my exertions, and still in my pajamas, I headed for my bedroom to take a restorative nap.

I cringed to see the bedroom door open.

Which could mean only one thing. Prozac had broken in.

I raced inside to check on my armoire. Surely there was no way she could get past two phone books and a packing carton.

Who am I kidding? That cat was a regular Houdini with hair balls.

Somehow she'd managed to dislodge the phone books and upend the carton, and was back at work perfecting her chef d'oeuvre on the side of my armoire. Several more scratches had been added to her masterpiece.

She gazed up at me with a proud swish of her tail.

Eat your heart out, Picasso.

A half hour later, I'd put all my DVDs back on my dresser, sealed the armoire tight as a drum in its carton, and stashed it away in the hall closet.

Score one for Prozac.

But this little game wasn't over.

Not by a long shot.

The next day dragged by interminably as I waited in vain for Heather to call.

I spent most of it working on a Toiletmasters brochure for their new "double flush" commode (don't ask), but my heart wasn't in it.

True, my heart's rarely in it when I'm writing about toilet bowls, but that day I was especially distracted.

When three o'clock rolled around and I still hadn't heard from Heather, I assumed it was a lost cause. She'd read my teen queen lyrics and was probably using them to scoop up Elvis's latest poops.

I was heading for the kitchen for a teensy Oreo break when I heard a knock at my door.

I opened it and saw the first bright spot in my otherwise gloomy day.

Standing there was Scott, my shiny new boyfriend, his Adam's apple looking extra kissable in the afternoon sun.

"Hi, there," he smiled, turning my knees to mush. "I was working a case in the neighborhood and I decided to pop by for a quick hello."

"Hi," I squeaked, trying not to sound too overjoyed.

"Actually," he said, stepping inside, "I wasn't really in the neighborhood. I drove all the way from Culver City. And I didn't want to just say hello."

With that, he wrapped me in his arms for a smooch.

This is a family novel, so I won't go in for tawdry details, but let's just say it was quite a while before we finally came up for air.

"Hope I'm not interrupting anything," he said.

"Not a thing," I replied, mentally tossing all thoughts of Heather and double-flush toilets out the window.

We were in the middle of an encore performance of our smooch when suddenly I felt something furry wedging its way between us.

It was Prozac, of course, who was using Scott's ankle as her own personal stripper pole.

"How's my little love bunny?" Scott asked, swooping her up in his arms.

She gazed up at him seductively.

Lonesome without you, big boy.

Talk about your shameless hussies.

"I'll pick you up tomorrow at seven," Scott said to me as Prozac licked his neck with abandon, "and we'll drive out to my folks together."

"Fine," I nodded, still a bit numb from his kisses.

For all I knew, he asked all his dates to meet his parents. I was probably making way too big a deal of this.

"I sure hope they like me," I said.

"Of course, they'll like you. They're gonna love you. Just like—"

Just like I do, were the words I was waiting for him to add. But much to my disappointment, all he said, was, "Just like everybody does."

So much for declarations of love.

"Wish I could stick around," he said, "but I've got to get back to work. My partner thinks I'm out getting donuts."

After planting a quick kiss on my nose, he peeled Prozac from his neck and headed out the door.

I trudged back to my computer with a sigh, forcing myself to wax euphoric over Toilet-masters' double-flush toilet. I was in the middle of describing its sleek lines and "comfort height" seat when the phone rang.

"Jaine, honey!" Heather's voice came zinging across the line. "So sorry I didn't get back to you sooner, but I've had a hectic day at the spa. So many pores, so little time! Anyway, hon, Taylor and I read your lyrics and we love them!"

Ka-ching! Five hundred clams in the bank!

"Not only that, Taylor insists that you come with us to the pageant this weekend. She wants you there for moral support. I'll pay for everything, of course. Room. Food. The works."

A weekend in Alta Loco at a teen beauty pageant? Not exactly a dream destination.

"I'll even throw in an extra five hundred dollars!" Heather chirped.

"What time do we check in?"

We agreed to meet in the hotel lobby the next day at 3 PM. I explained to Heather that I'd need to drive up to L.A. for dinner with Scott's folks, which was fine with her.

I hung up, feeling quite pleased with myself. Not only was I about to earn an extra five hundred bucks, but it was most gratifying to know that I'd made a connection with Taylor. Clearly the teen had been impressed with my talents and looked upon me as a role model and mentor.

It felt good having such a positive effect on a girl at such an impressionable age.

Just as I was basking in the glow of my own wonderfulness, about to award myself my own personal Medal of Honor, the phone rang.

"Jaine. It's me, Taylor." For some reason, she was whispering. "About this weekend—"

"I'm really flattered that you want me along, Taylor. Any advice you need, any moral support, don't hesitate to ask."

"Yeah, right, whatever. Just remember to bring M&M's, okay?"

Cancel that Medal of Honor.

Chapter 4

I set out for Alta Loco the next afternoon with a spring in my step, a smile on my lips, and enough M&M's to stock a movie concession.

All systems were go for my departure.

Lance had agreed to look after Prozac while I was gone and had already planned a special outing at a pet beauty spa for her and his dog Mamie.

I'd texted Scott to tell him I'd be driving to his parents' house from Alta Loco and asked him to send me their address. And packed away in my suitcase, ready to make a fab first impression, was my new gray silk blouse with the kimono sleeves.

What's more, I'd checked the hotel online and saw it had a Jacuzzi and sauna. With any luck, I'd be able to sneak off to the sauna and sweat off an extra pound or fifteen before dinner.

Now I picked up my bags and headed for the door.

"Thanks so much for taking care of Pro," I said to Lance, who was sitting on the sofa with her royal highness.

"No problem, hon. She and Mamie are going to have so much fun getting their aromatherapy baths."

I pitied the poor soul who tried to give Prozac a bath. Fur would fly, and it wouldn't be Prozac's.

"Will you miss me while I'm gone, sweet pea?"

Prozac glanced up from where she was nestled in Lance's arms and gave me a quizzical look.

And you are . . . ?

Really, in my next life, I've got to come back as a dog person.

I wasn't expecting the Ritz-Carlton, but I groaned in dismay when I pulled into the cracked blacktop parking lot of the hotel. A concrete bunker with sun-bleached stucco and rusted balconies, the place hadn't been updated in years. A red sign out front perched on rickety poles told me that I was at the AMADA INN. Even from thirty feet away I could see the faint outlines of a missing R. Clearly the place had once been a Ramada Inn, and whoever bought it hadn't bothered to spring for a new sign.

The inside wasn't any better. The carpet was threadbare, the lobby chairs worn thin by decades of tourists' tushes.

I did not, however, get to see much of the hotel furniture when I walked in the lobby to the Teen Queen pageant that day. The place was a sea of raging hormones. Everywhere I looked, I saw big hair, pouty lips, and jutting boobs.

And those were just the moms.

The teens were an assorted lot of pubescent

nymphs—some ready for their *Cosmo* close-ups, others still wrestling with braces and acne.

I looked around and spotted Heather and Taylor waiting on line to check in. Heather was decked out in skin-tight jeans and tank top, her long legs tottering on five-inch wedgies. And nestled in her arms, growling at anyone foolish enough to make eye contact, was her pooch, Elvis.

Taylor stood next to her, still in the same sloppy sweats she'd been wearing when I met her, still reading *Siddhartha*.

"Honestly, Taylor," I heard Heather say as I walked over to them. "I don't understand why you insisted on wearing these ratty old sweats."

"They're not judging me on checking in," Taylor replied with an exasperated sigh.

"Who knows?" Heather snapped. "Maybe they are. Maybe secret judges are lurking around to see how you behave when you're not on stage."

"Well, I don't understand why you had to bring that stupid calorie scale," Taylor shot back.

I looked down and sure enough, there was a small scale perched on top of Heather's matching leopard-print luggage.

"Because you can't afford to gain a single ounce, that's why!"

Time for me to break up this little mother-daughter spat.

"Hi, guys!" I said, wheeling over my CVS suit-case (only $29.99, plus a 25 percent off coupon on my next purchase of Dr. Scholl's foot pads).

"Jaine, dear!" Heather cried, wrapping me in her arms and giving me an air kiss.

Did you bring the M&M's? Taylor mouthed behind her back.

I shot her a surreptitious nod as Heather let me go.

"Look, Mom!" someone piped up behind us. "A dog!"

We turned to see a blue-eyed teen making koochy noises at Elvis, who rewarded her with a particularly nasty growl.

"Don't pet him," snapped the teen's mom, a wiry redhead with a pinched face and jutting chin. "He may have fleas."

"My dog does not have fleas!" Heather cried, whirling around to see who'd just insulted her pride and joy.

"If you say so," the redhead replied with a smirk.

"And watch where you're eating that ice cream," Heather warned the redhead's daughter, who was eating an ice cream cone just inches away from a rolling rack with several garment bags suspended from it. "There's a fifteen-hundred-dollar Vera Wang gown in one of those bags," Heather bragged.

"Really?" said the redhead. "You spent fifteen hundred dollars on a gown for your daughter?"

"Not only that," Heather added, pointing to

yours truly, "I hired a songwriter to write lyrics for the talent contest."

I stood there, trying to look as professional as possible, hoping no one would ask me to sing a medley of my hit tune, *The Toiletmasters Christmas Party Song*.

"My Gigi's a natural beauty," the redhead crowed. "She doesn't need a designer label or a songwriter to win this contest."

"Maybe not," Heather muttered under her breath. "But she sure could use a nose job."

"I heard that!" the redhead screeched.

"C'mon, Mom," Taylor said, grabbing Heather by the arm. "It's our turn to check in."

And indeed, a harried clerk was waving us over to the check-in desk. Not a moment too soon.

"They shouldn't allow dumb animals in this hotel," the redhead hissed in a stage whisper that could be heard clear across the lobby.

Heather whirled around, indignant.

"My Elvis is not a dumb animal!"

"I wasn't talking about the dog," the redhead sneered.

Heather shot her a filthy look.

Oh, dear. Something told me this was going to be a long weekend.

We rolled our luggage over to the Amada Inn's two dinky elevators, only to discover one of them was out of order.

Why was I not surprised?

Impatient clumps of moms and teens hovered near the working elevator, ready to charge in the minute the doors opened.

Heather grabbed her garment rack and was about to push her way through the mob when she suddenly stopped dead in her tracks.

"Omigosh!" she whispered, nudging me in the ribs. "A judge!"

She gestured to a skinny guy in a bow tie and round wire-rimmed glasses.

And indeed on the lapel of his blazer was a tag that read OFFICIAL JUDGE, MISS TEEN QUEEN AMERICA PAGEANT.

"That's Dr. Fletcher," Taylor said. "He's the principal at Alta Loco High."

"Let's go over and say hello," Heather said, eager to pounce.

"I can't say hello, Mom," Taylor protested. "He doesn't even know me. Alta Loco is a big school."

"Well, young lady, it's time he got to know you."

With that, she grabbed Taylor by the elbow, and hauled her over to the principal's side.

"Hi, there," she cooed, batting her false eye-lashes. "I couldn't help but notice you're one of the pageant judges."

He nodded warily. I'm guessing he knew a barracuda mom when he saw one.

"Allow me to introduce myself," Heather

prattled on. "I'm Heather Van Sant, and this is my extraordinarily talented daughter, Taylor."

All around her, the other moms were giving her the stink eye.

But Heather kept slathering it on with a trowel.

"You should hear my daughter sing," Heather crowed. "She has the voice of an angel."

"How nice," the principal replied with a wan smile.

For a minute, I was afraid Heather was going to make Taylor put on her Carmen Miranda outfit and belt out a tune right there in the lobby.

But just then the elevator door opened, and Heather sprang into action, determined to make her way on board.

"See you later," she said to the judge with a jaunty wave.

Before she could take two steps, however, she was intercepted by a gawky kid in a bellhop's uniform.

"Excuse me, ma'am," he said. "I'm afraid I can't let you on the elevator with your garment rack. It'll take up too much space. Just give me your room number and I'll bring it up to you when the crowds die down."

Reluctantly Heather gave him her room number.

"Be careful," she warned. "There's a fifteen-hundred-dollar Vera Wang gown on that rack."

The bellhop assured Heather he'd take the utmost care of Vera Wang.

By now, of course, the elevator was long gone.

Spotting Dr. Fletcher still waiting in the crowd, Heather sprinted back to his side to regale him with breathless accounts of Taylor's many accomplishments. She was in the middle of telling him about Taylor's performance as Turnip #3 in her elementary school production of *Farmer in the Dell*, when the elevator returned.

As soon as she heard the ding of the doors opening, she made a run for it, plowing her way past several indignant moms. Somehow she managed to get us on board. She held open a space for Dr. Fletcher, but he shook his head no.

"Ride up on an elevator with you? Are you kidding? I'd rather book passage on the *Titanic*."

Okay, so what he really said was, "Thanks, anyway. I'll wait for the next one."

But we all knew what he was thinking.

We spent what seemed like an eternity riding up in that damn elevator, packed like sardines and breathing the heady aroma of bubble gum and hair spray.

When at last we arrived at our floor, I bid Heather and Taylor adieu and headed for my room down at the end of the hall.

Alas, I regret to report it was not much bigger than the elevator.

I glanced around in dismay at the sagging double bed, crammed in between two battered nightstands. And I didn't even want to think about what kind of stains were lurking in the stiff patterned comforter.

Across the room—all three feet away—an ancient TV sat atop a dresser built some time during the Punic Wars. Over it all wafted a fog of stale cigarette smoke.

When I went to open the window, I discovered it was sealed shut.

I stood there a minute, admiring my view of the parking lot, then started to unpack, hanging what clothes I could fit on the four wire hangers dangling in the closet.

Oh, well. At least I could melt away some pounds in the Amada Inn's sauna. If I hurried, I figured I could squeeze in a quick session.

Stripping down to my bra and panties, I donned the threadbare bathrobe I found hanging in my closet and scooted out the door.

No way was I about to waste time waiting for the one and only working elevator. So I proceeded to clomp down five flights of stairs to the lower level, home of the Amada Inn's sauna, gym, and hair salon.

As I walked along the dimly lit corridor, I heard voices coming from a room to my right. I peeked inside and saw a small office with a desk and computer and a shelving unit stocked with rhinestone tiaras and tin trophies. Sitting on the top shelf was an elaborately studded tiara, bigger than the others, with what looked like a clock in the middle.

This had to be Pageant Headquarters.

Two nearly identical looking blondes were working in the office. One wore a red blazer; the other wore blue. Both had tortured their hair into helmet-like pageboys, not a strand out of place.

On closer inspection, I realized that one of the blondes, the one in the blue blazer, was the older of the two, and clearly the boss.

"Hurry up with that Krazy Glue, Amy!" she barked at her young assistant. "The rhinestones keep falling off the tiaras." She bent down to scrape some errant rhinestones from the carpet. "I swear, that's the last time I ever order tiaras from Ulan Bator."

"I found it!" the young assistant cried, holding up a tube of Krazy Glue.

"Good," the older woman snapped, thrusting a tiara in her hand. "Now start gluing."

Scooting past the pageant ladies, I came upon the Amada Inn gym, a sorry collection of outdated equipment. No wonder it was empty.

Beyond the gym was the hair salon. A sign on its front door informed me it was closed indefinitely for remodeling.

At last I reached the sauna, only to discover that it, too, was closed for repairs.

Did anything in this hotel actually work?

I thought about exercising at the gym, but nixed

that idea, given the fact that underneath my robe I was wearing only a bra and panties.

With a sigh, I headed back to the stairwell, passing the pageant organizers' office, where the young blonde was busy gluing rhinestones on a tiara, and the older blonde was yelling into her cell phone.

I rang for the elevator, and waited. And waited. And waited.

After a while I gave up and began the long trek back up the five flights of stairs to my room. Not nearly as easy as it was going down. By the time I got to my floor, I was ready to call room service for an oxygen tent. But of course, at the Amada Inn, I was sure there was no such thing as room service.

I staggered to my room, hoping that maybe I'd sweated off a couple of pounds climbing the stairs.

Once inside my little hideaway, I hurled myself on my bed, gasping for air, praying I wasn't sucking in too many carcinogens from the cigarette smoke in the air.

I was lying there, panting, when the phone rang.

Wearily, I picked it up.

"Jaine!" Heather's voice came on the line a panicked screech. "Get over here right away. The Vera Wang is missing!"

I raced down the hall to the room Heather was sharing with Taylor—much nicer than mine, by the way, with two double beds and a scenic view of the Denny's across the street—and found Heather stomping around on her five-inch wedgies, boob implants bouncing, outrage steaming from every pore.

"Someone stole our Vera Wang!" she cried when she saw me. "When the bellhop delivered our garment rack, the dress was missing."

Taylor looked up from one of the double beds, where she was trying to read *Siddhartha*, and sighed.

"Calm down, Mom. It's only a dress."

"It's a Vera Wang, for heavens sake! It cost me fifteen hundred dollars."

"It cost *Daddy* fifteen hundred dollars," Taylor muttered under her breath.

Heather headed over to the other bed, where Elvis was busy chewing on the strap of a huge leather tote bag.

"Naughty dog!" she tsked. "Mustn't eat Mommy's Gucci."

Wrestling it from his grasp, she fished around inside and pulled out her cell phone.

"I'm calling 911."

Taylor sprang from her bed and grabbed the phone.

"You can't call 911 for a missing pageant gown. 911 is for emergencies only."

"If a missing Vera Wang isn't an emergency," Heather huffed, "I don't know what is."

Taylor threw up her hands in disgust.

"Why did you have to go bragging about the dress to everyone, anyway? You might as well have pinned a sign on the garment bag that said 'Steal Me.'"

"I'm sure it wasn't stolen," I said, eager to calm them down. "I bet someone took it by mistake."

"It was no mistake," Heather insisted. "And I know exactly who took it. That redhead on line behind us. She had the nerve to call me an animal!"

"Only after you said her daughter needed a nose job," Taylor pointed out.

"It was the redhead, all right," Heather said, ignoring Taylor's voice of reason. "And I'm calling the cops."

Once again, she reached for her phone. And just as one of her acrylic tips was poised to tap 911, there was a knock on the door.

"I'll get it," I said. "Maybe they found your dress."

And indeed I opened the door to see the older blonde from the pageant office, carrying a garment bag. According to the tag on her blue blazer, she was CANDACE BURKE, PAGEANT DIRECTOR.

She glided into the room, tall and poised, an unflappable smile on her face. I'd bet my bottom Pop-Tart she was a former Teen Queen herself.

"Mrs. Van Sant," she said, holding out the garment bag, "we found your Vera Wang."

"Who stole it? The redheaded bitch?"

"No one stole it, Mrs. Van Sant," Candace cooed in slow even tones, as if talking to a cranky toddler. "The bellhop accidentally put it on the wrong garment rack."

Heather shot her a skeptical look.

"How did he 'accidentally' take a garment bag from one rack and put it on another?"

Another mollifying smile from Candace. Any minute I expected her to hand Heather a lollipop.

"In the hustle and bustle of loading the racks onto the elevator, the bag fell," she explained. "And when the bellhop picked it up, he put it on the wrong rack. It's that simple."

But Heather was not convinced.

"I still say the redhead stole it."

"Let's not make any accusations we can't back up," Candace replied, her smile turning a tad steely. "And what's this?"

She'd turned her gaze on Elvis, who'd abandoned Heather's Gucci tote and was now busy gnawing on the TV remote.

"We can't have your doggie damaging hotel property."

She walked over to Elvis, who began growling a most hair-raising growl.

"Be careful," Taylor warned. "He bites."

But Candace did not seem the least bit cowed.

"Oh, he won't dare bite me."

Then she beamed Elvis a laser glare.

I swear, it was like holding up garlic to a vampire. Instantly Elvis dropped the remote and shrank back into the pillow shams, whimpering.

Wow, this Candace dame was one tough cookie. I reminded myself to stay on her good side and keep my remote in perfect working order.

After having put the fear of God into Elvis, Candace pasted her pageant smile back on and bid us a fond farewell.

"See you soon at Mocktail Hour!" she said, heading out the door.

When she was gone, Heather plopped down on her bed, sulking. "I don't care what anybody says. That redhead stole the Vera Wang."

Taylor, meanwhile, had taken the gown out of the garment bag. She was about to hang it in the closet when she brought it up to her nose and sniffed.

"It smells," she said. "Of perfume."

She handed it to me, and I took a sniff. Sure enough, it had a sweet citrus scent.

"Aha!" Heather leapt up from the bed and grabbed the gown. "You're right." She sniffed. "It does smell of perfume." A triumphant look crossed her face. "I knew it! The redhead's daughter has been prancing around in your Vera Wang. For all we know, the redhead was wearing it, too!"

Her eyes burned with fury.

"Well, if she thinks she's going to get away with it, she's crazy!"

I could practically see the wheels in her brain spinning with plots of revenge.

"We're going to get even with that mean old redhead, aren't we, Elvis?"

But Elvis, tuckered from his encounter with Candace, was fast asleep, unaware of the storm clouds brewing above.

Chapter 5

Mocktail Hour was in full swing when I showed up at the Amada Inn's Grand Rooftop Ballroom, a not-so-grand cavern of a space with a panoramic view of the 405 freeway. All around me, precocious teens were swilling virgin daiquiris, virgin Marys, and virgin piña coladas.

Why did I get the feeling the drinks were the only virgins in the room?

A buffet table had been set up off to the side, manned by the mousy blond assistant I'd seen earlier in the pageant office, now wearing a bright red blazer and a nervous smile.

I gazed longingly at the glorious array of hors d'oeuvres on display: stuffed mushrooms, cheese puffs, Swedish meatballs, and franks-in-a-blanket.

I was dying for a frank-in-a-blanket, but in an effort to stay as svelte as possible for that night's dinner with Scott's parents, I didn't have a single one.

Okay, so I had one. Okay, two. Okay, four, if you must know. But I was famished from trekking up all those stairs from the broken sauna.

Next to me, Heather swatted Taylor's hand away from a stuffed mushroom. "Do you realize how many calories are in that thing?"

And Heather was not alone in her vigilance. Most of the moms were strong-arming their daughters away from the high calorie snacks.

But then from down at the other end of the table, I heard a loud, braying voice. "My Gigi can eat anything she wants, and never gain an ounce."

We turned and saw the redhead from the check-in line, with her daughter in tow, stuffing their faces with Swedish meatballs.

"There she is," Heather hissed, fire in her eyes. "That awful woman from the lobby. I'm going to find out if she took your Vera Wang."

She was just about to stomp off when Taylor grabbed her by the elbow.

"If you go over there and make a scene, I swear I'm going to quit the pageant."

"What makes you think I'm going to make a scene?" Heather sniffed, indignant.

"Because that's what you always do. Honest, Mom, if you go over there, I'm quitting."

Heather blinked, taken aback. It was clear Taylor meant business.

"Okay, darling," Heather cooed. "If that's how you feel, I won't go."

"Good." Taylor nodded, relieved.

"Jaine will."

Huh???

"What do you mean?" I sputtered.

"Wander over there and smell them. See if their

perfume is the same stuff we smelled on the Vera Wang."

"Look, Heather. I can't go around smelling people—"

"I'll pay you a hundred bucks."

"Just let me finish my frank-in-a-blanket."

And so seconds later I was ambling over to where the redhead and her daughter were sucking down hors d'oeuvres.

I sidled near them and took a sniff, but unfortunately all I could smell were Swedish meatballs. Somehow I had to zero in closer on their necks.

Then I got an idea.

I walked over to the redhead, whose name, according the name tag slapped on her chest, was Luanne.

"Omigosh!" I cried. "A bee!"

"What bee?" Luanne looked around, alarmed. "Where?"

I leaned in toward her neck and swatted the imaginary bee away, all the while taking a healthy sniff.

"Oh, no!" I said, turning to her daughter. "Now it's on your neck!"

I then repeated the process with Gigi, who, unlike her mom, was gazing at me with unabashed cynicism.

"I didn't see any bee," she said.

"Didn't you? I swear I saw one flying around."

"So then where is it?" she challenged.

"I don't know. It must have flown away. You know bees. Always flitting here and there. To and fro. Busy little critters. Pollinating flowers. Spreading nature's glory."

I tend to babble when I'm nervous.

But Gigi wasn't about to let this drop.

"What's a bee doing inside a hotel, anyway?" Then, turning to the nearby moms and teen queen wannabes, she asked, "Have any of you seen a bee?"

A chorus of no's filled the air. Accompanied by lots of suspicious stares.

"Oh, dear. I guess I was seeing spots again. It's been happening to me a lot lately. I really must go see my doctor. Well, see you later!"

And without any further ado, I slunk back to Heather and Taylor. I was beginning to think it would have been better if Heather had gone over and made a scene.

"Well?" Heather hissed as soon as I returned. "Did you smell anything?"

"Not a thing. Except Swedish meatballs."

"See, Mom?" Taylor said. "They didn't take my gown."

"I wouldn't be so sure of that. They probably showered off the evidence, knowing I'd be on to them."

The next fifteen minutes or so were spent mixing and mingling, pageant moms and daughters slugging down mocktails as they checked out the competition.

Heather, however, barely listened to the chatter around her, too busy shooting death rays at Luanne.

The mixing and mingling came to an abrupt halt when Candace strode over to a podium on stage at the front of the room.

"Attention, everyone!" she barked into a microphone. "Let's all take our seats!"

She pointed to the rows of folding chairs that had been set up for the occasion.

I followed as Heather nabbed us seats in the front row.

"Welcome," Candace said, when everyone had scurried to their seats, "to the Alta Loco division of the Miss Teen Queen America pageant. I'm your pageant director, Candace Burke."

She smiled coolly as pageant moms and daughters, eager to suck up to her, applauded wildly.

"Over there behind the buffet table is my assistant, Amy Leighton."

The mousy blonde in her red blazer waved from behind the table.

"And here are this year's distinguished judges."

Candace gestured to the stage where two men and a young woman were sitting behind a table. Hanging from the front of the table was a satin banner, with the words ALTA LOCO TEEN QUEEN

AMERICA embroidered in hot pink letters. The "i" in America, I could not help but notice, was dotted with a tiny tiara.

"First, let's all say hello to Dr. Edwin Fletcher, principal of Alta Loco High School."

I immediately recognized the skinny guy with the bow tie and wire-rimmed glasses Heather had practically knocked over in her efforts to promote Taylor. Now he gave a curt nod, his lips a thin grim line. Something told me he'd not be handing out a lot of tens.

"Sitting next to Dr. Fletcher is former Alta Loco Teen Queen, Bethenny Martinez."

A Hispanic beauty in her early twenties, blessed with creamy olive skin and lush chestnut hair, Bethenny flashed an Ultra Brite smile and waved to the girls, gliding her palm from side to side, much like Queen Elizabeth waving to the commoners.

"She's not so hot," Heather muttered, prompting all who heard her to wonder if she needed her eyes examined.

"Our third judge," Candace was saying, "is none other than Antoine 'Tex' Turner of Turner BMW, Alta Loco's number-one car dealership."

A hunky dude in western gear, Tex graced us with a high-testosterone grin.

"Howdy, gals!" he said, doffing his cowboy hat and revealing a headful of thick, Brad Pitt hair.

A soft murmur of approval rippled through the audience.

"And last but not least," Candace said, yanking her charges back from their fantasies, "I'd like to introduce your pageant emcee, star of stage, screen, and television—my hubby, Mr. Eddie Burke!"

At which point a short, stocky guy in a bad toupee came bounding out on stage, waving to the audience.

This was a star of stage, screen, and TV? Really? On what planet?

"I just flew in from New York," he announced, "and boy, are my arms tired."

Good heavens. Pterodactyls were telling that joke in *Jurassic Park*.

He waited in vain for some laughs, then took a seat at the end of the table next to Tex, where he proceeded to scratch his toupee, moving it ever so slightly askew on his head.

"We'll be doing Q and A with the judges and Eddie in a few minutes," Candace said, "but right now I want to remind you of our upcoming schedule of events.

"Tomorrow we're having the swimsuit and talent competitions, and on Sunday, the ball gown production number and final crowning, during which one lucky young lady will become Alta Loco's Teen Queen and receive this genuine Tiffany tiara!"

She held up the tiara I'd seen in her office, the one with the strange clock in the center.

"It's got a built-in clock, so the winner will always remember this very special 'time' of her life!"

"It sure doesn't look like Tiffany to me," Heather whispered.

She was right, of course. As I was to later learn, the manufacturer of this silver-plated headgear was an outfit in Taiwan called Tiphany Novelties and Erotic Toys.

But at that moment the teens in the audience were gazing at it with unadulterated lust.

"Remember, girls," Candace was saying, "the next two days are going to be the most important two days of your life. The Teen Queen America title has been the stepping stone to all sorts of fabulous careers in show business, modeling, and TV weathercasting.

"Why, just a few months ago Bethenny here," she said, gesturing to the former teen queen, "was cast in an exciting TV infomercial!"

Bethenny nodded modestly as the girls in the audience swooned with envy.

"Of course," Candace continued, "there can be only one winner of the Teen Queen Tiphany Tiara. But that doesn't mean the rest of you are losers. Just by being here today, you've shown you've got what it takes to be a proud competitor."

Not to mention a thousand bucks in entry fees.

"Win or lose, these next two days will give you the chance to learn, to grow, and, most important, to make new friends—friends you'll treasure for the rest of your life."

As Candace babbled on about the value of friendship, my eyes wandered over to the judges' table. Glancing down below the banner hanging from the front of the table, I saw that the former teen queen had slipped her foot out of her stiletto heel and was now rubbing her toes up against Tex Turner's ankle.

Somebody was making friends, all right.

Very good friends, indeed.

Chapter 6

A nd now," Candace chirped, "it's time for Q and A with the judges!"

My cue to make my exit for my dinner date with Scott's parents.

Getting up from my seat, I saw Candace frown in disapproval, and as I scurried up the aisle, I could practically feel her eyes burning holes in my back.

I'm surprised she didn't have me arrested for going AWOL.

Back in the broom closet posing as my room, I threw off my clothes and jumped into the shower, which I soon discovered had all the water pressure of a leaky faucet. I sudsed myself as best I could with a complimentary sliver of Amada Inn soap, and patted myself dry with one of the graying towels hanging limply from the towel rack.

Never had I felt less refreshed.

I slipped into my new silk slacks with the matching kimono-sleeved top, my one and only pair of Manolo Blahniks, and some dangly silver earrings.

Then I slapped on some lipstick and mascara and surveyed my mop of curls, which—having been unsuccessfully jammed into the Amada Inn's

Barbie-sized shower cap—had sprung out like a chia pet. I thought briefly about blowing it straight, but did not want to risk electrocution with the Amada Inn's antique hair dryer.

A final spritz of perfume, then I grabbed my purse and was out the door.

While waiting for the elevator, I checked my phone and found a text from Scott with his parents' address. I was surprised to see they lived in Malibu. When I first met Scott he told me he grew up in my hometown of Hermosa Beach, and I'd figured his folks still lived there. Somehow I didn't picture a cop's blue-collar family living in tony Malibu. Oh, well. Maybe they lived in a modest pocket of town, just like my duplex in the slums of Beverly Hills.

After I'd Googled directions to their house, the elevator still hadn't shown up. So I proceeded to clomp down four flights of stairs in my Manolos. By the time I got to the lobby, I was sweating like an Olympic gymnast.

All that time in the shower, for nothing.

Oh, well. There was nothing I could do about it. So I got in my Corolla and headed for the freeway.

Traffic, of course, was a nightmare. The only time traffic in L.A. isn't a nightmare is between 3 and 5 AM and when I'm going for a root canal. Then everything flows like mustard on a frank-in-a-blanket.

I sat in my ancient Corolla as traffic inched

ahead, simultaneously cursing and trying not to sweat into my kimono-sleeved blouse. It was a hellish hour and fifty minutes, but at last I made it to Malibu and found myself on a winding road lined with gated estates.

This sure as heck wasn't a modest pocket of town.

I pulled up at Scott's parents' address and peered through the gates. My jaw dropped when I saw what looked like a small castle in the distance.

Smiling awkwardly into a security camera, I pressed a buzzer, and seconds later, the gates swung open. Then I drove my Corolla up a tree-lined path, eventually reaching the castle-like home I'd seen from the road, a sprawling affair with enough wings to host a Teen Queen America convention.

Was it possible, I wondered, that Scott's parents worked as caretakers for a fabulously wealthy family?

Getting out of my Corolla, I groaned to see my beautiful silk top was a mass of wrinkles. If only I'd remembered to pull it out from under my seat belt. Now the darn thing looked like a road map of the Rockies.

I headed for the Willises' elaborate front portico, desperately trying to smooth out the creases. But it looked like they were set for life.

What's worse, when I checked my watch, I saw that it was close to eight. And I was supposed to have been there at seven.

I rang the bell, an hour late and draped in wrinkles.

Soon a sweet, cherubic woman came to the door, the same kind of rosy-cheeked woman I'd imagined Scott's mom would be.

Unfortunately, this was not Scott's mom.

It was the maid, Rosita, who greeted me with a warm smile and ushered me down a hall into a gargantuan wood-beamed living room, dotted with overstuffed furniture, French doors leading out onto a terrace, and a fireplace big enough to house a Cessna.

A regal woman with a slightly beaked nose unfurled herself from where she was sitting on one of the overstuffed chairs. Her black hair, streaked with gray, was swept back at the sides in perfect wings.

Like me, she was dressed in silk pants and flowy top. But unlike my Nordstrom special, hers had undoubtedly cost thousands of bucks. And needless to say, there was nary a wrinkle in sight.

Rosita announced my presence before skittering away down the hallway.

The woman with the beaked nose, who I could only assume was Scott's mom, looked me up and down with cold gray eyes.

"A pleasure to meet you . . . at last."

The latter said with a pointed glance at her watch.

"I'm so sorry I'm late. I got stuck in traffic. I hope I didn't hold things up."

"Not at all," she assured me. "We finished our hors d'oeuvres ages ago."

I glanced over at a glass-topped coffee table littered with the remains of cocktail hour munchies.

"I'm Scott's mother, Patrice," Ma Willis was saying, "and this is my husband, Brighton."

"Bri!" She called out to a red-faced guy sitting on a recliner, nursing a scotch and watching The Weather Channel on a TV mounted above the fireplace.

"Bri, say hello to Scott's friend, Jan."

"Um. Actually, it's Jaine."

"As if I give a rat's patootie."

Okay, so what she really said was, "Oh, right." But I could read between the lines.

Scott's dad tore himself away from a storm in Topeka and tossed me a halfhearted, "Hello, there."

"Sit down, Jaine," Ma Willis said, "and help yourself to whatever's left of the hors d'oeuvres. The pâté's gone, but I think there are a few crackers left. Dinner should be ready any minute. I'll go check with Rosita."

She slithered off, and I sat down on a sofa across from Scott's dad, who seemed to have totally forgotten my existence, his eyes still glued to that storm in Topeka.

By now, I was starving. It seemed like ages since I'd scarfed down those franks-in-a-blanket at the Amada Inn.

I checked the coffee table and found a few cheese rinds, some abandoned shrimp tails, and exactly one uneaten cracker.

I snapped it up eagerly.

I was looking around, wondering where the heck Scott was and hoping to find a stray bowl of nuts, when I noticed a half-finished glass of champagne in front of me.

For an instant I was tempted to slug it down, but I didn't dare. What if Pa Willis lost interest in The Weather Channel and caught me in the act?

I was staring at the champagne longingly when I realized there was bright coral lipstick on the rim of the glass.

Funny. Ma Willis's lips had been colored a deep blood red.

Suddenly I began to feel uneasy. Whose lips, I wondered, belonged to this coral lipstick?

I was about to find out, because just then Scott came walking in through the French doors with a lithe, blond, willowy creature. With startling blue eyes and sun-bleached hair pulled back in a headband, she practically radiated blue blood and old money.

Her simple jeans and T-shirt made my wrinkled kimono getup seem wildly over the top. She and

Scott were laughing gaily as they entered the living room—a little too gaily for my tastes.

"Jaine!" Scott cried, catching sight of me. "I'd like you to meet an old friend of the family. Chloe Landis."

"Lovely to meet you," the willow grinned, revealing a mouthful of impossibly white teeth.

"Scott and Chloe used to be engaged."

This newsflash delivered by Ma Willis, who came sailing into the room with a mischievous gleam in her eye.

"But that's all over now!" Scott hastened to assure me, shooting his mother a dirty look as he hurried to my side.

Impervious to his glare, Ma Willis smiled brightly and said, "Let's all head in for dinner, shall we?"

Then she turned to her husband, who still sat rapt in front of The Weather Channel. "Brighton!" she shouted. "Time for dinner! Turn off the damn TV!"

Stirring from his stupor, Scott's dad clicked off the TV, then pressed another remote. And before my astonished eyes, a painting that looked like an original Renoir came sliding down from the wall to cover the TV screen.

So this was how the one percent lived.

We trooped across the hall to a dining table set with an exquisite Battenberg lace tablecloth and enough crystal to stock a branch of Bloomingdale's.

Pa Willis took a seat at the head of the table while Scott and I sat down next to each other, across from Chloe, who sat by herself at the other side of the table. My fanny had no sooner hit the chair than Ma Willis hoisted me up by the elbow.

"Oh, no, Jaine!" she cried. "You can't possibly sit here. You must switch seats with Chloe, so you can have an ocean view."

And before I knew it, Chloe had whipped across the room to sit thigh by thigh with Scott and I was all by my lonesome at the other side of the table.

"But, Mom," Scott protested. "It's dark out. Jaine can't see the ocean."

"Maybe not," Ma Willis conceded. "But she can see the moon and the stars and our new patio furniture."

Scott shot his mom another dirty look, which she proceeded to blithely ignore.

"Want some wine, Jan?" Scott's father asked, holding out a bottle of cabernet.

I nodded eagerly. Something told me I was going to need a wee bit o' alcohol to make it through this dinner.

Pa Willis poured me a generous slug, and passed the bottle around to the others.

"So, Jaine," Ma Willis asked with an icy stare, "what is it that you do?"

"I'm an advertising copywriter."

"She wrote *In a Rush to Flush? Call Toilet-masters!*" Scott beamed proudly.

"Is that so?" Ma Willis replied, as if she'd just seen a rat prancing across her Battenberg lace tablecloth.

"How wonderfully kitschy," Chloe said, practically blinding me with her perfect smile. "Who are some of your other clients?"

I started reeling them off, eager to make a good impression.

"Oh, I've got Mattress King Mattresses, Ackerman's Awnings—"

"Where *Everything's Just a Shade Better!*" Scott piped up. "Jaine wrote that!"

"And there's Fiedler on the Roof Roofers," I continued. "And Tip Top Dry Cleaners."

"*We clean for you. We press for you. We even dye for you!*" Scott chimed in.

"Really?" Pa Willis said, suddenly jumping into the conversation. "Can you get this stain out of my tie?" He flapped his tie in my face. "I got pâté on it."

"Jaine *writes* for a dry cleaner's, Dad. She doesn't work there."

"Oh," Pa Willis said, disappointed.

"Jaine's really very talented," Scott insisted, my one-man cheering squad.

But Ma Willis was not impressed.

"Chloe used to model for Tommy Hilfiger," she pointed out with pride.

"Oh, Patrice," Chloe blushed. "That was ages ago."

"Now she's a marine biologist."

I smiled weakly.

"Okay, I give up. Chloe wins."

No, I didn't really say that. I just took a slug of wine and said, "How interesting."

A few painfully awkward moments passed, during which Pa Willis scratched at the pâté stain on his tie, Scott fidgeted with his fork, and Chloe smiled sweetly at Ma Willis.

At last, Rosita came hurrying in from the kitchen and started passing out bowls of soup.

Oh, foo. It was plain old consommé. Not a thing in it. Chicken noodle soup without the chicken and the noodles and the flavor.

Everyone slurped at it in silence.

I was dying to reach for the basket of rolls Rosita had set down on the table, but no one else was eating them, so I refrained.

Desperate to make conversation, I said to Ma Willis, "You have such a lovely home."

"It is, isn't it?" she replied. "Too bad we don't get to stay here more often. We spend most of our time at our country house in the Cotswolds."

"The Cotswolds?"

"It's in England, dear."

I knew that.

"We're avid horse people," Ma Willis explained. "We love to ride."

"Horses," Chloe added, clearly having pegged me as mentally deficient.

"I don't suppose you ride, do you, Jaine?" she asked, with a smug smile. "You don't seem the type."

I'd have given anything to wipe that smile off her face.

And out of nowhere I suddenly heard myself saying, "As a matter of fact I do."

"Really?" Scott asked, eyebrows raised in surprise.

Oh, what the hell. It was a long way from the Cotswolds. They'd never know the truth.

"Yes, I've been riding ever since I was knee high to a saddle."

With that, I threw caution to the winds and reached over to grab a dinner roll.

And that's when tragedy struck.

I watched in horror as my flowy kimono sleeve brushed against my glass of cabernet and knocked it over—spilling red wine all over the Willises' exquisite white lace tablecloth.

"Gosh, I'm so sorry!" I cried, watching the stain spread into a big red blob.

"Don't worry, Patrice," Pa Willis said. "Jan can clean it. She works at a dry cleaners."

"She *writes* for a dry cleaners!" Scott cried, exasperated.

"I'm afraid I've ruined your beautiful tablecloth." I moaned.

"No matter, dear," Ma Willis said, her voice dripping icicles. "There's another one at the Victoria and Albert Museum. We can go visit it when we're back in England."

The rest of the dinner passed in a mortifying blur. Rosita's pork chops tasted like ashes in my mouth. In the background, I could hear Ma Willis and Chloe chatting away, and every once in a while I looked up to see Scott shooting me an encouraging smile. But all I could focus on was the big red blob of wine on the tablecloth. I was so depressed, I could barely finish my second helping of julienne potatoes.

At last the meal came grinding to a halt, and I excused myself, explaining that I had a long drive back to Alta Loco. By now, I could not wait to get out of there. And I was sure that, as far as Ma Willis was concerned, the feeling was mutual.

"I'll walk you to your car," Scott said, jumping up to join me as I started to leave.

"I can't believe I spilled that wine on your mom's tablecloth," I said, as we headed out into the night.

"Accidents happen," Scott said, taking my hand in his. "It's no big deal."

"It is a big deal. Your mom hates me. She hated me even before I spilled the wine."

"She doesn't hate you, Jaine. She's tough with everybody. You should've seen her when she first met Chloe. She gave her the same frozen treatment she was giving you tonight. That's just her way. She'll warm up to you, just like she warmed up to Chloe."

"About Chloe," I said. "Are you sure it's really over between you two?"

"Never been surer. And by the way," he added, "I had no idea she was coming to dinner tonight. That was all Mom's idea."

"Does Chloe know it's over? She seemed awfully chummy."

"I don't know what's in Chloe's head, but I know what's in mine. There's only one woman in my life right now," he said, his big brown eyes gazing into mine. "And that woman is you."

With that, he took me in his arms, and leaned in for a kiss. At last. Something fun was about to happen.

But just as our lips were about to meet, floodlights snapped on all around us.

I whirled around to see Ma Willis standing at the front door, arms crossed over her chest, Chloe at her side.

"It's dark out there, Jaine," she said, with her patented icy smile. "We didn't want you to have another accident."

She hated me, all right.

Chapter 7

I drove home in a deep funk. I could not have made a worse impression on Scott's parents if I'd showed up with an AK-47 strapped to my elastic-waist pants.

Damn those kimono sleeves. They should come with a safety warning.

By the time I got back to the hotel, it was after eleven and I couldn't wait to climb into bed.

I let myself into my broom closet and was just about to get undressed when there was a knock on my door.

I opened to it to find Taylor standing there in her pajamas.

"You got the M&M's?" she whispered, like a spy in a John le Carre novel.

"Of course," I said, stifling a yawn as I ushered her inside.

"I thought my mom would never fall asleep," she groaned, flopping onto my bed. "She's been watching me like a hawk all day. She made me order the broiled fish at dinner and wouldn't even let me have a roll. I'm positively famished!"

"Here you go," I said, tossing her a bag of M&M's with peanuts.

She ripped into it eagerly and popped one in her mouth.

That's the difference between naturally skinny girls and the rest of us.

Never in a zillion years would it occur to me or you to eat M&M's one at a time. Would it?

"Want some?" she asked, holding out the bag.

"I really shouldn't," I said, grabbing a few. All of which went sailing into my mouth simultaneously.

"Say," she said, "would you mind awfully getting me a Coke from the vending machine? Regular, not diet."

"Sure," I replied, feeling a bit peppier after my dose of chocolate.

Grabbing my wallet, I headed down the hallway till I came to an alcove where the vending machines were located.

I was standing there, trying to iron out the creases in my dollar bill so it would fit in the vending machine slot, when I heard voices along the corridor.

At first they were muffled, but then I heard a man say, "But Candace. I don't have that kind of money. I'm just a high school principal."

It was Dr. Fletcher, he of the bow tie and grim lips. And apparently he was talking to Candace, our esteemed pageant director.

Who, by the way, seemed totally unmoved by his plea.

"Better find the money quick," she said. "I want

ten grand, or I'll tell everybody the truth about you."

By now I'd plastered myself against the far wall of the alcove, so as not to be caught eavesdropping on this little drama, and continued to listen to Dr. Fletcher throw himself on Candace's mercy as they headed down the hallway.

What was that all about? I wondered once their voices had faded away.

Clearly Candace was blackmailing Dr. Fletcher. But about what? It seemed hard to believe that the mild-mannered academic had any skeletons in his closet. On the other hand, I wasn't the least bit surprised to learn that Candace was doing a spot of blackmailing.

Somehow I sensed that behind her pageant smile beat the heart of a street thug.

Back in my room, Taylor was stretched out on my bed, gratefully chomping down on M&M's.

"So how was dinner?" I asked, plopping down on the bed beside her.

"Awful," she replied. "Mom spent most of the meal trying to smell everybody, looking for the Vera Wang thief. I thought I'd die of embarrassment. And I had to sit there eating that icky fish, while Elvis was eating steak tidbits. Can you possibly think of a worse meal?"

"Unfortunately I can," I said, images of Ma Willis flitting through my brain.

We spent the next fifteen minutes or so sucking up chocolate as Taylor shared her dreams of some day becoming a great writer.

"Just like Isabel Allende," she said. "Only American, of course. And taller. With a really cute husband."

When she'd had her fill of M&M's, she bid me a fond farewell and headed back to her room.

By now it was after midnight and even my sugar rush couldn't stem the tide of my exhaustion. I quickly got undressed and brushed my teeth, counting the seconds till my head hit the Amada Inn's rock-hard pillow.

But just as I was about to pull back the comforter, there was a knock on my door.

Could it be Taylor, back for some more M&M's?

With a sigh, I shuffled over to the door and opened it.

Imagine my surprise when I saw Lance.

"Lance! What are you doing here?"

"I'm going down to Palm Springs with Gary."

"Who's Gary?"

"The UPS guy! I finally got up my courage and asked him out. We had dinner tonight at the most divine sushi place, and over California rolls we decided to spend the weekend at Gary's condo in Palm Springs. Isn't that the most exciting news ever?"

At which point I heard a piercing yowl and

87

looked down to see a cat carrier. With Prozac inside. She looked none too happy.

Stuff a sock in it, willya, and get me out of this cage!

"I almost forgot," Lance said. "I came to drop off Prozac. Gary's allergic to cats."

I unlatched the carrier and Prozac came charging out, taking stock of her new surroundings. Alas, she was not impressed. I could tell by the dismissive thump of her tail.

I've seen bigger rooms in a Roach Motel.

Then she scampered onto the bed and curled up on its one and only pillow. I knew from past experience it would take an atom bomb to wrench it from her.

It looked like I'd be sleeping without a pillow that night.

"Here's her litter box," Lance said, lugging it in from the hallway. "And by the way, the clerk at the front desk said they charge an extra fifty bucks a night for pets."

Oh, groan. What would Heather say when she heard about this?

"Awfully close to the freeway, aren't you, hon?" Lance said, gazing out my window. "Wow, I can almost read that guy's speedometer! Oh, well. At least one of us will be staying someplace nice this weekend."

Then, checking his watch, he exclaimed, "Gotta run! Mamie's waiting for me in the car. I don't

88

suppose you'd consider taking care of her while I'm at Gary's, would you?"

"No, I would not!"

"Okay, okay. Just asking."

And off he scooted into the night, grinning the same idiotic grin he always grins when he thinks he's in love.

I only hoped Gary's condo had wood rot.

YOU'VE GOT MAIL

To: Jausten
From: Shoptillyoudrop
Subject: Only a Matter of Time

It's just as I suspected. Daddy's taken apart Nellybelle's engine and has the pieces scattered all over the garage. He'll never in a million years be able to put it back together again! And thank heavens he wouldn't dream of doing the sensible thing and calling a mechanic.

It's only a matter of time before the garbage men are carting it away.

Meanwhile, I'm off to pick up my dress for the fashion show—
XOXO,
Mom

To: Jausten
From: DaddyO
Subject: Only a Matter of Time

Dearest Lambchop—
You'll be happy to know I've been hard at work tinkering with Nellybelle's engine. It's only

a matter of time before I have her purring like a kitten!

Love 'n' snuggles from

Daddy

P.S. It's strange. I thought for sure your mom would tell me to call in a professional to fix Nellybelle like she always does when we have trouble around the house. But oddly enough, she hasn't said a word. In fact, she's been encouraging me to do the job myself. I guess at long last she's come to appreciate my skills as a handyman.

To: Jausten
From: Shoptillyoudrop
Subject: Gorgeous Dress!

Hi, Sweetheart!

I'm back from Pink Flamingo with my dress for the fashion show, and it's absolutely gorgeous! As nice as anything I've ever seen on the shopping channel. A white silk top with bateau neck and peplum waist over a black pencil skirt. Unfortunately, thanks to that fudge I ate the other night, it's a wee bit tight round the peplum waist.

I absolutely must lose five pounds in time for the fashion show. Time to get rid of all the sweets in the house. I'll put everything in the freezer out in the garage. We had it pad-locked last year after a raccoon clawed it open and ran off with our hamburger meat. Honestly, those raccoons are brazen little critters, aren't they?

I'll have Daddy change the combination on the lock so I can't possibly open it.

Instant weight loss guaranteed!

Tata for now—

Your about-to-be-much-thinner,

Mom

To: Jausten
From: DaddyO
Subject: A Guy Just Can't Win

Dearest Lambchop—

It looks like Mom's on one of her crazy diets again. She just stored all our desserts in the freezer in the garage and had me change the combination on the lock. She made me promise not to tell her the combination no matter how much she begged and pleaded. I give her less than 24 hours before she starts begging and pleading. Then she'll get mad at me if I don't tell her. And even madder if I do.

A guy just can't win around here.

You know I adore your mom, Lambchop, but I have to confess sometimes she can go a little nuts. Luckily there's at least one sane member in this family.

Well, gotta go and rub baby oil on Nellybelle's carburetor.

Love and hugs from

Daddy

Chapter 8

I slept badly that night, plagued by ghastly dreams, no doubt induced by the M&M's I'd inhaled before climbing into bed.

I was in the middle of a particularly harrowing nightmare where Ma Willis was chasing me around her dining room table with a giant bottle of cabernet, when I was jolted awake by what sounded like a jackhammer on my ceiling.

Was it possible the Amada Inn was actually doing construction work directly over my room?

When I called the front desk to complain, a weary clerk explained that it was just one of the pageant contestants practicing her tap dancing.

"I've been getting complaints all morning," he said.

"Aren't you going to do anything about it?"

"Sorry, ma'am. No way am I messing with a pageant mom. Not without a stun gun."

I hung up with a sigh and turned to see Prozac lolling on the pillow, which she'd been hogging all night.

"I'm glad one of us slept well," I snapped. "In case you're interested, my neck is stiff as a board."

If I expected any sympathy, I was sadly

mistaken. All my tale of woe elicited was a ginormous yawn.

Yeah, right, whatever. So when do we eat?

Then she leaped on my chest, yowling at the top of her lungs, clawing me for her breakfast.

It was then that I looked around and realized Lance had forgotten to bring cat food.

Damn that man!

I hauled myself out of bed and was just about to get dressed when my phone rang. It was the clerk down at the front desk.

"Can you please keep your cat quiet?" he said, rather snootily. "The people in the next room are complaining."

Oh, great. Pageant moms with prima donna teens were off limits. But lowly writers with prima donna cats were fair game. I certainly hoped the Amada Inn didn't expect to get five stars on Yelp from yours truly.

After throwing on some jeans and a T-shirt, I headed down to the lobby to get Prozac some chow from the breakfast buffet.

Between my stiff neck, my tap-dancing neighbor, and that irritating call from the front desk, I must admit I was not in the sunniest of moods. But I perked up considerably when I saw the breakfast spread: scrambled eggs, ham, bacon, Danish, and delightfully gooey sticky buns.

I was dying to grab a fork and dive into the stuff,

but first I had to get some food for my hungry princess.

I was just wrapping some ham in a paper napkin when Taylor came sidling up to me, flip-flops clopping, her hair in giant rollers.

"Skip the ham, Jaine," she whispered, "and get me a sticky bun. All my mom let me have for breakfast was some crummy wheat bran cereal."

"Actually," I said, "the ham's not for you. It's for my cat."

"Your cat?" She blinked in surprise. "I didn't see a cat in your room last night."

"She came after you left."

At which point Heather came sweeping over to us, clad in a body-hugging jog suit, diamond bangles dripping from her wrist. The only place she was jogging to in that getup was Van Cleef & Arpels. In her arms she held Elvis, who wore a baby blue T-shirt with the words PAGEANT DOG emblazoned across his tiny chest in rhinestones.

"Whatever you do, Jaine," she said, glaring at her daughter, "don't let Taylor have a sticky bun. Can you believe she wants to eat pastry less than an hour before the swimsuit competition?"

"It's not fair," Taylor pouted. "Even Elvis got to eat bacon!"

"You'll thank me when you're wearing that tiara," Heather said, oozing motherly righteousness.

"Which reminds me, Jaine," she added, turning

to me, "when you've got a few minutes, would you mind tapping out an acceptance speech for Taylor to deliver when she wins the contest?"

"But the contest hasn't even started yet," Taylor protested. "How can you be so sure I'll win?"

"Because you're the prettiest, most talented girl in the hotel. Don't forget," said the former Gilroy Garlic Queen. "You've got pageant genes in your blood."

Then Heather caught sight of the ham in my napkin.

"They've got plates for the food, you know. Right over there, at the end of the buffet."

"It's for her cat," Taylor said.

"Your cat?"

"My friend was supposed to watch her this weekend, but an emergency came up and he dropped her off at the hotel."

"Isn't that nice, Elvis?" Heather cooed. "A kitty for you to play with."

Elvis, clearly not eager to make friends, just bared his tiny fangs.

"And I just found out," I said, inwardly cringing, "that the hotel charges an extra fifty dollars a night for pets."

"Not a problem, hon." Heather smiled brightly.

Thank heavens she wasn't angry.

"I'll just deduct it from your paycheck."

Double damn that Lance!

I headed back upstairs with Prozac's breakfast,

and as I was about to let myself into my room, I realized I'd forgotten to put out the DO NOT DISTURB sign. Major mistake. Experience has taught me it's always best to keep Prozac away from a maid with a cart full of freshly cleaned towels.

I made a mental note to put the sign on when I left again.

Back inside, Prozac was hard at work scratching the Amada Inn's rickety chest of drawers.

"Prozac!" I cried. "What on earth are you doing?!"

She looked up from her endeavors with pride.

I like to think of it as Post Abstract Impressionism.

Snatching her up in my arms, I wondered how much extra I was going to be charged for room damages.

Then I fed her the ham—which she gulped down in no time—and left some water in a cereal bowl I'd nabbed from the buffet line.

Before hustling out the door, I gave her a stern talking-to, and I'm proud to say that when I left the room, she wasn't clawing the chest of drawers anymore.

Now she was the clawing the bedspread.

I was standing in the hallway, hoping the Amada Inn's only working elevator would actually show up, when I saw Bethenny, the former teen queen, tottering toward me on impossibly high heels, her curvaceous body jammed into a slinky black dress. Frankly, she looked less like a pageant queen than a call girl cruising for a john.

I thought back to yesterday's Mocktail Hour, when I'd seen her playing footsies with Tex Turner, the auto dealer. Something told me she and Tex were more than just fellow judges.

"Hi, there!" she said, flashing me her Ultra Brite smile. "Are you here with the pageant?"

"Sort of. I'm helping one of the contestants prepare for the talent show."

"Really?" she replied, eyeing me with pity. "Better stock up on tranquilizers."

Then, no doubt realizing she wasn't living up to her image as Teen Queen spokesperson, she quickly added, "Only kidding, of course. Pageants are such an exciting part of a girl's life! I remember the year I won," she gushed, launching into what sounded like a speech she'd given many times before. "What a thrill. It's the best thing that's ever happened to me, that's for sure. I've met so many wonderful people and done so many wonderful things. I'm just so darn grateful to Candace and her fabulous team!"

Another twinkly smile.

"Gosh, the elevator's slow, isn't it?" she said, her smile now straining at the edges.

She gave the button a vicious stab with a neon pink nail, and at last we heard the elevator ding.

The doors opened to reveal Candace and Tex Turner. Both of whom sprang apart hastily at the sight of us.

Candace's hair was mussed, her bright red lipstick smeared, and I couldn't help but notice a vivid swipe of that lipstick on Tex's cowboy shirt.

Clearly we'd just interrupted a smooch session.

Bethenny stared at them, fire in her eyes, as we got on the elevator.

Tex had the good grace to blush, but Candace eyed us coolly, as if she'd been up to nothing more than checking the schedule on her clipboard.

"Hello, you two!" she chirped brightly. "Ready for today's exciting contests?"

"Um, sure," I managed to say, holding up my end of the conversation.

But Bethenny just stood there, glaring at Candace.

I could easily picture those neon nails of hers gouging the pageant director's face to ribbons.

It seemed like a small eternity, but at long last we reached the lobby.

Tex and Candace hurried out of the elevator, but Bethenny seemed frozen to the spot.

"I can't believe Tex is cheating on me with that tramp of a pageant director," she hissed.

"Are you sure you're okay?" I asked, gently leading her out into the lobby.

"Yeah, I'm fine. But Candace won't be when I get my hands on her."

Uh-oh. Looked like more trouble in pageant paradise.

Chapter 9

Back at the buffet, I scarfed down a highly nutritious breakfast of coffee and a sticky bun, checking my cell every few minutes for a text from Scott. Alas, there were none. By the time I'd licked the last of the sticky bun from my fingers, I was pretty much convinced I'd never hear from Scott again, thanks to that god-awful dinner at his parents' house.

And so it was with heavy heart that I opened my emails and read the latest missives from my parents. Daddy was right, of course. It was only a matter of time before Mom would be begging him for a treat from the freezer. Poor thing. Dieting doesn't come easy to her.

Thinking how much Mom would enjoy it, I helped myself to another sticky bun and headed off for the swimsuit competition.

The less said about the contest, the better. All in all, it was a most depressing affair—so many perfect young bodies parading around, tummies flat as washboards, skin sleek as silk.

How come I never looked that good when I was sixteen? Oh, well. I only hoped a few of the lithe lovelies were hiding zits under their makeup.

Up on stage, Eddie, sporting a freshly teased toupee, was doing his idea of comic patter.

("Welcome, everyone, to the Miss Teen Queen America Contest, where a raving beauty is the girl who comes in last, haha.")

The three judges sat at a table facing the stage, supposedly making notes on the contestants.

But Dr. Fletcher wasn't paying much attention to the bevvy of beauties before him. Instead he was shooting desperate glances at Candace, who sat at a separate table with her assistant Amy. Once again I wondered what on earth Candace was holding over him.

And Dr. F. wasn't the only one staring at Candace. Next to him, Bethenny was practically breathing fire as she gave Candace the evil eye.

Of the three judges, only Tex seemed to be interested in the girls on stage—a little too interested, in my humble op, winking and smiling and doffing his cowboy hat at the ripest of the crop.

Meanwhile, at my side, Heather was conducting a running snarkfest, trashing each contestant, pointing out nonexistent skinny legs, big butts, and flat chests.

"None of them can hold a candle to my Taylor!" she boasted.

And when it was finally Taylor's turn to strut her stuff, I must admit she looked amazing. Just as I'd suspected, under her sloppy sweats, she was hiding a spectacular body.

Over at the judge's table, Tex doffed his cowboy hat with a flourish.

"Applaud!" Heather instructed me, jabbing me in the ribs.

I proceeded to clap loudly as Heather called out, "Woo hoo! Way to go, Taylor!"

It had been that way with all the moms, each of them bursting into applause when their daughters appeared, bolstered by hoots from their posse of friends and relatives.

Even Elvis, cuddled in Heather's arms, began yipping. Although I suspect he was just annoyed at being woken from his nap.

Up on stage, Eddie was saying, "And here's Taylor Van Sant from Alta Loco, a perfect 34-22-36."

From several rows behind us, I could hear Luanne cackle, "But unfortunately not in that order."

The other moms around her broke out in a round of giggles.

Heather whirled around in her seat, furious. For a minute I was afraid she was going to get up and slug Luanne, but just then Elvis whined for a dog treat and Heather restrained herself.

But only momentarily.

Heather was out for revenge, and she got it moments later, when Gigi showed up on stage. Then it was payback time.

As Gigi paraded her hot young bod in her swimsuit, Eddie said, "Gigi exercises every day, which is why she's got a flawless hourglass figure."

"Too bad it's all sinking to the bottom," Heather sniped in a voice that could be heard clear across the room.

Candace looked over and shook her head in disapproval.

But Heather didn't care. She just sat there, gloating.

Soon the last teen had strode across the stage in her swimsuit and the competition was over. A winner was announced.

Much to Heather's disappointment, it wasn't Taylor. But rather, a stunning blonde from Fullerton.

"She's not so hot," Heather and Luanne said in unison.

For once, they were on the same team.

"Those judges must be blind!" Heather said, as she zipped Taylor into her technicolor Carmen Miranda outfit.

I stood awkwardly at their side, holding Elvis, who was busy baring his fangs at me.

(Believe me, the feeling was mutual.)

We were in a large hall adjoining the banquet room, set aside as a makeup and changing room for the girls. Everywhere frantic moms were squeezing their daughters into skimpy outfits and going over last-minute rehearsals for the talent competition, filling the room with the sounds of singing, tap dancing, and the occasional bonk of a baton landing on the floor.

"I can't believe they gave the swimsuit prize to that loser," Heather sniffed in disgust, as she ruffled the flounces on Taylor's dress. "But don't feel bad, honey. Just because you didn't win the swimsuit competition doesn't mean you can't win the grand prize."

Taylor looked up from my song lyrics, which she was still busy committing to memory.

"Mom, I don't feel bad. I don't care if I win."

"Of course you care. You're just putting on a brave front. Now remember. At the end of your song, when you take the peach from your headdress and toss it to one of the judges, throw it to one of the men. Don't waste it on the bimbo teen queen—"

She stopped suddenly, staring across the room.

"My God! Can you believe how ridiculous she looks?"

We followed her gaze to where Gigi stood, dressed like Cleopatra in a diaphanous harem costume and black wig, her eyes thick with liner, an asp bracelet snaking up her arm.

In her hand she held a piece of paper from which she was reading. Thanks to my years as an English major, I recognized it as a bit of chatter from *Antony and Cleopatra*.

I listened as she mangled Shakespeare's lines with gusto:

Give me my robe, put on my crown! I have
Immoral longings in me. Now no more
The juice of Egypt's grape shall moist
   this lip:
Yeah, yeah, good Iris; quick. Methinks I
   hear
Anthony call!

The whole thing might have sounded a lot better
if she hadn't been chewing gum at the time.

"Yee-uck!" Heather exclaimed, just a little too
loudly, prompting some curses from across the
room. "Taylor's going to put that airhead to shame!
Wait till you hear her, Jaine. She's got the voice
of an angel. Which reminds me. I left her throat
lozenges in our room. I'll be right back. Stay calm,
honey. Deep breaths! Positive thoughts!"

The minute she was gone, Taylor turned to me,
a desperate gleam in her eye.

"Got any M&M's? I'm famished."

I was beginning to feel like a drug dealer
supplying a junkie as I dug into my purse looking
for the bag of M&M's I'd had the foresight to
stash there. I quickly retrieved them and handed
them to Taylor, who was famished, all right. She
actually put five in her mouth at once.

"I can't wait till this whole thing is over and I
can go back to my AP English class," she said,
chomping down gratefully.

She continued inhaling the chocolates until she

saw Heather heading back into the room, then stuffed the remaining M&M's in my purse and asked, "Do I have any chocolate on my teeth?"

"No, you're fine."

Breathing a sigh of relief, she pretended to be studying her song lyrics as Heather bustled to our side.

"Here we go! One-calorie cherry-flavored cough lozenges!"

"One whole calorie, huh?" Taylor said. "What a bonanza."

"Now let's try on your headdress," Heather said, choosing to ignore Taylor's dollop of sarcasm.

She lifted a cornucopia of plastic fruit and strapped it on Taylor's head.

"Mom, this thing weighs a ton!"

"Just pretend it's the winner's tiara. Keep your eyes on the prize, hon! Keep your eyes on the prize!"

"Yeah, right," Taylor sighed, gazing longingly at my purse.

Chapter 10

Fifteen minutes later, we were back in the Amada Inn's rooftop ballroom, waiting for the talent competition to begin.

Sitting alongside Heather in the front row, I had the uneasy feeling that there was something important I'd forgotten to do, but for the life of me, I couldn't think what it was.

Up on stage, Candace had wrestled the mike away from Eddie and was now tapping on it to make sure it was working.

"Welcome back, everybody," she said, her pageant smile firmly in place. "Before we get started with the talent show, I just want to remind all our contestants that we will be rehearsing the musical production number for tomorrow's crowning ceremony here in the ballroom from two to three p.m. this afternoon. So I expect to see you all back here at two o'clock. Promptly!"

She glared out at her subjects to drive home her point.

"Then the rest of the afternoon, it's fun in the sun! You're free to take advantage of all the fabulous facilities here at the gorgeous Amada Inn and rest up for tomorrow's grand crowning ceremony."

Fabulous facilities? At the Amada Inn? I could

only assume she was referring to the vending machines.

Having delivered her marching orders, Candace thrust the mike into Eddie's eager hands and headed back to her seat.

"And now," Eddie said, beaming from under his toupee, "one of the most exciting events of the competition, the Miss Teen Queen America Talent Show!

"Do your best, gals," he winked, "because there just may be a talent scout or two in the audience. Remember! Today, Alta Loco. Tomorrow, Hollywood!"

A vigorous round of applause filled the air as the pageant moms looked around the room for hidden talent scouts.

"For our first contestant," Eddie was saying, "let's all give a big hand to Betty Lynn Wallis, from Tustin, California, who's going to play Beethoven's *Moonlight Sonata* on her banjo!"

At which point a pretty young thing in a sequined tuxedo pranced out on stage and began playing Beethoven on her banjo, missing notes with wild abandon.

Poor Ludwig was undoubtedly spinning in his grave, but Tex the car dealer seemed to be enjoying it enormously, his eyes riveted on Betty Lynn's sequined chest.

And so it went, one wacko act after another.

Not content to merely sing or dance, the teen

queen wannabes (or, more likely, their moms) had felt compelled to jazz up their acts with some rather quirky twists.

One gal tap-danced to *America the Beautiful*. Another made animal balloons while roller-skating. And another (my personal fave) demonstrated the proper way to make a peanut butter and jelly sandwich.

Had there been any actual talent scouts in the audience, I'm betting they were gone soon after the peanut butter hit the jelly.

And then it was Taylor's turn.

"And now," Eddie crooned from the mike, "the song stylings of a peach of a gal, Miss Taylor Van Sant."

Taylor came sashaying out in her Carmen Miranda costume, her fruit bowl headdress perched on her head, shaking her hips to a Latin beat Heather had pre-recorded for the contest.

Frankly, I was surprised to see her perform with such gusto. I'd just assumed she'd sleepwalk through the whole thing, eager to get it over with.

I was beginning to think that Heather was right, that maybe Taylor actually had a shot at winning the grand tiara.

That is, until she opened her mouth.

That's when reality hit the fan, big time.

Taylor Van Sant was a gorgeous girl who looked quite fetching in a fruit bowl headdress, but alas, she couldn't even begin to carry a tune.

"I'm Taylor Van Sant and I'm here to say," she began to sing, in a voice that could shatter glass at fifty paces.

"What did I tell you?" Heather nudged me with pride. "Sings like an angel!"

A Hell's Angel, maybe.

Up on stage, Taylor was still caterwauling:

"—I want to be teen queen in the very worst way—"

From a few rows behind us I could hear Luanne guffawing, "You can't get much worse than that!"

Heather whirled around in her seat and hissed, "Shut up, you skank!"

Taylor continued to assault our eardrums, singing so badly, poor Tex was unable to focus on her cleavage.

At one point, Elvis, nestled in Heather's lap—no doubt thinking he was listening to the sounds of a dog in heat—let out a love moan in reply.

Thankfully, Taylor seemed oblivious to her own bad singing and continued to belt out her tune.

Aye aye aye aye
Taylor's so sweet
Aye aye aye aye
She can't be beat
Aye aye aye aye
Goodwill she'll preach
Aye aye aye aye
Taylor's a peach!

Then, as rehearsed, she reached for a peach on her headdress, specially designed to be detachable, and tossed it to the judges. Unfortunately she tossed it with just a tad too much gusto, bonking Bethenny on the head.

"Owww!" the former teen queen cried.

"I'm so sorry!" Taylor cried. "Are you okay?"

"We are now," Luanne shouted out. "Now that you've stopped singing."

"Of all the nerve!" Heather huffed, whirling around to face Luanne.

"I only speak the truth." Luanne smirked. "Earplugs, anyone?"

"Silence, ladies!" Candace raised an admonishing brow from where she sat on the sidelines. "Or your daughters will be penalized."

Heather and Luanne turned away from each other like two tomcats pulled apart in an alley. Meanwhile, Taylor was skittering off the stage, her headdress in her arms, darting sorrowful looks at Bethenny.

"I told you we shouldn't have come here," she said, plopping down next to us in the front row. "What if I gave Bethenny a concussion?"

"Oh, please," Heather said with an airy wave. "She doesn't have a concussion. Not with that thick skull."

After a brief intermission while Amy got Bethenny an ice pack, the chatter about Taylor's flying peach finally died down and the show continued to drag on, one quirky performance after another. I have to admit my mind wandered a tad, checking for texts from Scott, and still wondering what important thing it was I'd forgotten to do.

"And now," Eddie was saying, "performing Cleopatra's soliloquy from *Antony and Cleopatra*, here's Gigi Summers."

Clearly Luanne had spared no expense on Gigi's act. Two burly stagehands wheeled in a huge chaise longue littered with cushions. Stretched out among them in her Cleopatra outfit was Gigi, staring dramatically off into space.

When the stagehands had gone, she sprang to life and began reciting the speech we'd heard in the makeup room.

> Give me my robe, put on my crown! I have
> Immoral longings in me. Now no more
> The juice of Egypt's grape shall moist this
>   lip:
> Yeah, yeah, good Iris; quick.

Now she cupped her hand to her ear as if listening to something in the distance.

> Methinks I hear Anthony call!

At which point, a loud meow filled the air.
A very familiar meow.

Oh, lord. Could it be? Was it possible?

Indeed it was.

Before my horrified eyes, Prozac wandered out from behind one of the chaise longue cushions.

And at long last I remembered the important thing I'd forgotten to do: I failed to put the DO NOT DISTURB sign on my door when I'd left my room. When the maid came to clean, Prozac had undoubtedly bolted.

Now she blinked out into the audience.

Anybody seen the complimentary breakfast buffet?

"Prozac!" I cried.

"What's this cat doing here?" Candace asked, her voice hard as steel.

In fact, she'd just begun examining her privates.

"She's mine!" I admitted. "I'm so sorry."

But just as I was about to go to get her, a white ball of fur whizzed past me up to the stage. It was Elvis, undoubtedly miffed that another four-legged creature was hogging the spotlight.

He raced over to where Prozac was lolling on Cleopatra's chaise and started barking furiously.

If he thought he was going to intimidate Prozac, he was sadly mistaken.

On the contrary, Prozac looked down at him and sniffed.

Hey, I've smelled you before. You're the one Jaine's having an affair with!

And without any further ado, she leaped down

off the chaise, lunging at poor Elvis, who—
suddenly terrified—came skittering off the stage
as fast as his little legs could carry him.

Prozac, hot on Elvis's heels, now began chasing
him up one aisle and down another, both of them
yapping and meowing at the top of their lungs.

Wasting no time, I charged after them, and after
what seemed like a small eternity, I finally
managed to catch Prozac, scooping her up in my
arms before any fur could fly.

Heather came racing over to rescue Elvis, who
began baring his teeth most ferociously once he
was safe in her arms.

The next thing we knew, Luanne was at our
side.

"You!" she shouted at Heather. "You sabotaged
my daughter's act with your accomplice's cat!"

"I did no such thing!" Heather insisted.

"She had nothing to do with this," I said. "It's
all my fault."

"Look who's talking about sabotage," Heather
huffed at Luanne. "You're the one who stole my
daughter's Vera Wang gown."

"Don't be absurd! I didn't go anywhere near
your silly gown."

"Silly gown? It's a work of art compared to that
chintzy Cleopatra outfit your daughter's wearing.
She looks like a hooker at Caesars Palace."

"Well, at least my daughter has talent. She
doesn't sing like a leaky balloon."

"Leaky balloon?" Heather sputtered, her face a fiery red.

I just hoped it wasn't a cardiac flush.

"I've never heard worse singing in my life," Luanne sneered, now on a roll. "It was like asthma set to music."

That did it. Heather had reached her boiling point. Her daughter's angelic voice had been besmirched.

Holding Elvis under one arm, she hauled back with the other and whacked Luanne in the jaw, sending her sprawling to the ground.

In my arms, Prozac looked up, delighted.

Now that's entertainment!

At which point, Candace came stomping over.

"Okay, that's it," she snapped at Heather. "You're out."

"What do you mean?"

"Your daughter's disqualified. She's out of the competition. Pack up your things and go."

"But you can't do that!" Heather cried in protest.

"Yes, I can. It's in the official rules. Creating a public disturbance is grounds for disqualification."

"What about her?" Heather said, pointing to Luanne, who was still on the floor rubbing her jaw. "She started it."

"But she didn't resort to physical violence. Now pack up your things and get out."

"I demand my money back," Heather cried. "All my entry fees."

"Forget about it," Candace said, her face hard as nails. "That's in the rules, too. Entry fees are non-refundable."

"I'm not going anywhere," Heather said, hair extensions quivering with indignation. "I paid for two nights in this hellhole, and I'm damn well staying here. I'm calling my lawyer!"

With that, she grabbed Taylor by the elbow and headed for the door. But not before turning back and hissing at Candace:

"Better watch your back, lady. I'm gonna get you for this."

And off she stormed with Taylor, Elvis yipping in her arms.

"Damn!" I heard Candace mutter to Amy. "I'm going to have to call national headquarters about this. That woman is a walking lawsuit if I ever saw one. You'll have to take over for me at the dance rehearsal."

"Of course," Amy stammered, a trace of panic in her eyes.

"And you," Candace hissed at me, "get your scruffy little fleabag out of here."

Prozac swished her tail in indignation.

Hey, who're you calling "little"?

Candace shot me a filthy look, then headed up to the mike, cool as a vodka tonic, not a hair out of place.

"Let's not let that horrid display of bad manners spoil our fun," she said to the pageant moms, who were, on the contrary, in seventh heaven over this latest bit of drama. "But before we continue with the show, a change of plans about today's dance rehearsal. I've got some pressing matters to attend to in my office, so my assistant Amy will be pinch-hitting for me."

Amy smiled nervously at the crowd.

"And now, on with the talent," Candace said, passing the mike back to Eddie.

The last thing I heard as I headed out the door were the sounds of Chelsea Sternweiss from Riverside yodeling an aria from *Madame Butterfly*.

Chapter 11

I hurried over to where Heather and Taylor were waiting at the elevator, Elvis nestled in Heather's arms.

At the sight of Prozac, Elvis let out an angry yip. But Prozac just gazed up at him from hooded lids.

Cool it, powder puff. Can't you see I'm trying to nap?

Then, with a dismissive flap of her tail, she turned to me.

What a pill. I don't see what you ever saw in him.

Meanwhile, Taylor was whining, "Mom, can't we please go home?"

"Are you kidding? We're not going anywhere without my tiara—I mean, your tiara."

Oh, boy. I could see who was the real contestant in this pageant.

"One call to Daddy's attorney, and you'll be back in the contest before that pageant director knows what hit her."

Taylor sighed in defeat.

"No," Heather proclaimed, "none of us is going anywhere. And that means you, too, Jaine. Stick around, and I'll let you know the minute I have news."

Damn. It looked like I was in for another night in the Broom Closet Suite.

From my arms, Prozac meowed.

First dibs on the pillow!

Back in my room, I read Prozac the riot act about her disgraceful performance at the talent show.

"It's all your fault Taylor got kicked out of the contest. If you hadn't horned in on Gigi's act, Luanne never would have picked that fight with Heather, and Heather never would have wound up decking Luanne. You were a bad, bad, bad kitty! And Mommy's very disappointed in you."

She looked up at me with wide green eyes that could mean only one thing.

What's for lunch?

Yes, I could tell by the way she was doing her patented Feed Me dance around my ankles that she was feeling a bit peckish.

And she wasn't the only one.

It had been hours since my buffet breakfast, and I definitely needed a little pick-me-up. So I headed down to the Amada Inn's coffee shop, where I ordered a roast beef sandwich on rye for myself and a side order of tuna salad for Prozac.

Whatever the failings of the Amada Inn, I must admit they did a great job in the chow department. My roast beef sandwich (with a side of fries) looked positively scrumptious when I unwrapped it back in my room.

Prozac's little pink nose twitched with excitement the minute she saw me take it out of the box.

Yum! Roast beef! Just what I wanted!

"No, no, sweetheart. The roast beef's for Mommy. Look what I got you. Yummy tuna."

I held it out to her, but she sniffed in disdain.

No, thanks. Roast beef for me! And you're not my mommy.

Well, if she thought she was going to horn in on my roast beef, she had another think coming. I told her in no uncertain terms that she couldn't always have what she wanted. The roast beef was for me, the tuna was for her, and that's the way it was going to be.

I don't suppose you bought that, did you?

Of course, I let her eat the roast beef. I mean, what else could I do? She'd already poked her nose into the stuff. And besides, the tuna was really quite tasty. I even got to eat a few of the fries.

I was sitting there, munching on one of them, when my cell phone rang.

My heart did a little somersault when I saw it was Scott. I answered it, willing myself to be cool and collected.

"Scott! Thank heavens it's you! I thought you'd never call!"

Okay, so I've got to work on Cool and Collected.

"I feel horrible about last night. I made such a fool of myself."

"You did no such thing. You were perfectly charming."

"But spilling the wine like that—"

"Accidents happen. Nobody's blaming you."

Was he kidding? I could just picture Ma Willis stabbing pins in my voodoo doll.

"Anyhow," Scott was saying, "I called to see if you want to go to Santa Barbara with me on Wednesday. I've got the day off, and I thought we could drive up there for lunch."

"Just the two of us?" I asked. The last thing I wanted was a rematch with Ma Willis and Chloe.

"Just the two of us."

"Sounds heavenly."

And it did. After a weekend in the Broom Closet Suite, I'd be ready for a little treat.

"Great. I'll pick you up around ten?"

I hung up in a happy daze, already picturing myself whizzing up to Santa Barbara with Scott at my side. Just the two of us. No disapproving moms. No fabulously beautiful ex-girlfriends.

Damn that Chloe, anyway. Why the heck did she have to be so pretty—and thin? My goodness, I'd seen bigger thighs on Barbie dolls.

I stared down at my own two thighs, redwoods to Chloe's twigs, and groaned. I really had to whip myself into shape for my date with Scott. Was it possible, I wondered, as I popped the last of the fries into my mouth, to drop fifteen pounds by Wednesday?

And then I remembered the Amada Inn's gym, the one I'd passed by yesterday on my way to the sauna.

True, it had been a tad run-down, but then, so was I.

Within minutes, I'd changed into sweatpants and a T-shirt and was out the door, leaving Prozac sprawled on the bed, belching roast beef fumes.

This time, I was careful to hang up the DO NOT DISTURB sign.

So eager was I to get started on my workout that I didn't even wait for the Amada Inn's geriatric elevator to show up. Instead, I clomped down to the lower level and made a beeline for the gym.

Thank heavens it was empty when I got there. When it comes to exercise, I prefer to do my grunting and groaning in private.

Looking around, I saw three treadmills, two StairMasters, and a recumbent bike. I figured I'd get the best workout on the treadmill or the StairMaster, so naturally I headed for the recumbent bike. I mean, why exercise standing, when you can do it sitting? That's my motto, anyway.

After dusting off the seat (heaven knows when it had been last used), I climbed on board.

I was fully intent on pedaling my pounds away, but I hadn't counted on just how comfy it felt to lie back on that recumbent seat. If you recall, I'd been up since the wee hours, having been rudely awakened by the tap-dancing teen in the room above mine. And what with all the hoo ha of Prozac's surprise appearance at the talent show—not to mention Heather's brawl with Luanne, and trekking up and down the Amada Inn stairwell—I was tuckered.

I started off pedaling with vigor, but soon I felt my eyelids grow heavy. And before I knew it, I was out like a light, having the most wonderful dream.

There I was, cuddled on a chaise with Scott, wearing Taylor's Carmen Miranda outfit. (Somehow in my dream I'd magically morphed into a size two.) Scott was running his hands along my impossibly slim hips, setting my pulse racing with his smoldering gaze.

Then—just as he was leaning in to kiss me—guess who came sauntering out from behind the chaise in her two-hundred-dollar jeans and pristine white T-shirt? Chloe! How annoying was that?

Suddenly I felt like an overdressed rube with a bowl of fruit on my head. I was so darn angry at Chloe for breaking into my dream, before I could stop myself I was taking a peach from my headdress and throwing it at her. Only it wasn't plastic, but a real peach. And it sailed past Chloe and landed splat in the middle of Ma Willis's tablecloth which had sprung up out of nowhere, along with—gasp!—Ma Willis, who looked at the big peach blob on her priceless white tablecloth and started screaming at the top of her lungs.

I raced over to wipe off the stain, but the more I blotted it, the bigger it grew. And the bigger it grew, the louder Ma Willis screamed. Louder and louder until I woke up with a jolt and realized someone was actually screaming.

Jumping off the bike, I hurried outside into the hallway where I saw Candace, staring, horrified, into her office.

I followed her gaze and gasped.

There, lying in a pool of blood, face down, was mousy little Amy, her head bashed in with the prized "Tiphany" tiara.

Chapter 12

I t's all my fault!" Candace moaned, sinking to her knees. Gone was the tough martinet who'd ruled the pageant with an iron fist. In her place sat a frail, frightened woman.

"I don't understand," I said, kneeling down to talk to her. "How is Amy's death your fault?"

"The Coke," she said woodenly.

"What Coke?" I asked, wondering if the stress of the murder had sent her to la-la land.

"I spilled some Coke on Amy's red blazer at lunch," she explained. "So I gave her one of my blue blazers to wear. Amy always wore a red blazer, and I wore blue. Then I finished my phone calls sooner than I expected. So I decided to go to the dance rehearsal and left Amy behind to unload the trophies."

She pointed to a stack of cartons up against the back wall.

"We give out souvenir trophies to all the girls so they don't feel bad about losing. Anyhow, poor Amy probably had her back to the door unloading the trophies, so whoever killed her saw her blond hair and blue blazer and thought she was me. Especially in the hotel's crummy lighting."

It was true; the lighting in the office, just as in the Broom Closet Suite, was awfully dim.

"Everyone thought I was going to be in the office," Candace said. "I announced it over the mike. Whoever killed Amy was trying to kill me!" She put her face in her hands and moaned. "If only I hadn't spilled that Coke on her blazer!"

Looking down at Amy—dressed in Candace's blazer, her blond hair styled just like Candace's, working in the office at a time when only Candace was supposed to be there—I couldn't help but think that Candace was right, that Candace was the intended victim and that Amy had been murdered by mistake.

"What's going on here?"

Eddie came rushing up to us, his face flushed under his toupee.

"Amy's dead," Candace said, pointing to the corpse.

Eddie looked inside the office, and his face froze in shock.

And suddenly I wondered if he knew about his wife's affair with Tex. A short, stocky guy with a bad toupee, had Eddie flipped out at the thought of his wife making love with the hunky car dealer? Had he tried to kill her in a jealous rage?

Was that look of shock on his face because Amy was dead—or because he just realized he'd killed the wrong woman?

Eddie quickly recovered his composure and did what I should have done—called 911.

I stayed with them while Eddie tried to soothe Candace, patting her shoulder, assuring her everything would be okay. But Candace, swatting away his hand like a pesky gnat, was not about to be reassured. By the time the cops showed up, she was in an advanced state of panic, convinced someone was out to kill her.

"Call off the rest of the pageant, Eddie. We'll reschedule the crowning for another date."

"But the mothers will be furious."

"Who cares? I'm not going to stick around and wait for someone to take potshots at me."

Just then the detective on the case, a towering blond Brunhilde of a woman, came stomping over to join us. She stood before us, tall and big-boned, her blond hair scraped into a tight ponytail, muscles straining against the fabric of her uniform.

"Any of you have any idea who might have done this?" she asked, gesturing to Amy's body.

"I think I know!" Candace piped up. "It was that dreadful Van Sant woman."

"Who?"

"Heather Van Sant. One of the pageant moms. Just this morning she told me she was going to 'get' me! Isn't that right?"

Candace turned to me for confirmation.

"Well, technically, yes, but—"

"See? Heather's the one you want."

Brunhilde dutifully wrote down Heather's name in her notebook, then told us to go back to our rooms to await further questioning.

Just as I was about to head for the elevator, I heard one of the cops in the office say, "Looks like we have our time of death. The clock in the tiara stopped when the victim's head was bashed in. At two-thirty-four p.m."

My gosh. I'd shown up at the gym at a little after two. If only I hadn't fallen asleep, I might have heard the murder, seen the killer, solved the crime, and saved myself from my own little brush with death.*

(*Coming soon to a chapter near you.)

Pacing the floor of the Broom Closet Suite (a whole three and a half steps in each direction), I thought about the time of the murder. If it had taken place at 2:34 like the cops said, then Candace and all the teens except Taylor were in the clear. Because from 2 to 3 PM they were all at the dance rehearsal.

I just hoped Taylor wouldn't join her mother on Brunhilde's suspect list.

I continued to pace, wondering how long I'd be stuck in beautiful downtown Alta Loco, when there was a knock on my door.

It was Detective Brunhilde with her trusty notebook.

I ushered her inside and offered her the only seat

in the room, a battered armchair slathered with a fine layer of cat fur.

"Sit down, won't you?" I said, brushing off cat hairs as I spoke.

After eyeing the chair warily, she finally decided to risk it and sat down.

Meanwhile, Prozac looked up from where she'd been clawing the bedspread and sniffed in Brunhilde's direction.

Then, like a shot, she leaped off the bed and into Brunhilde's lap.

Brunhilde's face turned an interesting shade of purple.

"Get this little monster off me!"

Okay, so what she really said was, "What a cute cat."

But you didn't have to be a detective to figure out what she was thinking.

By now, Prozac was sniffing her like a bloodhound.

Hey, blondie. Got any knockwurst?

"Let me take her from you," I said, scooping Prozac in my arms.

A yowl of protest as I dumped her back on the bed.

Hey! I smelled knockwurst on her breath. Maybe she's got leftovers.

"Shall we get started with some questions?" Brunhilde asked, pencil poised over her pad.

"Ask away."

After getting my name and contact info, she got down to the nitty-gritty.

"You know anyone who might have wanted to kill Amy Leighton?"

I honestly couldn't think of a soul who'd want to kill Candace's mouse of an assistant.

"Not really."

"What about Candace? Can you think of anyone who might want to harm her?"

Take a number. There was Bethenny, who was furious with Candace for horning in on her affair with Tex. And Dr. Fletcher, Candace's blackmail victim. And of course, there was always Eddie, the cuckolded husband.

I told Brunhilde everything I'd seen and heard.

"Well," she said, foraging inside her ear with her pencil eraser, "you certainly are the observant little witness."

"Actually," I said, with a modest smile, "I've done some private investigating in the past."

"Really? And have you done this private investigating with the benefit of a license?"

"Not exactly," I admitted.

"Then I'd advise you to keep your nose out of this case."

"Yes, of course."

I barely refrained from clicking my heels together and shouting, "*Sieg Heil!*"

"By the way," she added, her eyes narrowed in suspicious slits, "I heard you and Ms. Burke had a bit of a run-in, something about your cat ruining the talent show."

"It wasn't a run-in. She told me to take Prozac back to my room, and I did. End of story."

"No lingering resentment on your part? Some people get awfully sensitive when it comes to their pets."

"I can assure you I didn't try to kill Candace."

"I'll be the judge of that."

Ouch.

"Well, that's about it," she said, getting up and brushing cat hairs from her tush. "You're free to go. We'll contact you if we need you."

"You mean I can check out of the hotel?"

"Yes. As far as I know, the rest of the pageant has been canceled."

Glory be. I'd be sleeping with a pillow tonight!

The minute Brunhilde left, I started packing. I was busy flinging my things into my suitcase when I heard another knock on my door.

This time I opened it to find Taylor, tears running down her cheeks.

"The police just questioned Mom," she said, stumbling into the room. "They think she was trying to kill Candace but killed Amy by mistake."

"Try not to panic, honey. They're questioning everybody."

"But they want Mom to come down to head-quarters for further questioning."

Yikes. That sure didn't look good.

"You've got to help!" she cried, wide-eyed with fear.

"You need some emergency M&M's?"

"No, you've got to prove Mom didn't kill Amy! I Googled you when Mom hired you, and I saw that you solved a whole bunch of murders."

At last—someone who appreciated my detecting skills.

"So will you help?" Taylor pleaded.

As overbearing as Heather was, I didn't believe she was a killer.

"Of course, honey. I'd be happy to help."

"Oh, thank you," she said, throwing her arms around me.

And with tears of gratitude glimmering in her eyes, she added: "I'll have some of those M&M's now, if you don't mind."

Out in the parking lot, I rolled my suitcase over to where Heather and Taylor were loading their BMW, Elvis peeking out from Heather's ginormous Gucci purse.

From her cat carrier, Prozac meowed.

How come Powder Puff gets toted around like a prince, while I've got to ride in this crummy cat carrier?

Ignoring her protests, I approached the BMW.

"Heather, I just wanted to thank you for picking up my hotel bill."

And indeed, I owed her a big debt of thanks.

When I went to check out, I discovered Heather had paid my whole tab, including the nightly pet fee, and three hundred dollars in extra charges for Prozac-induced damages.

Apparently my tattletale maid had felt the need to itemize every last cat scratch she'd observed.

"Don't worry about it, Jaine," Heather said with a wan smile.

"Are you guys okay?" I asked.

"Of course we're okay!" Heather said, trying valiantly to keep up her smile.

"But, Mom," Taylor protested, "they're taking you down to police headquarters!"

"Oh, honey. That kind of thing happens all the time. I'm not going to get arrested. Isn't that right, Jaine?"

"Right," I lied, picturing Heather being hauled off to jail, shielding her face with Elvis.

"Taylor tells me you're a part-time private eye," Heather said.

"It's just a hobby."

"But she's really good, Mom," Taylor piped up. "She's actually tracked down some dangerous killers."

Heather looked me up and down.

"Really? *You?*"

She shook her raven extensions in disbelief.

I wasn't surprised by her reaction. I get it all the time. Just goes to show you can't judge a detective by her elastic-waist pants.

"You think you can clear my name?" Heather asked.

"I'll certainly try."

"Thanks so much." Were those tears of gratitude I saw welling behind her Pradas? "Naturally, I'll pay you for your time."

"We'll work that out later," I said, feeling guilty for taking more money from her after she'd coughed up that extra dough for Prozac's room rampage.

I watched as they got in their BMW and drove off, then started over to my Corolla. I was trying to ignore Prozac's whining when suddenly I heard a piercing, "Yoo hoo!"

I turned to see Luanne sprinting to my side, Gigi in tow.

"I heard on the grapevine that the police think Heather killed Amy," Luanne said, breathless with excitement.

"Is that so?"

"It couldn't have happened to a more deserving gal!" she beamed.

I turned on my heels to go, feeling more than a tad irritated. I'd grown fond of Heather and resented this ferret of a woman who couldn't wait to see my client locked up behind bars.

"Wait!" Luanne cried, thrusting a scrap of paper in my hand. "Here's my phone number. I really liked the lyrics you wrote for Taylor. And I thought you might want to write some for my Gigi."

She turned to her gum-chewing prodigy.

"Wouldn't that be nice, honey?"

"Yeah, I guess," Gigi shrugged.

I shoved Luanne's phone number in my pocket, murmuring something about having a lot on my plate.

No way was I going to write for this woman. No way. No how. Never.

Not unless, of course, she offered to pay me.

YOU'VE GOT MAIL

To: Jausten
From: DaddyO
Subject: No Willpower Whatsoever

Frankly, Lambchop, I don't mind telling you that your mom has been driving me crazy. Ever since I changed the combination on the freezer lock, she's been bugging me to open it so she can have a little "sweetie."

Your mother is a wonderful woman, and you know I love her dearly, but she has no willpower whatsoever. She could learn a thing or two about self-control from your iron-willed DaddyO.

Well, time to work on Nellybelle. It's been a bit tougher than I thought, but I've made great strides. I should have her up and running any day now.

Love 'n' snuggles from
Daddy

To: Jausten
From: Shoptillyoudrop
Subject: The Most Infuriating Man

Your father is the most infuriating man. All I asked for was a teensy Oreo, and you'd think

I'd asked him to break into Fort Knox. Yes, I know I told him not to let me have anything from the freezer, but I wasn't talking about a single Oreo. I just needed a little sugar to get me through the morning. But would he give it to me? Nooo. He came on all Holier than Thou, blathering about willpower and self control, and all the while I could smell chocolate on his breath.

I just know he's been into my fudge.

Off to a meeting of the library board. I only hope they serve cookies.

XOXO,
Mom

To: Jausten
From: DaddyO
Subject: Don't Tell Mom

Good news, Lambchop! I'm almost done putting old Nellybelle's engine back together. Just a few tweaks and she'll be ready to roar! I can't wait to take her out for a spin in my new plaid golf cap! (Did I tell you it's got a pom-pom on top, just like they wear in Scotland?)

XOXO,
Daddy

P.S. Don't tell Mom, but I think I'll go have some fudge to celebrate.

To: Jausten
From: DaddyO
Subject: Don't Tell Mom, Part II

You'll never guess what just happened, Lambchop. I was walking by Mom's closet when I accidentally brushed against her dress for the charity luncheon and knocked it to the floor. If you ask me, it was very foolish of her to leave it hanging from the closet door, where any innocent bystander could knock it down.

Nevertheless, it fell to the floor, and naturally I picked it up. And I guess I must have had a little grease on my fingers from the fudge, because suddenly I realized I'd left a stain on the back of the white top.

Now an ordinary man in my position would have panicked. But not your daddy. You'll be proud to learn I kept my cool and came up with a brilliant plan in my hour of need. I raced to the garage and got some exterior white latex paint, and simply painted over the stain. Your mother will never even know it's there.

Another crisis averted by
Your loving
Daddy

To: Jausten
From: Shoptillyoudrop
Subject: Up to Something

Hi, sweetheart—I'm back from the library board meeting, where Lydia Pinkus (bless her!) served the most delicious butter cookies. And, keeping to my diet, I limited myself to just two. (Okay, three.) That's the last dessert I'm eating until after the fashion show, I swear!

Meanwhile, here at home, Daddy has been skulking around with the guiltiest look on his face, like a cat who just ate the goldfish. Plus, he wants to take me to dinner at Le Chateaubriand— and we don't even have a coupon for a free entrée.

He's been up to something. I just know it.
XOXO,
Mom

To: Jausten
From: DaddyO
Subject: Inscrutable as a Sphinx

Mom's back. At first I was scared she might discover what I'd done to her dress. But I've been cool as a cucumber, inscrutable as a sphinx.

She doesn't suspect a thing.
Love 'n' hugs from
Daddy

Chapter 13

How wonderful it was to be back in my own bed, with a pillow all to myself. No teens tap dancing on the ceiling. Just the sweet sounds of Mrs. Hurlbutt hollering at Mr. Hurlbutt across the street.

Prozac and I slept in the next morning, Prozac no doubt still tuckered from her riveting stage debut at the Amada Inn. It wasn't until close to nine that she finally clawed me awake for her breakfast.

Yes, the day started out pleasantly enough. That is, until I opened my emails and read the latest from Tampa Vistas.

Oh, well. I couldn't worry about Mom's fudge-stained dress, not when I had a killer to track down.

Settling down with my coffee and cinnamon raisin bagel, I checked the *L.A. Times* for news of the murder. Sure enough, there it was on page one of the city section. Under the headline DEATH BY TIARA were twin photos of Amy and Candace in their pageant blazers. As in life, Amy's smile was tentative while Candace beamed boldly into the camera.

According to the story, the police were calling Amy's death a probable case of mistaken identity, with the killer really gunning for Candace. Thank goodness there was no mention of Heather as a suspect.

When I called her a few minutes later to find out how things had gone at police headquarters, Heather told me they'd asked her "a million questions," served her appalling coffee, and warned her not to leave town.

At least she wasn't behind bars. And I planned to keep it that way.

I decided to start my investigation with Bethenny. I remembered the look of rage I'd seen on her face when she caught Candace in the elevator with Tex. She'd sure seemed homicidal to me.

Turning to my trusty pals at Google, I discovered that Bethenny had her own website, a colorful affair dotted with airbrushed photos of the former teen queen in various bikinis. I checked out what had to be a highly fictional bio (she claimed to have studied acting with Uta Hagen Dazs). Then, when I clicked on her APPEARANCES page, I saw to my delight that she was scheduled to preside over the opening of a bowling alley in Burbank the next day.

I made up my mind to be there.

But for now I intended to stay home and recuperate from the stressed-filled adventures of the past two days. I spent the next several hours still in my jammies, reading the newspaper and vegging out with the *New York Times* crossword puzzle.

Heaven, sheer heaven.

After a lazy afternoon watching *Frasier* reruns, Prozac snoozing at my side, I finally managed to pry myself from my bed and headed for the bathroom. Soon I was soaking in a mountain of strawberry-scented bubbles, simultaneously pondering the nature of good and evil and whether to order Chinese or pizza for dinner.

Pizza won.

I ordered sausage and pepperoni (with extra anchovies for Prozac), and a half hour later the delivery guy was at my door, handing me a piping hot pizza, the sausage and pepperoni swimming in a sea of gooey cheese.

Oh, yum!

I'd just settled down on my sofa and was about to dig into my first slice, when I heard someone knocking at my door.

My keen powers of detection told me it was Lance, mainly because he was shouting, "Open up, Jaine. It's me, Lance!"

Reluctantly abandoning my pizza, I trudged to the door and opened it. Lance came sailing in, clad in immaculate khakis and a pink rugby polo (his Palm Springs look).

"It's official!" he cried. "I've met Mr. Right!"

I stifled a yawn.

Lance meets Mr. Right about as often as he gets his roots done.

"Gary's such a fantastic guy. So smart and literate—he's really a screenwriter, just does this UPS stuff to pay the bills. And he's so ripped from lifting all those packages. I could watch him flex his calf muscles for hours!"

And he was off and running, singing Gary's praises, yammering about his eyes, his abs, his calves of steel.

Throughout Lance's paean to Gary, I nodded on autopilot, scarfing down pizza and tossing anchovy tidbits to Prozac. I was trying to decide whether to run out for Rocky Road or Chunky Monkey for dessert, when I heard him say: "So what do you think?"

Oh, hell. He'd just asked me a question. Usually he's so caught up in the saga of his own life, he doesn't stop for questions.

"Which is it?" he was asking. "The desert or the beach?"

"Um. The beach," I said, figuring I had a fifty percent chance of getting it right.

"I agree. Palm Springs is great, but I've always wanted to have a beach wedding."

Good lord. The guy had gone from calf muscles to wedding plans in the time it took me to scarf down a single slice of pizza. (Okay, three slices.)

I thought about telling him he was moving

way too fast, but I knew I'd just be wasting my breath.

Finally he ran out of steam and helped himself to a slice of pizza, plucking the sausage and pepperoni from his slice. The guy sure knew how to take the fun out of pizza.

"So," he asked. "How did your weekend go? How was the beauty pageant and your date with Scott?"

Now it was my turn to babble. In one long litany of woe, I told Lance all about my nightmare date at the Willises', how they turned out to be filthy rich with houses in Malibu and the Cotswolds, and how Scott's gorgeous ex-girlfriend had horned in on dinner; how I'd gotten a tad tootled and spilled wine on the Willises' priceless tablecloth; and, as if that weren't enough, how Prozac hijacked the talent show at the beauty pageant and got into a fight with Elvis, and how Amy wound up getting murdered and how I'd slept through the whole thing on my exercycle and how the cops suspected Heather who I knew couldn't have done it in spite of her big mouth and flying fists.

When I was all through, Lance stared at me with wide blue eyes.

"Scott's parents have a house in the Cotswolds? Maybe Gary and I could have our wedding there."

"Lance, did you not hear a word I just said? Someone got killed at the beauty pageant!"

"Oh, I heard that part, hon. Very sad, I know. Tsk tsk and all that. But life is for the living. And that means us. We really can't let Scott slip through your fingers, not if we want to have our double wedding in the Cotswolds."

"We're not getting married, Lance. At least, I'm not."

"Not with that attitude, you're not. You've got to think positive."

Then he put his arm around me.

"Don't worry, hon. I'm going to be by your side, guiding you every step of the way till you land Scott at the altar. I'll be the wise and urbane Henry Higgins to your wretched Eliza Doolittle."

"Thanks a bunch," I snarled.

"Not a problem, sweetie. That's what friends are for. Well, gotta run! I'm meeting Gary for drinks!"

And he sailed out the door, the most annoying man in the world.

The only thing that gave me the slightest bit of comfort was the piece of anchovy I'd stuck to the seat of his khakis.

Chapter 14

I tootled out to Burbank the next afternoon for the grand opening of the Strike It Rich Bowling Alley, a low slung bunker of a building with a huge neon bowling ball blinking merrily on the roof.

After parking in a lot half full of cars, I headed over to join the motley group of bowling enthusiasts gathered for the festivities.

A ribbon had been strung across the bowling alley's front doors. Bethenny stood in front of it, poured into a tight black tank dress, smiling at a sweaty guy who I assumed was the owner of the place. In her hands, she held a pair of giant scissors.

The sweaty guy, clad in a T-shirt that said BOWLERS DO IT IN ALLEYS, cleared his throat and spoke into a handheld mike.

"Welcome, everyone, to the grand opening of the Strike It Rich Bowling Alley, where we always have time to 'spare' for you!"

He and he alone chuckled at his lame gag.

"And now, to cut the ceremonial ribbon, let's give a warm welcome to former Miss Alta Loco Teen Queen, Bethenny Martinez."

Bethenny flashed her pageant smile at the crowd.

Nearby I heard a pimply-faced goon whisper to his pals, "She can bowl in my lane any time she wants."

I figured that he and his buddies, all wearing identical puce-colored bowling shirts, were in some sort of bowling club.

"Ms. Martinez," the owner was saying, "will you do the honors?"

Her pageant smile firmly in place, Bethenny leaned in to cut the ribbon, exposing a bit of her cleavage and prompting some heavy drooling from the bowling club.

Apparently someone had forgotten to sharpen the blades on the ceremonial scissors, because as much as Bethenny hacked away at the ribbon, she couldn't seem to cut it.

Eventually a questionable looking fellow from the bowling club whipped out a hunting knife and offered it to Bethenny, who finally managed to hack the ribbon apart.

A Strike It Rich photographer snapped a picture amid tepid applause, and we all headed inside, where Bethenny was scheduled to bowl the first ball.

Although Early Army Barracks on the outside, Strike It Rich's interior was quite elaborate. In addition to an armada of bowling lanes, polished to a high gloss, the place sported a plushly carpeted bar and spacious dining area.

Bethenny had swapped her stilettos for bowling

shoes and was now standing in the center lane, ready to bowl.

I'd pegged Bethenny as the kind of girly girl who'd just plop the ball down and let it wobble into the gutter. But, no. She pulled the heavy ball way back, biceps bulging, then sent it barreling down the lane.

Wow. That was some powerful arm. Powerful enough, if you ask me, to have clobbered someone to death with a Tiphany tiara.

The bowling goons cheered wildly as Bethenny scored a strike, then rushed over to her side to have her sign their bowling balls.

I waited patiently while she chatted up the crowd, signing bowling balls with smiley faces. One of the guys from the bowling club unbuttoned his shirt and bared his chest for her to sign.

"I'll never wash it again," I heard him say.

The scary thing was, he probably meant it.

When the crowd had at last broken up, I made my move.

"Hi, Bethenny," I said, trotting to her side.

She shot me a puzzled look. "Do I know you?"

"Yes, I'm Jaine Austen. We met at the pageant the other day."

Still clueless.

"At the elevators," I prompted.

At last, she remembered.

"Oh, yeah, right. Well, nice to see you." She started to scoot off, and I scooted right after her.

"Hey, wait up! I never did get a chance to tell you I'm a big fan of yours."

She whirled around, suddenly all ears. "You are?"

Time to trot out one of the fun facts I'd gleaned from Bethenny's website.

"Gosh, yes! Why, I've been following your career ever since I first saw you on the soap opera, *The Rich & The Entitled*."

"Where I played Diner #2 in the coffee shop?"

"Yes, you were so riveting in that scene eating your fries, I wasn't even looking at the actors with the speaking parts."

"I know!" she said, her eyes lighting up. "That's what everyone told me! That's why they didn't ask me back. The diva playing the lead got jealous."

"That's so unfair!" I said, with all the fake indignity I could muster.

"Well, it's been great talking to you," she said. "Would you like me to autograph a cocktail napkin?"

"I'd love that. And if you wouldn't mind, I've got some questions I'd like to ask you."

"About what?" she asked, eyes narrowed, suddenly suspicious.

Oh, hell. Somehow I got the feeling she wasn't about to open up to me about the murder. Not here. Not now. Not while she was still stung by the memory of getting dumped from *The Rich & The Entitled*.

"Actually, I'm a freelance writer, and I'd like to write a story about you for the *Los Angeles Times*."

"You write for the *L.A. Times*?"

"Indeed I do."

Which wasn't a total lie. I did write a check for them each month for my subscription.

"How wonderful!" she said, breaking out her pageant smile again. "Of course. Let's sit down."

She led me over to the bar area, which was pretty much deserted at that time of day.

"Sweetie!" She snapped her fingers at a brittle blonde behind the bar. "Stoli martini straight up with a twist."

These teen queens grow up so fast, don't they?

"What about you?" she asked me.

"I'll have a ginger ale," I replied, determined to stay clear-headed for our tête-à-tête.

"So tell me all about yourself," I said.

"Aren't you going to take notes?"

"Oh, right. Notes."

I whipped out my cell phone, and clicked on a nonexistent app.

"I've got a recorder built right in to my phone. Just speak up, and I won't miss a word."

Speak up she did. I spent the next forty minutes guzzling Strike It Rich beer nuts and listening to the saga of Bethenny's life: Where she was born (Azusa, California); how old she was when she won her first pageant (two); how she spent the years after winning Miss Alta Loco Teen Queen opening supermarkets and bowling alleys around the greater Los Angeles area; how she wrote about her experiences in her new book, *Bethenny's Beauty Secrets*; how she was currently grooming herself for a career on the stage studying acting with Uta Hagen Dazs; and how she was soon to appear in her first starring role in a convection oven infomercial.

"That's quite a story," I said, when she finally wound down and I'd licked the last of the salt from the beer nut bowl.

"Yes, it is, isn't it?" she beamed.

"I'm so glad we ran into each other that day at the pageant." Then, trying desperately to segue to the murder, I added, "What a shame about poor Amy."

"I know," Bethenny tsked. "I heard on the news that she was killed by mistake, that the killer was really aiming for Candace."

"I don't suppose you saw anyone going into the pageant offices at around two-thirty that afternoon, did you?" I asked.

"Nope. I was in my room, giving myself a facial. Skin like mine doesn't just happen, you know," she added proudly. "I give the recipe for my facial in my book, in case you're interested."

"Oh, I am. I can't wait to read it."

By now I'd lied so much, I was qualified to run for Congress.

"Do you have any idea who might have wanted to see Candace dead?" I asked.

"It pains me to say it," she said with a vindictive gleam in her eye, "but my money is on Tex Turner."

Hell hath no fury like a teen queen scorned.

"As you may have already guessed, Tex and I were romantically involved—until Candace came along."

All the more reason for Bethenny to want her out of the way.

"After I saw them in the elevator, I confronted Tex, and he told me he hadn't meant to get mixed up with Candace, but she'd come on so strong, he just couldn't say no."

"And that's why he wanted her dead? Isn't there a less violent way to end a relationship?"

"No, he wanted her dead because Candace was threatening to tell his wife about their affair."

"Tex is married?"

"Total ball and chain," Bethenny nodded. "He doesn't love his wife, but she's filthy rich. Which is why he's stayed with her all these years. His wife's bankrolling his car dealership, and he can't afford to lose her."

She gnawed pensively at her lemon twist.

"Tex had me wrapped around his little finger. He knew I'd never say anything to his wife about our affair. But not Candace. She was threatening to blow the whistle. Tex was scared senseless."

Whaddaya know? Looked like I had a shiny new suspect to add to my list.

"Well, I'd better get going," I said, slapping some bills on the bar to pay for our drinks. "It's been a pleasure."

"When will my story be in the paper?"

"Your story?"

"For the *L.A. Times*."

"Oh, right. Your story. I'll call you as soon as I have a date," I said, feeling a tad guilty about lying to her.

"Super!" Bethenny cooed. "And don't forget to come to my book signing. I've got a chapter on taming the frizzies you'll find very interesting!"

Okay, now I didn't feel so guilty.

I drove home, wondering if Bethenny was right about Tex. Had the hunky car dealer bludgeoned Amy to death in a bungled effort to save his marriage?

Or was Bethenny the killer?

She'd claimed to be in her room giving herself a facial at the time of the murder. Not much of an alibi, with nary a witness to prove it. And what about *Mrs.* Tex Turner? Had she found out about Tex's affair and come tearing over to the Amada Inn, intent on knocking off her husband's lover?

Back at Casa Austen, Prozac greeted me with a soothing purr and a loving ankle rub.

Oh, please. In my dreams. The minute I walked in the door, she came hurtling to my side with a bloodcurdling yowl that could mean only one thing:

Where have you been? Do you realize it's been an hour and a half since my last snack? Which, by the way, was a piece of pepperoni I found under the sofa. Don't you ever vacuum? So when do we eat? I'm starving!

After tossing her some Hearty Halibut Guts, I made a beeline for my computer to run a search on Tex's wife. I found tons of pictures of her and Tex at various charity events. She was an aristocratic-looking dame, pale and ash blond with a sharp nose and broad, bony shoulders.

Nancy Clark Turner was her name, heir to a hefty tobacco fortune.

One look at her steely eyes, staring out into the camera, and I figured she had the cojones to try to kill her husband's lover.

But just as I was about to add her to my suspect list, I pulled up a picture of her on *The New York Times* website, attending an opera in New York the day of the murder.

Three thousand miles away from the scene of the crime.

With a sigh, I crossed her off my suspect list and went to the kitchen to whip up a nice healthy poached chicken salad for my dinner.

Okay, so it wasn't a poached chicken salad. It

was a Hungry-Man dinner, with extra mashed potatoes, and apple cobbler for dessert.

Sue me.

Later that night, Prozac and I were in bed watching *Sunset Boulevard* (Prozac is a huge William Holden fan). I gazed at all my DVDs scattered on my dresser. So darn messy. All because Prozac couldn't keep her paws off my new DVD armoire. I made a mental note to buy some cat repellent and rescue my armoire from the hall closet at the earliest possible opportunity.

It was disgraceful, really, the way Prozac ruled my life.

From now on, I had to start putting my foot down and showing her exactly who was boss.

And I would, too. Just as soon as I finished giving her her after-dinner belly rub.

Chapter 15

A slick young guy in a pinstriped suit and hair stiff with gel came ambling over to me as I pulled into the lot of Tex Turner BMW.

"Time to get rid of the old clunker, eh?" he said, with a jolly laugh.

Clunker?! He had his nerve talking that way about my vintage Corolla!

"Actually I'm here to see Mr. Turner," I said, sliding out of the car, hoping he wouldn't notice the chocolate stains on my seat cushions.

"Tex doesn't handle day-to-day sales," Mr. Hair Gel informed me.

"I'm here on a personal matter."

"Really?" His eyes widened in surprise. "You sure don't look like Tex's type."

Clearly Tex was servicing a lot more than BMWs at his dealership.

"Tex is up in his office," Mr. Hair Gel said, and led me into the showroom—a sleek chrome and marble affair.

Three shiny new Beemers glistened on the showroom floor.

It was the middle of the week, and there were practically no customers. Just a dazed couple flailing to stay above water with a piranha salesman in one of the sales cubicles. The rest of the sales staff were either working on their computers or pretending to.

"Tex's office is upstairs," Mr. Hair Gel said, pointing to a stairway at the side of the show-room.

"Thanks."

"And if you ever decide to dump your clunker," he said, handing me his business card, "just give me a call."

"Will do," I lied.

I dropped his card into the detritus of old receipts and linty Lifesavers at the bottom of my purse, then scurried up the stairs to a reception desk. There I was greeted by a wide-eyed kewpie doll with tousled red hair.

I just hoped it wasn't tousled from a round of dipsy doodle with Tex.

"Hi, there!" she said, with a toothy grin. "Can I help you?"

"I'm here to see Mr. Turner. I'm Jaine Austen. From the Miss Teen Queen America Pageant," I added, hoping Tex would think I was one of the pageant officials.

The kewpie doll picked up her phone and dialed Tex's extension.

"Jaine Austen to see you, sir. From the pageant."

Apparently Tex bought my story because the kewpie doll hung up and flashed me a welcoming smile. "Come on in."

She stood up to reveal a knockout figure, clad

in a skirt so short it was practically a belt, and I followed her as she sashayed into Tex's office.

Unlike the showroom downstairs with its hip young metrosexual vibe, Tex's office was furnished in a woodsy cabin style, with a map of Texas on one wall, an autographed picture of John Wayne on another, and a shotgun mounted over his desk.

Tex sat behind the desk in his cowboy getup, boots propped up, his Stetson flung on a hat rack in the corner of the room.

"Thanks, Jolene," he said to the kewpie doll as she slithered out of the room, his eyes riveted firmly on her tush.

Man, what a lech. I was beginning to feel awfully sorry for Mrs. Tex.

"So, Miss Austen, you're from the pageant?"

He swung his feet off the desk and reached out to shake my hand. Then, taking a closer look at me, he said, "Hey, wait a minute! I know you. You're the one with the cat who barged in on the talent competition."

I nodded weakly.

"Quite a little ham you've got there," he winked.

"Don't I know it," I said, still cringing at the memory.

He gestured to a wet bar in the corner of his office.

"Can I get you something to drink? Water? Coke? Bourbon on the rocks?"

The last suggested as his eyes raked me over from top to bottom.

"No, thanks. I'm fine."

"Then what can I do you for?" he said with a most unsettling leer. "I see a beautiful gal like you behind the wheel of a shiny new Beemer."

"Actually, Mr. Turner, I'm here to talk to you about Amy Leighton's murder."

That sure wiped the leer off his face.

"Oh? What about it?"

"The police think Heather Van Sant may have killed Amy in a mistaken attempt to murder Candace."

"So I've heard."

"Anyhow, Heather has hired me to track down the real killer."

"You?" He blinked in surprise. "Don't tell me *you're* a detective?"

"Part-time, semi-professional."

Once more, his eyes raked me up and down. "Well, don't quit your day job."

And just like that, Tex Turner became my first choice for Suspect I'd Most Like to See in a Prison Jumpsuit.

"Heather isn't the killer," I said, ignoring his crack.

"How can you be so sure? After all, she threatened to 'get' Candace in front of a banquet room full of pageant moms."

"Pretty stupid thing to do if she'd planned to kill her."

"Maybe Heather's a stupid woman."

"Well, I don't think so, and I'm trying to get her off the hook. Did you happen to see anyone, anyone at all, heading toward Candace's office the afternoon of the murder?"

"Me? No. I was here in my office the whole afternoon. Drove back to the dealership right after the talent show."

"So you were nowhere near the Amada Inn at the time of the murder?"

"Of course not!" His eyes narrowed into suspicious slits. "I don't know what you're implying, Ms. Austen, but I had absolutely nothing to do with Amy's death."

Something told me I'd just fallen out of his flirt zone.

"Jolene, honey," he said, buzzing his intercom. "Come in here a minute."

Seconds later, Jolene came bopping back into the room.

"Yes, Mr. Turner?"

"Jolene, where was I last Saturday between two and five p.m.?"

"You were right here in your office, Mr. Turner."

Spoken like an actor, on cue. But just a little too quickly, a little too stiffly, her eyes darting uncomfortably around the room.

Little Miss Jolene was lying. Of that I was certain.

I didn't know what Jolene had seen on the afternoon of the murder, but she sure as heck hadn't seen Tex here in his office.

Tex bid me a not-so-fond farewell—"The next time you're in the market for a new car, try your local Toyota dealer"—and I headed out to the parking lot to wait for Jolene.

I had a strong premonition she'd be leaving the building shortly. How did I know? Maybe it was my years of experience as a part-time semi-professional PI. Or maybe it was because I heard her telling someone on the phone she'd be leaving for her lunch break in ten minutes.

And so I sat in my Corolla, waiting for Jolene to make her appearance.

Sure enough, ten minutes later, out she came.

I dashed out of my car and followed her as she made her way over to a bright yellow VW Beetle at the far end of the lot.

"Hey, Jolene!" I called out.

"Oh, hello, Ms. Austen," she said, turning to face me.

Was that a hint of fear I saw in her eyes?

"*Detective* Austen," I said, flashing her a USDA meat inspector badge I'd picked up years ago at a flea market. You'd be surprised how often I've been able to pass it off as a police detective's badge. Especially to gullible young kewpie dolls like Jolene.

"You're a cop?" She blinked in surprise. "I thought you worked with the beauty pageant."

"That's just an alias," I said, tossing my meat inspector badge back in my purse before she could get a better look at it. "I'm working under-cover. Alta Loco SVU."

"Wow." Her mouth hung open just a tad. "Just like on TV." Then she lowered her voice to a whisper. "Do you have a gun? Is it in a holster inside your blazer? Is that why your hips look so lumpy?"

Somehow I resisted the impulse to slap her silly.

"No, I'm not carrying a gun."

"Really? Then you might want to try wearing Spanx. They're great at getting rid of love handles and muffin tops."

"Thanks," I said through gritted teeth. "I'll make a note of that." Then, switching to my best undercover cop voice: "Getting down to busi-ness, I need to ask you a very important question."

"Okay." She shot me a nervous smile.

"Were you telling the truth in Mr. Turner's office?"

"Of course," she said, her eyes darting around the parking lot, looking anywhere but at me.

"He was here at the dealership between two and five p.m.?"

"Um . . . yeah," she said, picking at a cuticle.

"Are you prepared to swear to that in a court of law?"

"I guess." Her eyes were still darting madly, like a rabbit in a trap, or my ex-husband, The Blob, on our wedding day.

"You know the penalty for perjury, don't you? Fifteen to twenty. And aiding and abetting a murder? That's twenty to life. Accessory to murder? Even worse."

Of course, I was making all this up as I went along, but she didn't know that.

"But don't worry. It's not so bad in the slammer. Just watch out in the showers for gals named Spike."

That seemed to do the trick. The straw that broke the kewpie doll's back.

"Okay, okay!" she wailed. "I left the office to do some errands. So I'm not really sure Mr. Turner was here the whole time."

"How long were you gone?"

"From about two to three-thirty."

Bingo. That would have given Tex plenty of time to hustle over to the Amada Inn and bop Amy to death.

"Oh, God," Jolene said, raking her fingers through her mop of red hair. "If Tex finds out I told you the truth, I'll be in big trouble. What if he fires me?"

"Don't worry. He won't fire you."

"You promise?"

"I promise," I assured her, wondering how the heck I was going to keep my word.

I watched Jolene drive off in her yellow Beetle, a Garfield bobblehead nodding forlornly in her rear window. When I turned back to my Corolla, I saw Tex coming out from the showroom.

"Tex!" I cried. "Wait up!"

He looked around at the sound of his name, but when he realized it was me, he kept right on going, sliding into a fancy new BMW parked outside the showroom entrance.

But he wasn't about to get rid of me that easily.

Racing across the lot, I managed to reach his passenger window just as he'd turned on the ignition.

"Tex, I need to talk to you."

Apparently Tex wasn't in the mood to chat. Instead, he rammed on the accelerator and zoomed out of the parking lot like a bat out of hell.

Or, more to the point, like a man with something to hide.

Chapter 16

Heading home, I decided to make a very important pit stop. Well, two very important pit stops. The first at McDonald's, for a much-needed Quarter Pounder and fries. And the second at Pet Palace, a gargantuan pet supply store.

Lest you forget (I sure hadn't), I still needed to find a way to keep Prozac's claws off my shiny new DVD armoire.

After perusing the various pet repellents on display, I finally chose a can of something called Cat-Away. The copy on the spray can assured me that its pleasant pine scent formula was non-toxic and guaranteed to keep my cat off my furniture for at least thirty days. Just a spritz once a month, and all would be well in DVD land.

I hurried home, eager to put it to the test.

Back in my apartment, I took the DVD armoire out from where I'd stashed it in the hall closet and hauled it back into my bedroom. Then, ripping the tape from the carton, I pulled out the cherrywood beauty and set it down between my TV and my dresser.

At which point, Prozac, who had been hard at work napping on the living room sofa, came prancing into the room.

She gazed at the armoire with delight.

Goodie! My scratching post is back!

"Forget it, kiddo."

Scooping her up in my arms, I marched her straight back into the living room and plunked her down on the sofa. Then I trotted back to the bedroom, closing the door firmly behind me.

Seconds later, she was outside the door, yowling at the top of her lungs.

Let me in this minute, or I'm calling the ASPCA!

Ignoring her cries, I lovingly loaded all my DVDs onto the armoire's gleaming cherrywood shelves. Then I inspected Prozac's scratches, grateful to see that they were all on the side of the armoire. At least the front was still pristine.

Now for the magic moment.

I pulled off the cap on the can of Cat-Away and gave it a spritz.

Instantly, I recoiled in nausea.

Yikes, it stank. With a capital P.U.

This was Cat-Away's idea of a "pleasant pine scent"? The only pine in this stuff had been rotting in a city dump.

Oh, well. It would be worth it, I figured, if it kept Prozac's claws off my armoire. I continued to spray, holding my breath. When at last I was finished, my bedroom was awash in the aroma of pine needles and rotting garbage.

Then I opened the door to Prozac, who came charging in, Attila the Hun on uppers.

She took one sniff and stopped dead in her tracks.

Yay! It was working!

Then, just as I was blessing the wonderful folks at Cat-Away, Prozac went bounding over to the cabinet as if it were a bowl of freshly opened Minced Mackerel Guts.

Sniff. Sniff. Sniff. She couldn't get enough of the stuff.

Even worse, she actually started to gnaw on a corner of the armoire, gazing up at me in ecstasy.

Not only is it a scratching post, it's a swell chew toy, too!

Damn it all!

I banged the can of Cat-Away down on my dresser in disgust.

Then I wrenched Prozac away from her new chew toy and hauled her out into the living room amid yowls of protest.

Back in my bedroom, which was still reeking of Cat-Away, I threw open the windows, wondering how long it was going to take for the smell of rotting garbage to dissipate.

With heavy heart, I removed all my DVDs from the armoire and tossed them back on my dresser. Once again, I shoved the armoire back into the shipping carton, taped it up, and dragged it to the hall closet.

Prozac glared at me from where she was sulking on the sofa.

Killjoy.

She wasn't the only one in a snit.

I stalked past her to the shower to wash off my eau de Cat-Away, already plotting my next maneuver in what would go down in family history as the Great DVD Armoire Wars.

YOU'VE GOT MAIL

To: Jausten
From: DaddyO
Subject: Good as New!

Wonderful news, Lambchop! Nellybelle's all fixed, purring like a kitten, as good as new!

This afternoon I'm putting on my plaid golf cap (the one with the pom-pom on top) and taking her on the road!

Love 'n' hugs from

Mr. Fixit, aka Daddy

To: Jausten
From: Shoptillyoudrop
Subject: Purring Kitten

Your dad could barely contain his excitement this morning, strutting around the kitchen in that ridiculous plaid golf cap of his. He claims he's finally put Nellybelle's engine back together again.

When he dragged me out to the garage to show me his "purring kitten," I saw a piece of metal lying on the ground.

"You've got a part left over," I said.

"It's just a tiny part," he said. "It can't be very important."

He's taking it for a spin after lunch. I doubt he'll make it past the driveway.

XOXO,

Mom

To: Jausten
From: Shoptillyoudrop
Subject: Hellish Day

You won't believe this, but the golf cart is working! Daddy's been driving all around Tampa Vistas, wearing that ridiculous plaid golf cap and honking his *La Cucaracha* horn. He even took it out on the golf course, honking the horn and destroying everyone's game.

The phone has been ringing off the hook with complaints about that dratted horn.

He woke up poor Mrs. Thorndahl who's recuperating from gallbladder surgery, ruined the transcendental meditation class on the clubhouse greens, and had every dog in the neighborhood barking nonstop all afternoon.

I'm so mad I could spit!

XOXO,

Mom

To: Jausten
From: DaddyO
Subject: Wonderful Day!

Dearest Lambchop—

Nellybelle made her grand debut today, and everyone loved her! Everywhere I went people were shouting hello. At least I think that's what they were shouting; it was hard to hear over *La Cucaracha*.

Your mother claims people have been complaining about Nellybelle, but I simply can't believe that's true. A few old fussbudgets may have objected to her exuberant horn, but any-one with a spirit of adventure was sure to be impressed with her sleek lines and aerodynamic design. I can promise you, the vast majority of the people who saw her loved her.

Gotta run, there's someone at the front door.

Love 'n' snuggles from

Daddy

To: Jausten
From: DaddyO
Subject: Colossal Nerve!

You won't believe what just happened, Lambchop. That old battle-axe Lydia Pinkus showed up with a petition from seventy-five neighbors demanding that I stop riding around honking Nellybelle's horn.

She rambled on about how I was in violation of the Tampa Vistas noise pollution ordinance and ordered me to cease and desist playing *La Cucaracha* on Nellybelle.

"I'd urge you to comply with this request," she had the nerve to say, "or your golf cart will be towed away at your own expense."

Of all the unmitigated gall! I thought this was America, the land of the free and the home of the brave.

Whatever happened to freedom of speech? Freedom of press? The right to bear golf carts??!

No way am I backing down. I'm going to fight this thing all the way to the Supreme Court if need be!

Love 'n' hugs from
Your irate,
Daddy

To: Jausten
From: Shoptillyoudrop
Subject: No Pork Chops

I just told Daddy if he doesn't get rid of that stupid horn, he could forget about any pork chops for dinner tonight.

To: Jausten
From: DaddyO
Subject: On Second Thought

On second thought, Lambchop, I've decided not to aggravate your mom. I'll take down Nellybelle's horn. I'll miss *La Cucaracha*, but I'll still have my plaid golf cap with the pom-pom on top!

They'll never take that away from me!

Love 'n' snuggles from

Daddy

Chapter 17

I left my windows open all night, so by the next morning just the faintest trace of Cat-Away lingered in the air.

Still miffed at me for taking away the armoire, Prozac clawed me awake with a vengeance.

But I didn't care. I sat up and greeted the warm spring morning with a smile. Today was the day Scott was taking me for a drive up to Santa Barbara. I'd gotten a text from him last night reminding me he'd be picking me up this morning at ten.

After feeding Pro some Luscious Lamb Innards, I settled down to a skinnifying breakfast of half a cinnamon raisin bagel—absolutely dry, no butter, no jam. (Okay, so I had a smidgeon of jam. The tiniest dab, really. I had to have *something* to keep the raisins company.)

Then I checked my emails, shuddering to read about Daddy running amok in Nellybelle, blasting all of Tampa Vistas with his *La Cucaracha* horn.

I cheered up considerably, however, when I opened an email from Phil Angelides, my boss at Toiletmasters, with an assignment to update a brochure for Big John, their line of supersized commodes.

I still had two hours to go before Scott was due to show up, so I used the time wisely to get started on the Big John brochure.

Oh, who am I kidding?

Of course I didn't use my time wisely. I spent the next hour and a half trying on outfits for my date with Scott.

I tried leggings and skinny jeans, baggy jeans and capris. Tank tops and tunics, cardigans and pullovers. I tried the sporty look, the nautical look. Casual-elegant and boho chic.

By the time I was through, I had half my closet piled up on my bed.

I finally went with the first outfit I'd tried on, jeans and a T-shirt.

All that fuss for jeans and a tee.

Oh, well. On the plus side, I discovered an uneaten Almond Joy in the pocket of my nautical blazer.

Before I knew it, it was 9:40. Less than twenty minutes to put myself together for my big date! Frantically, I threw on some makeup, blew out my bangs, sprayed on some perfume, and grabbed a cardigan to drape over my shoulders.

Then I checked myself out in the mirror over my dresser. I must admit, I looked pretty darn good. My bangs had blown out nice and straight. All I needed was a spritz of hair spray in case Scott and I took any romantic strolls along the beach in Santa Barbara.

I reached for the can and gave myself a spritz.

And suddenly I was overwhelmed with the familiar yet nauseating odor of pine needles and rotting garbage.

Cat-Away!

I'd left the can on my dresser yesterday, and in my haste I'd grabbed it by mistake.

I was a walking, talking city dump.

At which point, I heard a knock on my front door. Oh, hell! It was Scott! Right on time.

With sinking heart, I headed for the living room.

Prozac looked up as I walked past her and sniffed with interest.

Hmmm! Someone smells yummy!

Sure enough, it was Scott at the front door, looking *tres* adorable in chinos and a blue and white striped oxford shirt, his cropped brown curls extra shiny, his Adam's apple eminently kissable. I thought I smelled aftershave, but it was hard to tell in the miasma of my Cat-Away.

"Hey, there," he said, with what had to be the sexiest grin in the Western hemisphere.

But when he leaned in to kiss me, he sprang back like I'd just zapped him with a stun gun.

"Whoa! Your hair stinks!"

Okay, so what he really said was, "New shampoo?"

"Actually, it's cat repellent."

178

"Cat repellent?" He blinked in confusion.

"I sprayed it on by mistake."

Prozac looked up from where she was examining her privates.

She's always doing stuff like that. She once tried to shave her legs with Reddi-wip.

"Maybe I should just pop in the shower and wash it off," I said.

"Oh, no. That'll take way too long. You'll be fine. I'll leave the windows open in my Jeep. I'm sure the smell will blow away in no time."

I only hoped he was right.

"Ready?" he asked.

"Ready!" I replied with a carefree toss of my smelly curls. "Santa Barbara, here we come!"

Or so I thought.

True to his word, Scott rolled down the windows in his Jeep, and by the time we hit the freeway, the wind had whipped my hair into the ever-popular finger-in-the-electric-socket look.

If the Cat-Away was bothering Scott, he showed no signs of it, chatting about how much he'd always liked Santa Barbara—the beaches, the mission, the carousel at Chase Palm Park, and the people-watching on State Street.

"I made us lunch reservations at the El Encanto hotel," he said.

Holy Moses. The El Encanto was a nosebleed-expensive resort high in the hills of Santa

Barbara, with a spectacular view of the city and the ocean beyond.

The closest I'd ever gotten to it was the travel section of the *L.A. Times*.

"How lovely," I said, kicking myself for not going with the Casual-Elegant look.

I could just see me in my T-shirt and electric-socket hair walking into the lobby. Would they even let me in?

But then Scott put his hand on my knee and said, "You look sexy like that. With your hair sort of wild."

Omigosh. He thought I looked sexy!

Suddenly my worries vanished. I was about to have lunch at the famed El Encanto with Scott at my side, Santa Barbara at my feet, and my sexy hair blowing in the wind.

I was debating whether to order a ladylike salad or go for the gusto and get a burger, when Scott's car phone rang.

"It's my mom," he said, checking the number on his screen.

Oh, foo. What was Ma Willis doing, intruding on our lovely ride?

"Scott, darling," Ma Willis's aristocratic drone came over the speaker. "Guess who's here! Grammy Willis! She's having one of her good days, so your father brought her over from the nursing home to have brunch with us. And she's dying to see you!"

"I'd love to see her, too, Mom"—at this, he pantomimed shooting himself—"but I'm driving up to Santa Barbara with Jaine."

"With who?"

"Jaine Austen, the gal who came to dinner the other night."

"That imbecile?"

Okay, so what she really said was, "Oh." But I could hear the disdain dripping from that single syllable.

"Can't you just stop by for a few minutes and say hello? It would mean so much to Grammy. Heaven knows how many days she's got left, with that pig valve in her heart."

Scott turned to me with a helpless look. *Do you mind?* he mouthed.

Of course I minded. But what could I tell him? That I'd rather spend the afternoon sniffing Cat-Away than visit his folks?

"No, I don't mind," I lied with a feeble smile. "Not at all."

And so off we went on our unexpected detour to the Willises' Malibu Manse, or as I would soon come to think of it, Hell House.

"I'm really sorry about this," Scott said, as we started back to Malibu. "But Grammy Willis is ninety-six and pretty frail. She's been living with an artificial valve in her heart that could give out any minute."

"Your mom seems very fond of her."

"Oh, no. Mom can't stand her. Never could. Grammy can be rather difficult. Having a 'good day' for Grammy means she hasn't thrown her Metamucil at her nurses."

Oh, swell. Just what I needed. Another hostile family member to confront.

"Mom's using Grammy to guilt me into stopping by. She and Dad spend most of their time in the Cotswolds and when they come to town, Mom tends to get a bit clingy.

"But I guess you'll just have to get used to that," he said, putting his hand on my knee again, and sending my G-spot spinning.

Whoa! Did that mean Scott and I had a future together?

Let's all say a little prayer, shall we?

Twenty minutes later, Scott was parking his Jeep in the driveway outside Hell House.

I checked my hair in his rearview mirror. By now, I looked like the love child of Medusa and Little Orphan Annie. But at least it didn't seem to smell too bad.

Frantically I tried to tamp it down as we made our way to the front door.

"Don't worry," Scott assured me, ringing the bell. "You look great."

What a sweetie, huh? He could tell I was worried, and right away, he reached out to reassure me.

Basking in the glow of his smile—not to mention the memory of his hand on my knee—I was indeed reassured.

That is, until the door opened. That's when everything fell apart.

Standing there framed in the doorway was Chloe, her willowy model's bod clad in the weensiest of bikinis.

Oh, crud. Who invited *her?*

"Chloe!" Scott said, echoing my surprise. "I didn't expect to see you here."

"Your mom phoned to tell me Grammy Willis was here and I raced right over to see her. You know how crazy I am about the old darling."

So Ma Willis had invited Chloe over to make her move on Scott. That woman was determined to bust us up.

"C'mon in, you two," she said, beaming at Scott. "We're having brunch out on the patio." Then, with a halfhearted smile in my direction: "So nice to see you again, Jan."

"It's Jaine," Scott pointed out.

"Yes, of course, silly me," she said, looking anything but silly. I could practically see the cogs in her brain spinning, trying to figure out how to pry Scott away from me.

She started her campaign by walking in front of us, flaunting her fabulous tush as she led the way through the house.

Scott didn't seem to notice, but c'mon. The guy

was only human. And Chloe's bod had Man Bait written all over it.

"Ick!" she said, suddenly sniffing the air. "Something smells awful. Like rotting garbage."

Damn! Apparently the Cat-Away was still clinging to my follicles.

"Do you guys smell anything?" Chloe said, turning to face us.

"No!" Scott piped up. "We don't smell a thing!"

Then, grabbing my elbow, he hurried me through the living room and out to the back of the property—an eye-popping expanse of real estate about the size of Romania. The patio had more furniture than my whole apartment: sofa and easy chairs, dining table, chaises, plasma TV, and gourmet kitchen with a six-burner oven.

Beyond the patio was an infinity pool, a tennis court, and off to the side a yard the size of your average NFL football field.

All overlooking the Pacific, and landscaped in Garden of Eden splendor.

Ma and Pa Willis were sitting at a glass and wrought-iron dining table, Ma tanned and sinewy in tennis whites, Pa's eyes glued to The Weather Channel on the plasma TV. Sitting alongside him was a tiny, dried-up bird of a woman, clutching a highball glass in her clawlike hand.

Grammy Willis, I presumed.

"Hi, Grammy!" Scott said, hurrying to her side.

She shot him a blank stare.

"Another vodka tonic, young man," she said, holding out her glass. "And this time don't be so stingy with the vodka."

"Grammy, I'm not a waiter. It's me. Scott. Your grandson."

She squinted at him through cold rheumy eyes.

"Oh," she said, recognition finally setting in. "Where the hell have you been? How come you never visit me in that dump of a nursing home they've got me locked up in?"

"Grammy, I saw you just last week," he said, bending down to peck her on her papery cheek.

Her gaze flitting between him and Chloe, she asked, "So when are you lovebirds getting married?"

"Now, Grammy," Chloe said. "That's all over. Scott and I aren't getting married. We're just friends now. Isn't that right, Scott?" she purred, practically blowing him a kiss.

"That's right," he said. Then, taking me by the hand, he added, "I'd like you to meet my friend, Jaine Austen."

Grammy wrinkled her nose.

"My God! What smells so awful?"

"See?" Chloe piped up. "I *told* you I smelled something."

Oh, hell. By now I was crimson with embarrassment. Clearly everyone was smelling my eau de Cat-Away.

"I don't know what you guys are talking about," Scott said. "I don't smell a thing."

"I'm not surprised," Chloe said, smiling indulgently. "You always did have a terrible sense of smell, honey."

Did you hear that? She called him "honey"! It was all I could do not to bean her over the head with my purse.

"Remember the time I was wearing Chanel No. 19 and you thought it was Chanel No. 5?"

The chucklehead just wouldn't shut up.

"Wait a minute!" Grammy Willis cried. "It's coming from her!"

Needless to say, she was pointing a bony finger at yours truly.

Now all eyes were riveted on me, Scott's wide with pity.

I had to put an end to this. Now.

"Actually," I said, with as much dignity as I could muster, "it *is* coming from me. This morning I accidentally sprayed my hair with cat repellent."

"Really?" Ma Willis smirked. "How very droll."

"Sprayed her hair with cat repellent? The girl's a lunatic!" Grammy Willis bellowed into her vodka.

"Would you care to wash your hair in one of our cabanas?" Ma Willis offered. "And while you're there, you can change into a bathing suit. I think we have one in your size—the one Cousin Caroline wore before her tummy tuck surgery."

Well, wasn't she the hostess with the mostest?

"Jaine doesn't have time to wash her hair and change into a bathing suit," Scott said with an exasperated sigh. "We're going to Santa Barbara."

"If you insist, darling. But you can't leave without a teeny bite of brunch."

And before I knew it, she had her steely arm on my back, propelling me to the dining table.

"Just don't put her next to me," Grammy muttered. "P.U.!"

Ma Willis obligingly sat me at the other end of the table, far from Grammy Willis—and everyone else, too. Except Scott, of course, who sat down next to me. Without missing a beat, Chloe picked up her plate and eased into the seat on the other side of him.

You'd think that after all the trauma of stinking up the joint, I'd have lost my appetite, but you'd think wrong.

The piece of quiche Ma Willis had given me looked dee-lish—studded with bacon and gooey cheese and nestled in a golden flaky crust.

I barely restrained myself from inhaling it in three bites.

"Have a mimosa, dear," Ma Willis said, handing me a champagne flute. "And don't worry. It's a glass tabletop," she smirked. "So you can spill all you want."

It was all I could do not to spill it down her tennis skort.

But I just forced a smile and took a healthy glug of the mimosa. And another. And another. Which, I must say, had quite a calming effect.

So I hardly even minded the next twenty minutes of endless chatter about family members about whom I knew nothing.

"Well, it's been fun," Scott said, at last pushing back his chair, "but Jaine and I really have to go."

"So soon?" Ma Willis cried.

Was she kidding? It felt like we'd been there since the dawn of time.

"Can't you stay for a quick game of Frisbee?" Chloe implored.

"Daddy's been looking forward to it all week. Haven't you, Brighton?" Ma Willis nudged her husband, whose eyes were still glued to The Weather Channel.

"Huh?" Pa Willis said, wrenching himself away from a storm in the Midwest.

"You've been looking forward to playing Frisbee all week," Ma Willis repeated slowly, as if talking to a five-year-old.

"Oh, right," he said, at last remembering his lines. "Of course. Frisbee. Wonderful weather for it. Would you believe they've got six inches of snow in Minneapolis?"

"Please, Scott," Chloe begged, batting her eyelashes at him. "Just one game?"

Scott had chugged down a mimosa himself, and I could sense his resolve weakening. One of his passions, I'd found out when we first met and he'd hired me to write an online dating profile for him, was playing Ultimate Frisbee.

"How about it, Jaine?" he asked. "Want to play?"

Puh-leese. No way was I about to run around flashing my thighs in front of the Willis clan.

"I can't, Scott."

"Why on earth not?" Ma Willis wanted to know.

"Um, old water skiing injury," I said, rubbing my knee.

"Pity," she clucked in faux sympathy. "But you don't mind sitting out a game, do you, hon?"

Daggers lurked behind her smile.

"No, of course not."

"Are you sure?" Scott asked.

I could see he really wanted to play.

"Go ahead. I'll be fine."

"You can keep Grammy Willis company!" Chloe chirped.

"Just one quick game," Scott promised, running out to the yard with the others, "and we'll be on our way."

Of course, the game wasn't the least bit quick. It seemed to stretch out interminably as I sat on the patio with Grammy Willis, several chairs between us.

"Don't get too near me," she warned me cordially. "You stink."

189

So there I sat, glugging down another mimosa, watching morosely as Chloe scampered in the grass in her bikini, flaunting her bod in front of Scott like a Vegas lap dancer.

"Aren't they a handsome couple?" Grammy Willis bellowed. "Good breeders." Then she lowered her voice to a boozy whisper. "I hear some ghastly girl with a big tush is trying to come between them."

And so it went. Grammy Willis sucking down vodka as she trashed her nurses and the tramp with the big tush, Chloe flirting mercilessly with Scott, Ma Willis looking on happily, and Pa Willis gazing up at the clouds, no doubt trying to predict any oncoming precipitation.

By now I'd given up any hope of going to Santa Barbara.

I was sitting there, daydreaming about pushing Chloe over the cliff to the ocean below, when suddenly the Frisbee came sailing over to the patio and landed at my feet.

"Give it here, Jean!" Chloe waved at me, eagerly.

"All righty," I said.

Oh, how I wanted to give it to her.

I picked it up and threw it at her with all my might, wishing it were a javelin. I was so darn steamed, I guess I must have hurled it with just a bit too much fervor.

Now I watched in horror as it sailed past Chloe

straight to Pa Willis, who, unfortunately, was still gazing up at the sky. Which is why he didn't even bother to duck when the Frisbee came whizzing at him and hit him smack dab in his eye.

On the plus side, at least the Frisbee game was over.

On the minus side, Pa Willis was rushed to the emergency room for stitches. Scott drove me home and then hurried off to the hospital to be with his dad. He told me not to blame myself, assuring me that it was just an unfortunate accident. But he sounded a tad distant, and I couldn't help wondering if he meant it when he said he'd be in touch.

Chapter 18

Would you believe I had to wash my hair five times before I finally got rid of the Cat-Away smell? When the last of the stuff had finally gone down the drain and the air was safe to breathe again, I hunkered down at my computer to work on the Big John brochure, determined to forget about my ordeal at Hell House.

Easier said than done. As much as I tried to concentrate on Toiletmasters' extra-large commode, images from my nightmarish brunch kept flashing through my brain: Ma Willis sneering down her patrician nose. Chloe flaunting her fabulous bod. Grammy Willis pointing her finger at me and telling everyone I stank. Worst of all, I kept seeing that damn Frisbee sailing through the air and bonking Pa Willis in his eye.

But with grit and determination (not to mention a few inspirational Oreos), I managed to finish the brochure updates and shipped them off to Phil at Toiletmasters.

After rewarding myself with a chicken burrito for dinner (tossing chicken bits to Prozac as I ate), I lolled away the rest of the night sprawled out in bed, mindlessly watching an *I Love Lucy* marathon on TV.

I fell asleep somewhere in the middle of the

episode where Lucy sets fire to her nose while trying to impress William Holden. I was soon lost in a dream where I set fire to Chloe's bikini (most satisfying). When I awoke, it was after eleven, and the evening news was on.

I was lying there, trying to dredge up the energy to get up and brush my teeth, when suddenly a picture of Candace flashed on the screen.

Sitting up with a jolt, I turned up the volume to hear a spray-tanned news anchor say:

"Candace Burke, the beauty pageant director whose assistant was killed just this past weekend in what the police are calling a mistaken attempt to murder Ms. Burke, was attacked tonight by an assailant in a jog suit and ski mask. Reporter Mario Prieto is live on the scene."

The camera cut to Candace standing outside her front door, her arm bandaged, Eddie hovering protectively at her side.

Standing across from them with a microphone was a baby-faced reporter who looked like he'd just come straight from his Junior Prom.

"Can you tell us what happened, Ms. Burke?" he asked, eagerly.

"I was coming home from the market," she said, clearly shaken at the memory, "when someone jumped out from behind the bushes and lunged at me with a knife."

"Was it a man or a woman?" Baby Face wanted to know.

"It was hard to tell in the dark. Whoever it was stabbed me in the arm"—here the camera zoomed in on her bandaged arm—"but I fought them off with pepper spray."

"She always carries it for protection," Eddie piped up. "Some of those pageant moms can get a bit confrontational."

"I ran into the house and called 911," Candace said, "but by the time the police showed up, my attacker was gone."

"Did you get a look at the assailant, Mr. Burke?"

"No," Eddie said. "Unfortunately, I wasn't home at the time of the attack."

"Do you have any idea who was behind the ski mask?" Baby Face asked, turning back to Candace.

"I have a good idea who it was," she said, "but upon the advice of my attorney, I can't say anything further."

It looked like she still believed the culprit was Heather but wasn't about to risk a defamation lawsuit.

"All I can say is that I'm sick at the thought that someone out there wants to kill me." At this, she began to blink back tears.

"That's enough for now," Eddie said. "My wife's had quite a stressful evening."

And indeed, a look of sheer panic shone in her eyes.

Candace was afraid, all right. And she had good reason to be.

Clearly whoever had tried to kill her at the pageant had just returned to finish the job.

Chapter 19

P lease don't fire me, Mr. Turner!" Jolene was
wailing.

I'd driven out to Turner BMW the next morning
and barged into Tex's office, despite Jolene's
protests that he wasn't there.

He was there, all right, feet propped up on his
desk, avidly watching something on his laptop
screen.

I figured it was porn.

"I'm sorry I couldn't back up your alibi," Jolene
cried, "but Detective Austen said if I didn't tell
her the truth, I'd be arrested as an accessory to
murder and spend the rest of my life in jail
taking showers with a gal named Spike!"

"Detective Austen, huh?" Tex asked with an
arched eyebrow.

"Yes, from the Alta Loco SVU! Isn't that right,
Detective?"

Jolene turned to me, and I nodded weakly.

"You mustn't blame Jolene," I said. "She really
did try to protect you."

"Don't worry, Jolene," Tex assured her. "You're
not fired. You're way too valuable for me to let
go." This uttered with his eyes firmly riveted on
her boobs. "Go back to your desk, and try to
calm down."

"Oh, thank you, sir!" she said, rushing out the door.

Somehow Tex managed to tear his eyes from her chest and turned to me.

"So you're a police officer, huh?" he smirked. "Last time we spoke, you were a part-time, semi-professional private eye. That's a mighty big career move in just two days. Mind if I see some ID?"

I was trapped, and I knew it. No way was Tex about to be fooled by my USDA meat inspector badge.

"Okay," I confessed, "so I'm not a cop."

"No?" He grinned triumphantly. "Well, I think I'll just call the police and have you arrested for impersonating an officer."

He reached across his desk for his phone.

"While you're doing that," I said, whipping out my cell phone, "I think I'll call your wife and tell her about your affairs with Candace and Bethenny."

Not surprisingly, he put down his phone.

"Where on earth did you get the idea I've been fooling around with Candace and Bethenny?"

"Oh, please, Tex. I saw you and Candace in the elevator at the Amada Inn. I could practically see the mattress burns on your back. And Bethenny told me all about your affair with her. I don't know when you started boinking her, but if she was still a minor, you could be facing jail time."

"So what do you want?" he asked, glaring at me.

Suddenly I was the one in the driver's seat.

"I want to know where you were the afternoon of the murder."

"I already told you. I was here in my office."

"Nowhere near the Amada Inn?"

"Absolutely not. And even if I was having an affair with Candace, why would I want to kill her?"

"To shut her up. According to Bethenny, Candace was threatening to tell your wife about your affair."

"Bethenny certainly is the little chatterbox, isn't she? Now I'm sorry I gave her such a good deal on her Beemer."

"Bethenny told me your wife's money is what's keeping Turner BMW afloat, and that you can't afford to lose her. So I'm wondering if you stopped by Candace's office to bludgeon her to death and killed the wrong pageant blonde by mistake."

"Interesting theory, but it's simply not true. I was here the entire afternoon, spying on my salesmen."

"Spying on your salesmen?"

"I have hidden cameras in all the sales cubicles."

With that, he swiveled his laptop so I could see the screen. Grainy images of Tex's minions in their cubicles flashed in constant rotation.

"A bit voyeuristic," Tex said, "but a very effective management tool."

He snapped the lid of his laptop shut and looked me straight in the eye.

"I didn't try to kill Candace," he said. "I may not have any witnesses to back up my alibi, but that's the truth."

Call me crazy, but in that moment, it seemed as if he was on the level. But then again, he was a car salesman. So who knew?

"If you ask me," he said, "you should be questioning Eddie. Talk about your long-suffering husbands. He's always resented Candace. Living in her shadow. Working as her gofer.

"And let's just say for a minute that Candace and I *had* been having an affair," he added with a sly smile. "What if Eddie found out about it? Maybe he was so angry at this final humiliation, he went berserk and tried to kill her. Makes sense to me."

Me, too.

A whole lot of sense, indeed.

Eager to point the finger of suspicion at someone else, Tex gave me Candace and Eddie's address and phone number. For a guy who claimed he wasn't boffing Candace, he sure knew a lot about her.

Soon I was tootling over to Casa Burke, which I found on a leafy street not far from Turner

BMW. Most convenient for an impromptu lovers' tryst, n'est-ce pas?

After parking my car down the street from their house (no sense announcing my arrival), I called the number Tex had given me.

The phone rang for quite a while before Eddie finally picked up. Putting on my best *Law & Order* voice, I said, "This is Captain Roth from the sheriff's department, calling for Candace Burke."

Then I held my breath, hoping Eddie would buy my Officer of the Law impersonation.

Thank heavens he did.

"I'm afraid she's not here right now. Can I ask what it's regarding?"

"Just a follow-up on her attack the other night. I'll call back later."

Before he could ask any more questions, I hung up.

All systems were go. The coast was clear. Now that I knew Eddie was alone, it was time to move in for the kill.

Getting out of the Corolla, I made my way to the Burkes' house—a pristine white Cape Cod surrounded by a velvety lawn, with lush hydrangea bushes lining the path to the front door.

Like Candace herself, the place was groomed to perfection.

I rang the bell, hoping Eddie hadn't been lying and that Candace wouldn't open the door and ask me what the hell I was doing there. I couldn't very well tell her I suspected her hubby of trying to knock her off.

After a few seconds, Eddie came to the door, unshaven and haggard. Clearly the attempts on Candace's life had taken their toll on him. Either because he loved Candace dearly, or because he'd tried to kill her twice and failed both times.

"Listen," he said wearily, "if you're from the press, I've said all I've got to say. Please leave me alone."

With that, he started to slam the door in my face.

"No, wait! I'm not a reporter. I'm Jaine Austen. We met this weekend at the pageant."

He squinted at me, trying to remember.

At last the dawn came.

"You're the one with the crazy cat who pranced on stage in the middle of the Cleopatra act."

I braced myself, waiting for him to start chewing me out. But instead he broke out in a wan smile.

"Most entertaining moment of the whole damn day, if you ask me."

What a darling man! He couldn't possibly be a killer, could he?

"So what are you doing here?" he asked.

"Actually, Heather Van Sant has hired me to investigate the murder at the pageant. I know Candace suspects Heather of trying to kill her, but I don't believe Heather's guilty. And I'm trying to clear her name."

"*You're* a private eye?" he asked, blinking in disbelief.

"Part-time, semi-professional," I said briskly, eager to cut off any chatter about my credentials. "Mind if I come in?"

"Now's not a great time," he said. "I'm awfully tired."

"Please," I begged. "Just a few minutes. It could save an innocent woman from going to jail."

I shot him the look Prozac uses on me when she's angling for a belly rub, all soft and gooey and Damsel in Distress.

"Oh, okay," he conceded. "But just a few minutes."

I followed him inside, past a living room decorated in peaches and pale green (a perfect setting for Candace's cool good looks), into a wood-paneled den.

Unlike the light and bright living room, the den was clearly Eddie's domain. Dark and gloomy, the room reeked of cigarettes. Piles of papers were scattered on a scarred wooden desk, while an ancient TV sat hulking across from a cracked leather sofa and rumpsprung oatmeal recliner.

All very Early Archie Bunker.

The walls were lined with show-biz head shots and publicity stills of Candace and Eddie in their bygone days as aspiring actors. Among the photos was a community theater poster of Candace as Blanche DuBois in *A Streetcar Named Desire*. And another of Eddie as Ebenezer Scrooge in *A Christmas Carol*.

"Have a seat," Eddie said, gesturing to the sofa.

I sat down, and as I did, tufts of stuffing came popping out from the cracks in the leather. Surreptitiously I tried to shove them back in.

But Eddie didn't even notice. He was staring at the photos on the wall, lost in his memories.

"Those were good times," he said, pointing with pride to a head shot of a much younger version of himself, beaming out at the world with an unlined face and a headful of long-gone hair.

"That's me when I was opening for Steve Lawrence and Eydie Gorme in Vegas. Best six weeks of my life," he said, gazing at the photo with longing.

"Candy and I both started out trying to make it big in show biz. Candy got a couple of commercials and I got some stand-up gigs. But neither one of us really took off," he said, plopping down on the recliner. "So Candy started this pageant thing, and I went along for the ride. It's been fun for her."

"And you?"

"Not so much. But it's the only game in town," he shrugged. "So what can I do?"

Kill your wife for the insurance money? I asked

myself, wondering if indeed the Burkes had life insurance policies.

"Steve Lawrence said I was the funniest comic he'd ever worked with," Eddie said, his eyes growing misty at the memory.

Either Steve was an awfully kind fellow or he'd worked with some pretty lousy comics.

"If you'd like," he said, "I can show you my press clippings."

Yuck, no!

"Better yet, I think I've got a tape of my act somewhere!"

I'd rather suck sofa stuffing!

"Sounds great, Eddie. But I really need to talk to you about the murder before Candace comes home. I know how much she dislikes Heather, and I want to get an unbiased account of what happened from you."

"Oh, don't worry about Candace. She's at her hypnotherapist's. She'll be gone for at least an hour."

"But I promised I wouldn't take up much of your time."

"This won't take long. And you'll love it. Trust me. It's hilarious."

If you learn nothing else from this little story, class, learn this: Never trust a comic who tells you he's hilarious.

Before I knew it, Eddie was shoving a tape in a beat-up VCR. And for the next twenty minutes, I sat there with a smile plastered on my face, forcing myself to chuckle at jokes that had been around since Henny Youngman was in diapers, praying Candace wouldn't come walking in the front door.

At last the routine ground to a halt.

"Wonderful!" I exclaimed, frightened my face had frozen into a permanent grin. "But now, about the unfortunate incident at the Amada Inn . . . ?"

"Oh, right," he said, reluctantly returning to reality.

"Did you happen to see anyone near Candace's office at the time of the murder?"

"No, I was in my room rehearsing my material for the crowning ceremony."

So much for an airtight alibi. For all I knew, he was tiptoeing down the hallway to bludgeon his wife to death with a tiara.

"Can you think of anyone who would want to see Candace dead?" I asked.

"No," he said, shaking his head. "I honestly can't. I know Candace can be tough on the outside, but underneath, she has a heart of gold. She's a kind, caring, philanthropic woman. Everyone who really knows her loves her."

Spoken with all the warmth and emotion of a robot on downers.

If this was the best he could do as an actor, no wonder he never made it in show biz.

Somehow I had to jolt him out of his pre-written script.

So I took a deep breath and blurted out, "Did you know your wife was having an affair with Tex Turner?"

His face crumpled.

"Yes, I know," he said with a resigned sigh. "It wasn't her first, and it won't be her last. But I didn't try to kill her in a fit of passion if that's what you're thinking. If I was going to do that, I would've done it years ago."

The stiffness had left his voice; the robot was gone.

At last, he seemed to be speaking the truth.

I thanked him for his time and got up to go. By now I was pretty much convinced he wasn't the killer, and I was just about to cross him off my suspect list when my purse brushed against the mountain of papers on Eddie's desk, sending them cascading to the floor.

"I'm so sorry!" I said. "How clumsy of me."

Then suddenly I noticed something buried underneath the pile of paperwork—a black ski mask.

Right away I flashed back to Candace's attacker, the one who jumped out at her from the bushes and came charging at her with a knife. According to Candace, he'd been wearing a ski mask.

Good heavens. Could Eddie have been her assailant?

"My ski mask!" Eddie cried. "I've been looking

all over for this. It's a souvenir of my one and only TV role, as Mobster Number Three in a very bad cop show.

"C'mere," he said, taking me by the elbow and leading me over to a photo on the wall—a still shot of three hoodlums in a dark alley.

"That's me!" He pointed to one of the hoodlums, a stocky guy dressed in black and wearing a ski mask.

"I thought I'd lost this baby," he said, dusting off the mask. "I've really got to clean my desk more often."

As we bent down to pick up the scattered paper, I was beginning to wonder if Eddie was a lot better an actor than I'd thought. Was that ski mask of his just a souvenir? Or had he reprised his role as Mobster Number Three and slipped it on to stab his cheating wife to death?

We'd just finished piling the papers back on Eddie's desk when I heard someone coming in the front door.

"I'm back!" Candace called out.

Frankly, I was relieved to hear her, glad I was no longer alone with her possible killer.

But when she walked into the den, I barely recognized her. Her face was blotchy; her hair no longer shiny and sculpted, but hanging limp on her shoulders. Dressed in sloppy sweats, she was a ghost of her former self.

"How'd the hypnotherapy go?" Eddie asked.

"Hypnotherapy?" Candace blinked, dazed. "It went okay, I guess. The doctor said he put me under, but I swear I was awake the whole time. If I don't sleep tonight, I'm going back on Valium."

"Candace hasn't been sleeping well," Eddie explained. "She keeps blaming herself for Amy's death."

"Of course I blame myself for her death. If I hadn't spilled that Coke on Amy's blazer, she wouldn't have been wearing mine, and the killer never would have mistaken her for me.

"What's she doing here?" she then asked, nodding in my direction.

"Jaine came to ask some questions about the murder."

Candace turned to me with weary eyes.

"What're you—some sort of PI?"

"Unbelievable, right?" Eddie piped up.

"A lot more believable than your crummy toupee," were the words I yearned to utter.

"But I heard you were a songwriter," Candace said.

"I write all sorts of things. I do advertising, resumes, industrial films—"

"Yeah, right. Skip the sales pitch. Why are you so interested in the murder?"

"Heather Van Sant has hired me to help clear her name. She insists she never tried to kill you. And I believe her."

"You know what?" Candace said, slumping down onto the rumpsprung sofa. "You could be right. At first I was sure Heather was the killer. But now, I don't know. Anyone could have done it. Someone out there is trying to kill me and I have no idea who it is."

She put her head in her hands and choked back what sounded like a sob. Then, in a frightened voice, she said: "I think someone's been following me."

"What?" Eddie cried, alarmed.

"A van's been on my tail the past few days."

"What kind of van?"

"I don't know. It was big. And black."

"Are you sure you're not just being paranoid?" Eddie asked.

"I'm not being paranoid. Someone's been following me! What on earth am I going to do?"

I glanced over at the ski mask perched on Eddie's desk.

For starters, I felt like telling her, try sleeping in separate bedrooms. Better yet, separate states.

"Don't worry, honey," Eddie said, putting his arm around her. "Everything's going to be okay."

"Just like it was the other night when the killer came at me with that knife?"

Was it my imagination or did I see Eddie blush?

"I should've never let you out alone at night,"

he said. "And it's not going to happen again. I'm going to hire a bodyguard to protect you whenever you leave the house."

That was all very well and good, but who was going to protect her when she was alone with Eddie?

Chapter 20

I took off from Alta Loco, haunted by the memory of that ski mask, and wondering if Eddie had indeed flipped out and tried to kill Candace. He had absolutely no alibi for the time of the murder. According to him, he'd been in his room working on material for the pageant crowning ceremony. Since Eddie seemed to lift his material directly from *1,000 Jokes for Any Occasion*, I hardly saw the need for much preparation.

But Eddie wasn't my only suspect without an alibi. Neither Bethenny nor Tex had witnesses to their whereabouts at the time of the crime. Had Bethenny really been giving herself a facial as she'd claimed? Had Tex really been spying on his employees?

Those were the thoughts swirling around my brain as I slogged through traffic—that, and whether to stop off at McDonald's or KFC for lunch.

KFC won out, and one mini-bucket of chicken bites later, I was driving over to Pet Palace. In my latest foray in the DVD Armoire Wars, I'd decided to buy Prozac a scratching post. Surely once she got her paws on a pole of thick, plush carpeting, she'd lose interest in my armoire.

After surveying various models, I decided to go for broke and spent way too much money on something called a Kitty Condo, a multi-tiered structure with platforms and ladders, and three carpeted beds, one in turquoise referred to as "the pool."

Lowell, my helpful Pet Palace clerk, rang up my sale, and asked if I'd care to pay thirty dollars extra for assembly. I assured him that I was perfectly capable of assembling a simple Kitty Condo and headed home.

A half hour later, I was sitting on my living room floor, surrounded by assorted Kitty Condo parts, cursing in languages I didn't even know I knew.

The diabolical fiends at Kitty Condo were sadists of the highest order, providing their unsuspecting customers with instructions so indecipherable, they may as well have been written in Sanskrit. What's worse, they had the gall to leave out steps four, six, and twelve in their "Easy Seventeen-Step Assembly."

Somebody ought to report those people to the Better Business Bureau.

(But I'm busy right now writing this book, so you do it, okay?)

Thoroughly disgusted, I decided to take a chardonnay break.

I was sitting on my sofa, sipping some of Chateau Costco's finest, when Lance showed up.

He sailed into my living room in a designer

suit and tie, fresh from his job fondling ladies' bunions at Neiman Marcus.

"Hi, sweetie. I just stopped by to tell you about my fantastic dinner date with Gary, the UPS guy. Is this a good time for you?"

"Not really."

"Well," he said, plopping down on the sofa, "we went to the most charming little Italian restaurant in Century City, Obika Mozzarella Bar. Mozzarella to die for! We shared a margarita pizza and a bottle of wine, and the rest was dating history. I swear, Gary looked so handsome, I hardly even noticed our stunning waiter.

"And how about you, hon? How are things with you and Detective Sublimely Wealthy?"

"Not so hot."

"Oh, no!" he said, taking my hands in his. "Tell Uncle Lance everything! Spill your little heart out."

And I did. I told him all about the Great Frisbee Fiasco. How Scott and I had been planning to drive up to Santa Barbara but had been hijacked to brunch at Hell House; how Chloe was waiting for us in her bikini; how I'd sprayed my hair with Cat-Away and stunk up the whole brunch; how I was stuck with Grammy Willis while Scott romped on the lawn playing Frisbee with Chloe; and how I accidentally bopped Pa Willis in the eye with the Frisbee and sent him to the hospital for stitches.

When I was through, Lance tsked in pity.

"Poor Jaine," he said, gazing down at my hands, still clutched in his. "When's the last time you had a manicure? Your nails are a wreck."

"Did you not hear a word I just said? I sent Pa Willis to the hospital."

"Of course I heard. Another Jaine date gone bad. So what else is new? If only you'd let me know before the date, I could've given you some pointers. Pointer Number One: Never spray your hair with cat repellent. It's things like that, Jaine, that make it so hard to forge meaningful relationships in life.

"But don't worry, sweetie. I'll help you win Scott back. I'll think of something. We're going to have that double wedding in the Cotswolds if it's the last thing I do!"

That spoken with all the fervor of Scarlett O'Hara vowing never to go hungry again.

I shuddered at the thought of what idiotic scheme he might come up with.

"Hey, what's all this?" he said, finally noticing the Kitty Condo parts scattered behind the sofa.

"A scratching post for Prozac. It's utterly impossible to assemble."

"I'll be happy to help you with it, hon."

"You will?"

What an angel!

"Yes, of course. But not now. I'm meeting Gary at the movies in an hour. Must go home and make myself fabulous. An easy job, I know, but still, one mustn't shirk one's duties. A lesson you'd be wise to learn, Jaine."

And with that, he went sailing back out the door.

I barely restrained myself from hurling my glass of chardonnay at him.

Instead I finished it and turned my attention back to my Kitty Condo.

I think the wine really helped.

Less than an hour later, it was completely assembled.

All it took was patience, tenacity, and a house call from Lowell at Pet Palace.

Chapter 21

Alas, Prozac showed no signs of moving into her Kitty Condo. From the moment Lowell and I first showed it to her, she'd given it the cold shoulder, avoiding it much like I avoid the health food section of my local supermarket.

The next morning after breakfast, she'd hopped on the sofa as she usually does, barely giving the condo a glance.

But I couldn't worry about the condo, not when I still had a murder to solve.

It was high time I resumed my investigation and paid a visit to Dr. Edwin Fletcher, principal of Alta Loco High School.

You haven't forgotten that touching little scene near the vending machine at the Amada Inn, have you? The one where Candace had threatened to tell the world the truth about Dr. Fletcher unless he coughed up ten grand?

Sure sounded like blackmail to me. And a most emphatic motive for murder.

I called and told him I was investigating the case on behalf of Heather. Fortunately he agreed to see me, and after hanging up, I headed to my bedroom and slipped into my dress jeans, spanky white tee, and navy blazer. Hoping to make an extra special impression on the good doctor, I pinned my Phi Beta Kappa key on the lapel of my blazer.

Yes, I said Phi Beta Kappa.

Impressed? You should be.

I was quite proud of that key, having nabbed it for only two bucks at the same flea market where I bought my USDA meat inspector badge.

I was almost ready to go. But before I left, I had one very important chore to do—"decorate" the Kitty Condo.

If there was one thing that would get Prozac to try out her new home-away-from-home, it was chow.

I very cleverly loaded the condo with kitty treats: Chopped Chicken Chunks, Tasty Tuna Tidbits, Little Liver Lumps, and the ever-popular Seafood Entrails Party Mix. Surely my feline chowhound wouldn't be able to resist the lure of all those goodies.

"Bon appétit!" I cried as I left my apartment, confident that when I returned, she'd be all settled in to her new home, lounging in the condo pool.

Minutes later, I was in my Corolla and once again trekking down the 405 freeway to Orange County. If this kept up, they'd soon be naming a lane after me.

At a little after eleven, I pulled into the parking lot of Alta Loco High, an ersatz mission-style building with a red tile roof and Moorish archways.

Entering through massive double doors, I made

my way along a wide linoleum corridor, breathing in the heady aroma of Mr. Clean and old gym socks. Down at the end of the hall, I found the administrative offices. There I was greeted by Dr. Fletcher's secretary, a stocky prison warden of a woman with blunt-cut gray hair and a most intimidating unibrow. The nameplate on her desk read IRMA COMSTOCK.

After I cleared my throat to get her attention, she looked up from where she was hard at work on the Daily Jumble.

"What is it?" she snarled in welcome.

"I'm Jaine Austen. Here to see Dr. Fletcher."

"Jane Austen? Like the writer?"

"It's Jaine with an 'i.' You see, my mom was reading *Pride and Prejudice* when she was pregnant with me, and—"

"Yeah, whatever," she said, clearly uninterested in my mother's reading habits. "Follow me."

Hoisting herself up from her swivel chair, she led me into the good doctor's inner sanctum, then promptly stomped back to her Daily Jumble.

I looked around the large imposing room, no doubt designed to intimidate unruly students. Arched windows let in the bright sun, back-lighting Dr. Fletcher, whose slim body was dwarfed behind a huge desk. The walls were lined with framed degrees from UCLA and Berkeley, as well as a slew of awards for Alta Loco High, "A California Distinguished School."

Completing the honors was a large leaded-glass paperweight with a metal plaque proclaiming Dr. Fletcher "Principal of the Year" from the Alta Loco Chamber of Commerce.

"Ah, Ms. Austen," he said, springing up to greet me. "So nice to see you."

He leaned forward to shake my hand, sending a blast of citrusy aftershave in my direction. Something about that scent seemed familiar.

"Sit down, won't you?"

He gestured to one of two chunky leather chairs facing his desk.

"I see you're Phi Beta Kappa," he said, eyeing my blazer lapel as I took a seat.

I smiled modestly.

"You must be very proud. That takes a lot of hard work."

Not if you shop at the right flea markets.

"I'm afraid I won't be able to spare you much time," he said with an apologetic smile. "I'm working on a speech I have to deliver at the school assembly at two this afternoon."

Looking down at his desk, I saw a legal pad, upon which he had been making notes in a painstakingly precise hand.

"Of course," I assured him. "I understand. Just a few questions."

"Go ahead," he said, hands clasped in front of him on his desk like an obedient student.

"First off, can you think of anyone who may

219

have wanted to kill either Amy or Candace?"

"Absolutely not. Amy was such a mousy little thing. I can't believe she had any enemies. And as for Candace, she may have alienated a few pageant moms—after all, emotions run high at these events—but I doubt anyone hated her enough to kill her."

"Even you?"

"What on earth do you mean by that?" His eyes, pale gray behind his wire-rimmed glasses, grew wide with surprise.

Now was my time to pounce.

"The night before the murder, I overheard Candace threatening you. She said she was going to tell everyone the truth about you."

He managed a bark of a laugh.

"Oh, that." His hands were now clasped so tight, they were practically melded together, knuckles white with strain. "It was nothing, nothing at all. I promised Mother I'd give up smoking, and I fell off the wagon. Candace caught me taking a puff out in the courtyard and was threatening to tell her."

Oh, please. What a crock of poo poo. Candace had been threatening to blab to the world, not just his mommy, and was demanding ten grand for her silence. Surely a stolen cigarette wasn't worth ten grand. I wasn't buying his story. Not one bit.

And I was just about to tell him so when once

again I became aware of his citrusy aftershave. And suddenly I remembered where I'd smelled it before! On Taylor's missing ball gown after Candace had returned it to her!

Omigosh. Was Dr. Fletcher the one who'd nabbed Taylor's Vera Wang? Was this pillar of the educational community a cross-dresser? Was this the secret Candace had been threatening to expose?

Something told me I was on to something.

"Do you mind my asking where you were at the time of the murder?"

"In my hotel room," he said, with an angry glare.

Doing what? I wondered. *Saying Yes to the Dress?*

"Any witnesses?"

"Afraid not. Now if you'll excuse me, I've really got to get back to work."

With that, he pressed a button on his intercom, instantly summoning the formidable Ms. Comstock.

"Show Ms. Austen out, will you?" he instructed her.

Before I knew it, Ms. Comstock had me in her steel grip, and minutes later I was back out in the parking lot.

But not for long. Dr. Fletcher wasn't about to get rid of me that easily.

I whiled away the next couple of hours in my Corolla, playing Scrabble for One and checking in vain for a text message from Scott. I hadn't heard from him in days, and by now I was convinced that my Frisbee fiasco had pretty much put the kibosh on our relationship.

At a little after two, when I knew Dr. Fletcher would be busy delivering his speech at the student assembly, I headed back to his office.

The ever-charming Ms. Comstock looked up from the Daily Jumble she was still trying to solve.

"Can I help you?" she grunted, glowering at me from under her massive unibrow.

I sprang into action, using a plan I'd carefully devised in the parking lot.

"I seem to have lost my Phi Beta Kappa pin, and I'm afraid it must have fallen off in Dr. Fletcher's office."

"You're Phi Beta Kappa?" She blinked in disbelief. "Someone who spells Jane with an 'i'?"

Look who's talking. The lady who took three hours to finish the Daily Jumble.

"Yes, I am," I said, fingering my bare lapel, which was indeed missing its Phi Beta Kappa pin, due to the fact that I'd taken it off and stashed it in my purse.

"Mind if I look around for it?"

"Okay," she said, eyeing me warily, "but make it snappy."

Quickly I trotted into Dr. Fletcher's office.

Much to my dismay, I realized that Ms. Comstock was trotting right behind me.

But I was prepared for just such a contingency.

"By the way," I said, "do you happen to know who drives a brown Dodge Dart?"

"That's my car."

Of course, I already knew that. While in the parking lot, I'd seen the Dodge Dart in question parked in a space with Ms. Comstock's name on it.

"I think I saw a kid heading for your car with a can of spray paint."

Her unibrow furrowed in dismay.

"Oh, hell! Half of these hoodlums oughta be in jail."

And with that, she was off like a shot.

It wouldn't take her long to discover there was no kid in the parking lot with a can of spray paint, so I had to hurry.

I started rummaging around the room, praying that Dr. Fletcher was deep enough into his crossdressing to leave evidence of it here in his office. I checked out his closet, hoping I'd find a red-carpet gown, or at the very least a tasteful little black dress. But, alas, all I found was a raincoat and umbrella.

Then I raced over to his desk, riffling through his drawers, uncovering the usual pens and paper clips, as well as a stash of vitamins, granola bars, and some "Bullworker" upper body exercise ropes.

If Dr. Fletcher was a cross-dresser, it looked like he was in great shape under his underlovelies.

I continued my search, but all it yielded were some attendance sheets and a pamphlet on locker room hygiene.

But then, at last, I hit pay dirt. In the bottom right drawer, I found a dictionary. How odd, I thought, to keep a dictionary in a drawer. Most people keep them on their desks, or on a bookshelf. Why was this one hidden away where no one could see it?

Lifting it out of the drawer, I opened it up and found my answer.

There, pressed between Flamboyant and Flaubert, was a black lace garter belt. And a handful of photos. All selfies of Dr. Fletcher, dressed in women's outfits: There he was in capris and a halter top. Dressed for success in a pencil skirt and white silk blouse. Very Betty Crocker in a shirtwaist and apron.

And finally, the belle of the ball, in Taylor's Vera Wang gown! True, he hadn't been able to zip it all the way up. But that didn't seem to bother him as he smiled into the camera, sporting a blond shag wig, batting false eyelashes, his lips a bright Revlon red.

No doubt about it. Dr. Fletcher was a cross-dresser, and Candace had been ready to expose him, right down to his black lace garters.

And I had to admit he looked pretty darn good

as a woman. That Bullworker had really paid off; his arms were well toned, not a hint of middle-aged flab anywhere. Gazing at the photos, I felt a twinge of envy. It's a tad depressing when a guy in his fifties looks better in capris than I do. I was standing there, admiring his sylphlike waist when suddenly I heard an angry voice booming:

"What the hell do you think you're doing?"

I looked up to see Dr. Fletcher glowering in the doorway.

Slamming the door shut behind him, he walked toward me, eyes smoldering, hands clenched into tight fists. No longer the mild-mannered academic, but a goon in lace panties.

"I thought you were giving a speech at assembly," I stammered.

"It was a short speech. Now your turn. What the hell are you doing here?"

"Er . . . looking for my Phi Beta Kappa pin?"

"I doubt you'll find it in my dictionary. Let's cut the crap, shall we?"

"Okay," I said, gathering my courage. "I know Candace was blackmailing you, and it wasn't about your smoking habits."

I held up his girly photos to drive home my point.

Dr. Fletcher let out a soft sigh.

"If you must know, Candace caught me trying on Taylor Van Sant's gown and threatened to

225

tell the school board unless I forked over ten grand."

"Sounds like a perfect motive for murder," I pointed out.

"Forget about it, Sherlock. I didn't try to kill her. I cashed in a CD and paid her off. And if you don't believe me, you can check my records at Bank of America."

I believed him, all right. I just wondered if he paid her off *after* he screwed up his attempt to kill her.

"I'm paying Candace for her silence, but I'm not about to pay off anybody else." He picked up the heavy glass paperweight from his desk. "If you know what's good for you, you'll keep your mouth shut about what you've seen here today. We wouldn't want anything to hurt that brainy little Phi Beta Kappa head of yours," he said, sliding his finger along the sharp edge of the glass. "Would we?"

If he thought he could scare me by waving a lethally blunt instrument in front of my face, he was absolutely right.

"Not a problem," I assured him, backing out the door. "My lips are sealed."

Looking down, I realized I still had his black lace garter dangling from my arm.

"Ciao for now," I said, tossing it to him. "By the way, you looked great in those capris!"

Then I darted out of his office, where I

proceeded to bump smack dab into Ms. Comstock.

"There wasn't any kid in the parking lot with spray paint," she snarled, looking none too happy.

"Oh? Really? I must've scared him off. Lucky I was there, huh?"

Seeing no need to prolong our little chat, I put my fanny in overdrive and scooted off.

"Hey," she called out after me. "Did you find what you were looking for?"

"Did I ever!"

Chapter 22

A gal can work up quite an appetite snooping around for ladies' underlovelies, and by now I was starving. So I headed over to the nearest McDonald's for a Quarter Pounder and fries.

I was just licking a dollop of ketchup from my fingers when my cell phone rang. I grabbed it eagerly, ketchup be damned, hoping it was Scott.

But alas, it was Heather Van Sant.

"Hi, Jaine. How's everything coming along with your investigation?"

"Fine," I assured her, gulping down a fry.

"Wonderful! Let's set up an appointment for you to stop by the house and give me a detailed progress report."

Oh, foo. I was hoping to hop on the freeway and avoid rush-hour traffic. And I really didn't want to have to drive back down to Alta Loco tomorrow. Surely, I could give her a progress report over the phone.

"And while you're here I can pay you for the lyrics you wrote. And give you a retainer for your detective services."

"I can be there in ten minutes."

Heather came to the door in a sports bra and bike shorts, her exposed midriff tight as a snare drum.

"Forgive the gym rat look," she said, flicking an imaginary piece of lint from her fat-free hip. "I'm expecting my personal trainer."

She led the way inside, hot pink sneakers squeaking on the hardwood floor.

In the living room, I was surprised to see Taylor, slouched in an overstuffed armchair, chewing gum and reading *Steppenwolf.*

"Hey, Jaine," she said, looking up from her book.

"Taylor, what are you doing here? Shouldn't you be in school?"

"I've been keeping her home these past few days," Heather said. "Poor darling needs to decompress from the trauma of the murder."

Taylor, not looking the least bit traumatized, blew a ginormous bubble with her gum.

"That better be sugarless," Heather snapped, eyeing the bubble. Then, gesturing to the sofa, she said, "Have a seat, Jaine."

I cased the sofa for small animals, and sure enough, there was Elvis, doing his impersonation of a throw pillow.

"Look, Elvis!" Heather called out, waking him from his snooze. "It's Auntie Jaine."

Elvis glared up at me, fangs bared, as I sat down next to him.

"He's crazy about you," Heather gushed, oblivious to the look of sheer malice he was lobbing in my direction.

"Here's your money," she said, picking up a check from the coffee table. "A thousand for the lyrics and for coming with us to the Amada Inn. An extra hundred for sniffing Luanne and Gigi at Mocktail Hour. And a thousand for your retainer. Is that enough?"

Enough? I came *thisclose* to throwing my arms around her and showering her with baby kisses.

"This'll be fine," I said, staring at the zeros in a happy daze.

"So," she asked, sitting next to Taylor in a matching overstuffed armchair. "What have you discovered so far?"

"Tell us everything!" Taylor chimed in.

And I told them. About how furious Bethenny had been when she'd learned Candace was having an affair with Tex. How Tex might have wanted to kill Candace to save his marriage. And how Eddie might have wanted to bump her off to avenge his honor. And finally I told them how Candace had been blackmailing Dr. Fletcher.

The only thing I didn't mention was Dr. Fletcher's penchant for ladies' frocks. As far as I was concerned, what the man did in his private life was his business, and I wasn't about to destroy his career over a pair of black lace garters.

"That's great!" Heather cried when I was finished. "So many suspects!"

"You have to go to the police!" Taylor said, equally pumped.

"I will, as soon as I have some evidence connecting one of them to the crime. All I have now is motive."

Both mother and daughter slumped down in their seats, deflated.

"But don't worry," I said. "I'm bound to come up with something soon."

Total horse poop on my part, but they looked so dejected I had to say something.

"Well," I said, getting up from the sofa, "I guess I'd better be going."

"Don't go, Jaine!" Heather said. "Mario should be here any minute. He's the best personal trainer in all of Alta Loco. You can work out with us."

A workout? Oh, glug. I'd rather play kneesies with Elvis.

"I really should hit the freeway before rush hour," I demurred.

"Pish tosh!" Heather said with a dismissive wave. "Nothing personal, hon, but if those hips of yours get any wider, they're going to need their own zip code."

"Mom!" Taylor chided.

"Jaine knows I'm only saying it because I care about her. Really, hon. You must take exercising seriously. Why, I couldn't believe my eyes when I saw you asleep on that exercycle at the Amada Inn!"

The minute those words came out of her mouth,

she realized she'd made a mistake and blushed bright red clear down to her cleavage.

"Hold on, Heather. The only way you could've seen me asleep on that exercycle is if you'd been in the hallway outside Candace's office at the time of the murder."

"Okay, so I went to see Candace," she said, with a defiant toss of her hair extensions. "I wanted to confront her about kicking Taylor out of the pageant. But when I got to her office, I saw her lying there, dead. At least I thought it was her. Later, of course, I learned it was Amy. The minute I saw the body, I panicked and ran back to my room. But I swear, I didn't kill her!"

And suddenly, for the briefest instant, I wondered if she was telling the truth. Had Amy really been dead by the time Heather got to Candace's office? Or had Heather killed Amy by mistake, a homicidal pageant mom willing to mow down anyone standing in the way of her daughter's crown? And had she hired me, not to prove her innocence, but to throw suspicion in someone else's direction?

I was pondering this unsettling scenario when suddenly I heard a man's voice boom:

"Hello, everybody! Where are the two most beautiful women in Alta Loco?"

If this was Mario, the personal trainer, they weren't kidding about the "personal" part.

But the guy who came sailing into the room

was no personal trainer. A tall, imposing guy with Slavic cheekbones and pale hair slicked back, he wore the nosebleed-expensive suit of a CEO or Mafia chieftain.

"Hi, Daddy," Taylor said.

"Hello, dollface," he said leaning down to kiss her cheek.

I detected a trace of an accent in his gravelly voice.

"Jaine," Heather said, "I'd like you to meet my husband Nicky. Nicky, this is Jaine Austen, the gal I was telling you about. The private eye."

"Nikolai Vanzantsnikov, at your service." He took my hand and shot me a smile—almost blinding me with the gold fillings glinting in his teeth, not to mention the diamonds twinkling in his massive pinky ring.

"Nicky's originally from Russia," Heather explained. "He shortened his last name for business purposes. It'll make it so much easier when Taylor breaks into show biz."

Taylor rolled her eyes at this unfounded burst of optimism.

Meanwhile, the Russian husband still had my hand in his. For a minute I thought he was actually going to bring it to his lips and kiss it, but he refrained and instead stared into my eyes with laser-like intensity.

"You, I like. You remind me of my Aunt Olga. Strong lady. Once punched a bear unconscious."

Gosh, Heather was right. I really did have to trim down if I reminded him of his Aunt Olga, the bear puncher.

"You find the killer?" he asked.

"Not yet, but I'm doing my best."

"Don't worry. If you don't find killer, I will. Nicky Vanzantsnikov will never let his wife go to jail for crime she did not commit. I tell Heather all along, don't waste time on silly Alta Loco beauty pageant."

At last, a parent with some common sense.

"Skip local idiots and enter our darling daughter in Miss America pageant."

So much for common sense.

"I cannot believe this Candace lady, disqualifying my Taylor. Bad lady. Deserves to be punished. You know what they say . . ."

"Never cross a guy with gold fillings and a diamond pinky ring?"

Okay, so I didn't really say that. Not out loud, anyway.

"What goes around comes around," Nicky intoned with a solemn nod. "Something tells me this Candace lady, she will pay for what she did."

His blue eyes narrowed into icy slits. At that moment, I had no trouble picturing him tying a cement block to an enemy's ankle and tossing said enemy in a convenient river.

And suddenly a whole new scenario began to play out in my mind. What if Nicky was the killer? What if Heather called him in tears when Candace kicked Taylor out of the pageant, and he came running over to the Amada Inn, pinkie ring blazing, determined to wreak justice?

I drove home that afternoon, stuck in traffic and nagged with doubts.

It seemed hard to picture Heather as a killer.

But Nicky? The guy had hit man written all over him.

Chapter 23

I returned home to find Prozac on the sofa, just where I left her, hard at work clawing a throw pillow.

Looking over at the Kitty Condo, I saw all the treats were gone.

How maddening! The little rascal had eaten everything and ignored the scratching post.

"Prozac," I said, snatching the throw pillow from her. "Why aren't you playing on your Kitty Condo?"

She gazed up at me with undisguised disdain.

Oh, please. If that thing is a condo, I'm a Pomeranian.

I threw open the window to get rid of the stink of the Little Liver Lumps still lingering in the air, then stomped off to my bedroom to slip into something more comfortable.

If only there was some way to get Prozac to use the damn condo, I mused, as I changed into flip-flops and a *Cuckoo for Cocoa Puffs* sleep tee.

And then it hit me.

In a burst of brilliance worthy of S. Freud, I decided to try a little psychology on my fractious furball. Like most divas, Prozac often wants what she can't have.

"Okay," I said, hurrying out into the living

room, "since you don't want the Kitty Condo, it's mine, all mine. And you can't play with it."

With that, I got a bag of Oreos from the kitchen and put it on one of the condo platforms.

"Gosh, this is fun," I said, sitting down next to the condo and plucking one of the Oreos from the bag. "Cookies taste so much better when they're served from a carpeted platform! Yum!"

Prozac eyed me with disdain.

I've seen better acting on Duck Dynasty.

Then I got down on all fours and began clawing at the scratching post.

"Mommy loves scratching the post. See how much fun Mommy's having? Mommy's scratching. Mommy's clawing!—Dammit, Mommy just broke a nail!"

Then from outside I heard a familiar voice.

"Jaine?"

I looked up and saw Scott staring at me through the open window.

Oh, hell! There I was on all fours in my *Cuckoo for Cocoa Puffs* sleep shirt, my tush in the air, my thighs on display in broad daylight, scratching a cat post.

"Scott!" I cried, mortified.

"Can I come in?"

"Of course!"

I scrambled to my feet, cursing myself for changing into my dratted sleep shirt. Then I headed for the door, conscious of my bare thighs, picturing Chloe's fat-free beauties with nary an ounce of cellulite to mar their perfection.

When I finally screwed up enough courage to open the door, I found Scott standing there, looking *tres* hunky in his detective suit and tie.

"I suppose you're wondering what I was doing just now," I said, blushing I don't know how many shades of red.

"Not really," Scott said with a mischievous grin. "I was too busy admiring the view."

Oh, hell. He'd undoubtedly seen my tush in all its glory.

"Actually," I said, yanking down my sleep shirt, "I was trying to get Prozac to use her new Kitty Condo. Without much luck, I'm afraid."

Meanwhile, Prozac had leapt off the sofa and was now rubbing herself, ecstatic, against Scott's ankles.

She gazed up at him worshipfully.

I'll play in your condo any time you want, big boy.

"That's enough, Pro," I said, prying her off his ankles and plunking her down on the sofa, where she proceeded to shoot me one of her death ray glares.

(Really. If looks could kill, I'd have been wearing a toe tag.)

"Why don't I go put on some jeans?" I said, eager to cover my thighs.

"Don't!" Scott said, pulling me into his arms. "You look fine just the way you are. More than fine."

Then he smiled a smile that could melt titanium, and the next thing I knew we were locked in a steamy embrace. By the time we came up for air, my thighs were a distant memory. All I could think about was Scott and his heavenly kiss.

I was all set for Round Two of our smoochfest, when Scott said, "I'm sorry I haven't called sooner. It's been crazy busy at work."

"That's okay," I said, eager to resume our lip lock.

But he kept on talking.

"The reason I stopped by is because I wanted to ask you to brunch at my parents' house on Sunday."

Oh, god. Not another brunch at Hell House. I didn't care how kissable he was, I couldn't face his parents. Not again. Not ever.

"I don't think so, Scott. Not after what happened with your dad's eye."

"Don't be silly. Nobody blames you for that."

Yeah, right. I was surprised Ma Willis hadn't taken out a restraining order against me.

"Look," he said, as if reading my thoughts, "I know my mom has been rough on you, but like I already told you, she's that way with all my dates. It just takes time to win her over."

In my case, I was guessing a millennium or so.

"And besides," he added, his Adam's apple bobbing most appealingly, "it's my birthday on Sunday. And I'd hate to spend it without you."

And without further ado, my heart melted. Yours would have, too, if you could've seen his Adam's apple.

"Of course, I'll come," I cooed.

"Wonderful!" he said, once again taking me in his arms.

At last! Part II of our smoochfest was about to begin. But just as our lips were about to meet, there was a knock on my front door.

Grrr. Of all the rotten timing.

Reluctantly I tore myself away from Scott and opened the door to find Lance, holding an elaborate display of white silk roses and tulips.

"Hi, Jaine!" he said, barging right in.

Oh, for heaven's sakes. Such an aggravating man. Surely he must have seen us through the window playing kissy face. What the heck was he doing barging in like this?

"Scott," I said, barely containing my annoyance, "you remember my neighbor, Lance Venable."

"So nice to see you again," Lance said, then turned to me, holding out the flowers. "These came for you while you were out."

"Really?"

I found this hard to believe as this exact same floral arrangement had been on Lance's coffee table for the past three years.

"Yes, *really,*" he said, plucking a card from the flowers. "Read the card."

I opened the tiny envelope, which, by the way, was devoid of a florist's name, and pulled out a card.

"With love always, from Cyril," I read aloud.

Who the hell was Cyril supposed to be?

I was about to find out.

"An old boyfriend of Jaine's," Lance said to Scott, setting the flowers on my dining room table and arranging them just so. "Head over heels in love with her. Jaine has that effect on men. I don't know what it is about her, but she's just irresistible."

Over on the sofa, Prozac was coughing up a hair ball. Or pretending to. No doubt her comment on me as a femme fatale.

Meanwhile Lance was singing my praises to Scott, touting me as if I were Helen of Troy, Cleopatra, and Scarlett O'Hara all rolled into one.

I knew what this was all about. Lance said he was going to think of a way to help me woo Scott.

And this was it. He'd come up with "Cyril."

Clearly he was trying to make Scott jealous.

My first instinct was to put an end to this nonsense and tell Scott the truth. But then I saw a look in Scott's eyes, a look of uncertainty, the same look I got in my eyes when Chloe came sashaying by.

I liked that look a lot—on Scott.

"Well, I guess I'd better leave you two lovebirds alone," Lance was saying.

So happy was I with the result of his little scheme that I actually meant it when I said, "Thanks so much for stopping by."

"Poor Cyril," I said when Lance had skipped off to his apartment. "It was sweet of him to think of me."

"I hope I don't have anything to be concerned about," Scott said, eyeing the silk flowers uneasily.

"Oh, no. Not at all. It's all over between us. Just like it is between you and Chloe."

There it was again, that uneasy look in his eyes. He felt threatened, all right. And just like Prozac going after some Little Liver Lumps, he moved in to protect his territory.

Once again I found myself swept up in his arms.

It turned out I didn't have to worry about Scott seeing me in my ratty old T-shirt, after all. Because thirty seconds later, I wasn't wearing it anymore.

YOU'VE GOT MAIL

To: Jausten
From: Shoptillyoudrop
Subject: Just When I Thought It Was Safe

Just when I thought it was safe to answer the phone again, I got a call from Lydia Pinkus this morning, telling me she saw Daddy running around her front lawn in his underwear in the middle of the night!
    XOXO,
    Mom

To: Jausten
From: DaddyO
Subject: In the Doghouse

I'm afraid I'm in the doghouse with your mom, Lambchop. And it's all because of that battle-axe Lydia Pinkus. What the heck was she doing looking out her window at 2 AM, that's what I want to know. Why wasn't she asleep like any normal human being?
    But I suppose I'm getting ahead of myself.
    Yes, it's true I was running around in my underwear on Lydia Pinkus's lawn, but there's a perfectly logical explanation. You see, last

night, I was still feeling a little miffed about the whole *La Cucaracha* affair, smarting at the indignity of having to silence my trusty golf cart horn forever. I couldn't sleep and decided to go out to the garage freezer for a little ice cream.

So I got out of bed, threw a robe over my boxer shorts, and headed outside. I was just walking up the driveway where I'd parked my golf cart when I remembered I'd left my beloved golf cap on the front seat. And at that very moment, I looked over and discovered that I wasn't the only one who liked my cap. There behind the wheel of my golf cart was a raccoon, with my golf cap clutched in his little paws, nibbling at my pom-pom!

I raced over to grab it from him, but as soon as he saw me coming, he was off like a rocket with my cap in his mouth. Well, I couldn't very well let him steal my golf cap, could I? So I started running after him. I chased that damn critter three and a half blocks all the way to Lydia Pinkus's townhouse. Somewhere along the way—I think it was in Mrs. Thorndahl's front yard—my robe got caught on a rose bush, and I had no choice but to leave it behind.

Which is why, when I finally caught up with the raccoon in Lydia's front yard, I was wearing nothing but my boxers. I don't know why she's making such a stink over it. I happen to have rather shapely legs, if I do say so myself.

But I digress. Back to the scene on Lydia's lawn. By now I was close enough to grab my cap from the raccoon, but when I reached out to get it, he started hissing quite fiercely. And I must confess that your old Daddy got a wee bit scared. What if he attacked me? What if I wound up in the hospital getting a series of highly painful rabies shots?

I was just debating what to do when Lydia came out on her balcony and started hollering. At the sound of her voice, I swear that raccoon cringed in fear, dropped the cap, and skedaddled out of there.

I'm telling you, Lambchop, the battle-axe is one scary lady.

United at long last with my golf cap, I put it on and headed back home.

No big deal, really. I don't see why everybody is making such a fuss.

Love 'n' hugs from
Your much maligned,
Daddy

To: Jausten
From: Shoptillyoudrop
Subject: Lost His Marbles

Daddy just told me what happened last night. Can you believe a grown man chasing a raccoon for a silly golf cap?

Honestly, I think your father has lost his marbles.

On the plus side, though, he's feeling so guilty, he let me have some Oreos from the freezer.

XOXO,

Mom

To: Jausten
From: DaddyO
Subject: Low Profile

Your mom's had a few Oreos, and is feeling a lot calmer. Best to keep a low profile today.

Love 'n' hugs from

Daddy

P.S. I'll say one thing for that raccoon. He had excellent taste in hats.

Chapter 24

If you think I'm going to tell you what happened with me and Scott, you've got another think coming. My mom sometimes reads these little stories of mine when she's all out of Janet Evanovich books, and I'm not about to let myself in for one of her lectures on The Dangers of Dipsy Doodle.

(If you're reading this, Mom, I slipped out of my sleep shirt into a nice comfy chastity belt.)

Let's just say a good time was had by all, and I was still floating around in a romantic glow the next morning as I scarfed down my cinnamon raisin bagel.

So happy was I that I didn't even flinch when I opened my emails and read about Daddy chasing a raccoon through the streets of Tampa Vistas in his boxer shorts. Indeed, my prevailing sentiment at the time, I believe, was:

That Daddy! What a scamp!

I polished off my CRB in no time and was just about to nuke another when there was a knock on my door.

My heart leapt.

Could it be Scott? Back for a return engagement?

Fluffing my hair and wiping bagel crumbs from

my robe, I hurried to the door and swung it open, only to find a big blond lunk of a woman looming in my doorway.

Oh, hell. It was Brunhilde, the detective investigating the murder.

Needless to say, I was not exactly thrilled to see her.

Lest you forget, when last we met, she'd sort of suspected me of being the killer—making noises about how I might have wanted to kill Candace to avenge her bad-mouthing Prozac.

Was it possible she still suspected me? Had she somehow gathered evidence tying me to the crime? What if I'd inadvertently touched something and left fingerprints in the pageant office when I was comforting Candace after the murder?

Oh, God. What if Brunhilde was here to arrest me for a crime I didn't commit? Wouldn't you know I'd be hauled off to jail, just when everything was going so well with Scott!

But I couldn't allow myself to panic. I had to stay cool and collected.

"Mind if I come in?" Brunhilde asked.

"Please don't arrest me!" I shrieked. "I swear I'm not the killer!"

Okay, so I've still got to work on cool and collected.

"I repeat," Brunhilde grunted. "Mind if I come in?"

"Of course. Have a seat," I said, gesturing to the sofa, where Prozac was in the middle of her post-breakfast snooze.

Brunhilde sat down as far as she could get from my little angel, who woke up from her nap and began sniffing the air with interest.

Mmm. Bratwurst!

Like a flash, she was at Brunhilde's side, her little pink nose twitching with glee.

Sauerkraut! And Heineken, too! Hey, this gal's a one-woman Oktoberfest!

Brunhilde flinched in annoyance. Clearly she was not a cat person, so I quickly scooped up Prozac and plopped her on the floor.

Upon which, the little darling shot me a filthy look.

Well! Of all the nerve!!

With an angry swish of her tail, she stalked off toward my bedroom, throwing in an ear-piercing yowl for good measure.

That cat sure knows how to milk the drama out of an exit.

Turning back to Brunhilde, I resumed our little tête-à-tête.

"As I was saying, I assure you I didn't kill Amy."

"That's not why I'm here."

"Really?"

A wave of relief washed over me.

"According to Tex Turner, you've been running

around impersonating a police officer. An offense punishable by up to three years in prison, I might add."

Dammit. I was back to doing time again.

"I didn't mean any harm," I stammered. "I was just trying to question his secretary."

"I already told you to leave the police work to us," she said, with a most unsettling flex of her biceps.

"Yes, sir—I mean, ma'am. I promise, no more impersonating a police officer. Cross my heart."

"And what about Phi Beta Kappa members? I hear you've been passing yourself off as one of those, too. Dr. Fletcher checked the membership rolls. And you're not listed."

Good heavens. You'd think people would have better things to do with their time than to go ratting me out to the cops.

"Look, Ms. Austen," Brunhilde said, hauling herself up from the sofa, "I warned you once to keep your nose out of this case. And I don't want to have to do it again. The next time I get a complaint about you, I'm coming back with an arrest warrant."

"You have my word! My nose is officially out of the case!" I lied, fingers firmly crossed behind my back.

Yes, I know I should have stopped my investigation right then and there. And I gave it some serious thought. For a whole thirteen seconds. But when it comes to murder, I'm a lot like Prozac with a throw pillow.

I just can't seem to let go.

I promised myself there'd be no more impersonations. But they couldn't arrest me for asking questions, could they? There's such a thing as freedom of speech in this country, right?

All of which is why, when Luanne Summers called me later that morning and offered me a job writing novelty lyrics for Gigi, I got in my Corolla and tootled down to Alta Loco.

My nose was back in business again.

Chapter 25

I expected to find Luanne and Gigi in an Alta Loco McMansion, complete with swaying palms and gurgling fountain.

But much to my surprise, the address Luanne gave me turned out to be a rundown apartment building a stone's throw from the freeway. A one-story structure built over a carport, its gray clapboard exterior was blotched with water stains and flaked from years in the sun.

Luanne came to the door in skinny jeans and oversized tee, her fingernails painted an eye-popping lime green.

"Come in," she said, ushering me into her living room. Even though the apartment was at the front of the building, facing away from the freeway, I could hear the dull roar of the cars seeping through her windows.

"Excuse the crappy digs." She gestured to her mismatched thrift shop furniture. "My husband got all the good stuff in the divorce. Silly me, I signed a prenup.

"But that'll all change once Gigi gets discovered," she added with a confident nod. "You know, pageants are a gateway to the world of acting and modeling."

Luanne had clearly been drinking the pageant Kool-Aid.

Meanwhile, Gigi, the future actress/model in question, was in the middle of the living room in shorts and a tank top, awkwardly twirling a baton.

"Hi, Ms. Austen," she said, when she saw me.

"Be careful you don't break that lamp!" Luanne shouted, as the baton came perilously close to a ceramic-based table lamp.

"Gigi's learning a new talent," Luanne explained. "We want to make more of an impression at the next pageant. Not that she wasn't wonderful as Cleopatra, right?"

"Absolutely," I lied.

Frankly I thought the table lamp could have given a better performance.

"These batons have wicks at the end, so you can set them on fire," Gigi gushed, with all the glee of a budding pyromaniac.

"Yep, my little girl is learning how to juggle flaming batons!" Luanne beamed with pride.

Instantly my mind was flooded with images of the Amada Inn going up in smoke.

"I'm sure to win next time!" Gigi said, her big blue eyes shining with determination.

"You bet you will, honey!" Luanne assured her. "Now keep on practicing while Ms. Austen and I have a little chat about your novelty lyrics."

I followed Luanne to a cramped dining alcove and took a seat at a scarred wooden table littered with mail and assorted pageant brochures.

Up against the wall was a clothing rack stuffed with glittery gowns and costumes. Gigi's pageant wardrobe, no doubt.

"I want something fun and bouncy that Gigi can sing while she's twirling the batons," Luanne said, settling down onto a rickety chair across from me. "Work 'fire' in the lyrics, of course, and Gigi's many talents. So what do you think? Can you do it?"

Not without the help of my good friend Jose Cuervo.

"Well, I—"

"Good! I knew you'd say yes!"

Then, somewhat uneasily, she added, "So how much was Heather paying you?"

"Five hundred dollars."

She gulped in dismay.

"That's a little steep. I don't make much at my job at the nail salon."

For the first time I noticed a rhinestone embedded in the pinky of her lime green nails. No doubt her own handiwork.

"By the way," she said, pulling out a slip of paper from the pile of junk on her table and sliding it across to me, "here's a coupon for ten percent off your first visit to the salon. Which, if you don't mind my saying, you could really use. What do you cut your nails with? A chain-saw?"

Of all the nerve! I happen to use a pair of vintage manicure scissors I picked up at the same flea market where I got my USDA inspector badge and Phi Beta Kappa pin.

"Anyhow," Luanne was saying, "I don't make much, but I've got a savings bond left over from the divorce settlement. Maybe I could cash that in."

"No!" I shouted. "I couldn't possibly let you do that."

I thought of all the money she was pouring into these pageants. Heaven knows how much that Cleopatra barge had set her back. And the rack of costumes. That had to be a few thou right there. The woman was living on the edge to support her crazy pageant dreams. I wasn't about to let her dip into her savings. No way.

Then I had an idea.

"I'll write the lyrics for free," I said, "if you'll answer some questions about the murder at the Amada Inn."

"The murder? Why do you need to know about the murder?"

I wasn't about to tell her I was helping Heather. I wanted her to cooperate, not stab me with a flaming baton.

"I'm afraid I'm a suspect."

"You?" She blinked in surprise.

"The detective in charge of the case thinks I'm some sort of animal nut who may have tried to kill Candace because she insulted my cat."

All of which was true.

"But I thought Heather was their prime suspect," Luanne said, not bothering to hide her disappointment.

"Not anymore."

"Damn. If anyone deserved to be dragged off to prison, it's that godawful woman."

"So can you answer a few questions?" I asked.

"If I do, you'll write Gigi's lyrics for free?"

"Absolutely."

"Go ahead," she shrugged. "Ask away."

"First off, can you think of anyone who'd want to kill either Amy or Candace?"

"I can't think of a soul who'd want to kill Amy. Poor little thing," she clucked. "Talk about being in the wrong place at the wrong time. I'm sure the killer was out to get Candace."

"Do you have any idea who that could be?"

"I still say Heather did it. You saw how furious she was with Candace at the talent show."

"Anybody *other* than Heather come to mind?"

"Nope."

Luanne had clearly tried and convicted Heather of the crime, so I decided to switch to another line of questioning.

"I don't suppose you saw anyone near the pageant offices at the time of the murder?"

Was it my imagination, or did Luanne squirm in her seat ever so slightly?

"I'm afraid not. Gigi and I went to our hotel room right after the talent competition and stayed there until we heard about Amy's death."

"So you were in your hotel room the entire time?"

"Yes," she said firmly. "The entire time."

But there was a look in her eyes, something sly and cagey, that made me wonder if she was telling the truth.

"Isn't that right, Gigi?" she called out to her daughter. "I was with you in our hotel room at the time of the murder. Wasn't I, honey?"

Gigi, who'd been twirling her baton with carefree abandon, now jumped as if hit by a blow dart, sending her baton flying across the room into the table lamp, which toppled to the floor with a crash.

"I told you to watch out for the lamp!" Luanne cried, racing over to assess the damage. "Damn. The base is cracked."

"I'm sorry, Mom." Gigi watched Luanne put the lamp back on the table, avoiding my eyes, about as skittish as Prozac on her way to the vet.

"So, Gigi," I said, joining them in the living room. "Your mom was in your hotel room with you at the time of the murder?"

"Um. Yes. Absolutely."

Gigi lied about as well as I cook.

Not for one minute did I believe her. And so I decided to tell a little fib of my own.

"Funny you should say that. Because I was just talking with someone who swears they saw your mom in the hallway outside Candace's office."

My ruse worked.

"What do you mean?" Luanne squeaked.

"Just what I said. I have a witness who saw you at the scene of the crime."

And suddenly all the starch went out of her.

"Okay," she said, crumpling down on the sofa, "so I left our hotel room. I went to see Candace. I paid her three hundred bucks to make sure Gigi won the talent contest. But then she gave the prize to some klutz who tap-danced to *America the Beautiful.*"

So Candace had been accepting bribes, and reneging on them. Yet another motive to mow her down.

"I went to her office to have it out with her and get my money back. But when I got there, she was already dead. At least I thought it was her, lying there in that blue blazer. I didn't realize it was Amy until later."

"But my mom didn't kill her!" Gigi piped up. "I swear. She'd never do that."

"I bet I know who the killer is," Luanne said.

"Who?" I asked eagerly.

"Bethenny Martinez. I ran into her in the hallway outside Candace's office. She's the one who ratted me out, isn't she? If you ask me, she's the killer."

Yikes. First Heather. Then Luanne. And now Bethenny. All of them at the scene of the crime. That hallway was beginning to look like the 405 at rush hour.

"Well, thanks for all your help," I said.

"You do believe I'm innocent, don't you?" Luanne asked, gnawing at her pinky with the embedded rhinestone.

"Um, sure," I lied.

"And you're still going to write the lyrics for Gigi?"

Oh, foo. Why on earth had I suggested that idiotic idea?

"Of course," I said.

"Don't forget to make them fun and peppy, throw in 'fire,' and try to rhyme something with Gigi. So far all I've got is Fiji."

I promised I'd do my best and left her trying to seal the crack in the table lamp with clear nail polish.

Heading out into the bright afternoon sun, I felt a wave of pity for Luanne, with her DayGlo nails and cheesy furniture, trying so hard to make a go of things.

But then, just as I was walking past the carport, I noticed a beat-up black van with the vanity plates: GGS MOM. It had to be Luanne's car. And I suddenly remembered: Hadn't Candace said she'd been tailed by someone in a black van?

Had Luanne been the one following Candace?

Was my struggling manicurist with the rhinestone in her pinky the killer, after all?

Chapter 26

It was time to pay another visit to the former Teen Queen.

I needed to find out if Bethenny had really been at the scene of the crime, as Luanne claimed—or if Luanne had merely made a wild accusation to cast suspicion away from herself.

Back home, I got on Bethenny's website and was delighted to see that she was going to be signing copies of her new book, *Bethenny's Beauty Secrets*, at a Krispy Kreme doughnut joint out in Burbank the very next day.

A book signing at a doughnut shop? How odd. But I wasn't complaining. Any event involving doughnuts is always high on my To Do list.

So the next day, after a light lunch of Cheerios and a banana, I headed out to Burbank.

I must confess that on the drive over, I didn't even think about the murder. I was too busy debating about whether to get a chocolate glazed or strawberry jelly doughnut for dessert. Chocoholic that I am, at first I leaned toward the chocolate. But then I kept thinking of the strawberry jam oozing from a plump jelly doughnut. True, I'd get chocolate with the chocolate doughnut, but I'd get more to eat with the jelly.

What a quandary, huh?

I debated the issue with all the intensity of a Supreme Court justice, and still hadn't made up my mind when I pulled into the Krispy Kreme parking lot in Burbank.

Walking into the brightly lit shop, I was greeted by the sweet smell of cinnamon and sugar and chocolate.

I'm hoping that's the way it smells in heaven.

I expected to find Bethenny seated at a table, surrounded by a crowd of fans waiting to buy her book. But when I looked around, all I saw were two customers at the counter: an old man, and a young mom with a toddler.

For a minute I wondered if I'd come to the wrong Krispy Kreme.

Then I heard someone call my name.

"Hi, Jaine!"

I turned to see a pretty Latina behind the counter in a Krispy Kreme polo and visor, her hair in a thick ponytail.

Good heavens. It was Bethenny! Did she actually work here?

Apparently so, because the next thing I knew she was handing a bag of doughnuts to the old guy and asking, "Would you care to buy a book with that? *Bethenny's Beauty Secrets*. I wrote it. I used to be Miss Alta Loco Teen Queen."

She pointed to a stack of books by the napkin dispenser.

There on the cover was Bethenny in her teen

queen tiara, holding a hair dryer in one hand and a mascara wand in the other.

The old man blinked at her, puzzled.

"I came here for doughnuts. Why would I want to buy a book?"

"It has some great beauty tips."

"Does it tell how to get rid of toe fungus?"

"I'm afraid not."

"Then what good is it?" he said, grabbing his doughnuts and shuffling out the door.

Bethenny sighed and turned to her next customer, the mom with the toddler, who bought a chocolate glazed doughnut, and—after thumbing through the pages of Bethenny's book—declined to buy it.

Now it was my turn. This was it. My moment of truth. What would it be? The joy of chocolate? Or the mounds of jam inside that hunk of dough?

"I'll have a chocolate glazed doughnut."

Of course, you knew chocolate would win.

"And a jelly doughnut."

I don't know what happened. The words just sprung out of my mouth before I could stop myself.

"And throw in a cinnamon apple, too," I said, spotting a last-minute inspiration.

It's official. I can't take me anywhere.

"And would you care to buy a copy of my book?" Bethenny asked, with a pitifully hopeful look in her eyes.

Was she kidding? I'd rather buy diet rice cakes. But there was no way I could turn her down, not with her staring at me like Bambi tied to the railroad tracks.

"Of course," I said.

"That's great!" Bethenny beamed. "Thanks so much! It's twenty dollars."

Twenty bucks to get beauty tips from a Krispy Kreme pusher? Oh, well. There was no backing out of it now.

I paid for the book, which Bethenny autographed with a smiley face.

"Do you suppose you could take a break for a few minutes?" I asked, looking around the now empty store.

"Sure, just let me ask my manager."

"Hey, Brandon," she called out. "Okay if I take a break?"

A pimply kid who couldn't have been more than seventeen poked his head out from the kitchen door. "Okay, but just for a few minutes."

"Want some coffee?" Bethenny asked when he'd retreated. "It's on the house," she whispered confidentially.

"Sure. Thanks."

She poured us both coffee, and grabbed a plain doughnut hole for herself.

Can you believe there are people out there who eat a single doughnut hole at Krispy Kreme?

Me, neither.

Of course, that's why Bethenny was a size two and I'm a size none-of-your-business. Perhaps there was a lesson to be learned here. So as we settled down at a table, I made a solemn vow to eat just one of my doughnuts (chocolate glazed, of course) and save the rest for later.

"Thanks again," Bethenny said, "for buying the book. You're the first person to buy one all day. And probably the last," she sighed.

"I'm sure sales will pick up," I offered lamely.

"Oh, please. I couldn't even get my own mother to buy a copy."

She stared down at the book on the table between us and shook her head in disgust. "Why on earth did I ever think people would be interested in anything Miss Alta Loco Teen Queen had to say?"

Good question.

"I'm sorry I ever entered the pageant in the first place. It cost my parents a fortune, and what did I get for it? A couple of bowling alley openings, a stupid infomercial, and a tacky clock tiara. Damn thing didn't even come with batteries. I had to go out and buy them myself.

"And to top things off," she said, taking a desultory sip of her coffee, "I just wasted five hundred dollars to publish a book no one's ever going to read."

I tsked in pity at her tale of woe. I also stared enviously at her doughnut hole. Which she hadn't even begun to eat. By now, of course, I'd wolfed down my doughnut, and was dying for more. It took every ounce of willpower I possessed not to reach over and nab her ball of powdered dough.

But this was crazy. I had to stop obsessing about doughnuts and focus on the task at hand.

"Speaking of the pageant," I said, "I ran into Luanne Summers, who said she bumped into you outside Candace's office at the time of the murder."

"Oh?" Bethenny said, stirring her coffee so vigorously I thought she'd snap the wooden stirrer.

"Didn't you say you were in your hotel room the whole time giving yourself a pedicure?"

"A *facial,*" she snapped. "I said I was in my hotel room giving myself a facial."

"So which was it?" I asked. "The facial, or Candace's office?"

A tense beat while she continued to whip away at her coffee. Then she took a deep breath and said, "Both, if you must know. After minimizing my pores, I made a little trip to Candace's office. I wanted to tell her to keep her paws off Tex Turner. But when I got there, I saw the corpse on the floor and ran like a bunny. Smack into that blabbermouth Luanne.

"But I'm not the killer," she said with a defiant swish of her ponytail, "if that's what you're wondering."

Maybe her acting lessons with Uta Hagen Dazs were paying off. Because it sure sounded like she was telling the truth.

"Oh, no! I wasn't wondering that at all," I stammered. "Just making conversation. Guess I'd better be going," I said, pushing back my chair. "Good luck with your book."

"Hey, wait!" she called out as I started for the door. "When is the story coming out?"

"What story?"

"The one about me you're writing for the *L.A. Times*."

Darn. I'd forgotten all about that little fib. I didn't have the heart to tell her there wasn't any story. Not now, when she was feeling so low.

"They haven't set a date yet. I'll call you as soon as I know."

Feeling more than a tad guilty, I scooted out the door with my two remaining doughnuts, which, you'll be happy to learn, were still unsullied in the Krispy Kreme bag. And they stayed that way for a whole three and a half minutes until I got on the freeway and dug into them with gusto.

Chapter 27

Much like an unsuspecting gazelle romping in the jungle, unaware of the cougar in the tree above waiting to pounce, I came home to find a message from Ma Willis on my answering machine.

"Jaine, dear. Scott told me he's invited you to our little birthday brunch tomorrow. What a ghastly idea! Well, I suppose we're going to have to put up with you. Just try not to break anything. Dress casual, avoiding all kimono-sleeved blouses. And don't bring a gift. You couldn't afford to buy anything decent, anyway."

Okay, so that's not what she said. But I could tell that's what she meant. For those of you who insist on accuracy, the actual words she uttered went something like this:

"Jaine, dear. Scott told me he's invited you to our little birthday brunch tomorrow, and I couldn't be more delighted. Dress casual. And please don't bring a gift. Your presence is the only present we need. See you tomorrow!"

As much as I had the warmies for Scott, I'd totally forgotten about the brunch, banishing it to the dusty corner of my mind reserved for IRS audits and root canals, still shuddering at the thought of my other meals at Hell House.

Damn. In less than twenty-four hours I'd be back with the Willis gang. (And, no doubt, the impossibly perfect Chloe.) My stomach, still stuffed with doughnuts, sank.

Why the heck had I eaten the damn doughnuts, anyway? The last thing I needed were those extra calories clinging to my thighs at Scott's party.

"Pro, honey," I moaned to my pampered princess, now snoring on the sofa. "How am I ever going to lose fifteen pounds in twenty-four hours?"

Her big green eyes flew open.

Do you mind? I'm in the middle of a very important nap.

Determined to work off some of those doughnut calories, I decided to go for a nice long walk. I was just heading for the bedroom to change into my sweats when I heard a familiar knock at my front door.

It was Lance, who came sailing into my living room with a garment bag slung over his arm.

"Jaine, sweetie. Wait till you see what I've just bought!"

Inwardly, I groaned. I simply did not have time to deal with Lance and his fashion choices.

"Actually, I was just about to go for a walk and get some exercise."

"You, exercise?" he chuckled. "That's a good one! Hahahaha!"

"I fail to see what's so amusing about me exercising."

"Oh, please. You get winded brushing your teeth. Now seriously, you've simply got to see my new tweed jacket!"

With a flourish, he unzipped the garment bag and took out a thick tweed jacket, heather brown with tawny suede elbow patches.

"Isn't it gorge? I bought it for my wedding trip to the Cotswolds."

"Wedding trip? To the Cotswolds?"

"Yes, indeedie!" He plopped down next to Prozac on the sofa. "Gary and I had dinner at Obika Mozzarella Bar again last night—the best pumpkin ravioli ever, by the way—and guess what? Some hotshot producer at Fox is reading Gary's screenplay! We celebrated with a bottle of the most yummy pinot noir and I swear, Gary came *thisclose* to popping the question."

Unbelievable, n'est-ce pas? Lance is the only guy I know who can take pumpkin ravioli and turn it into a wedding proposal.

"Gosh, it's going to be so much fun being married to a screenwriter. Just think of all the 'A' list parties I'll be invited to! And don't worry, sweetie. I'll send you selfies from all of them!"

"How very thoughtful."

"And speaking of the Cotswolds, how's everything going with your hottie detective?"

"I'm going to another brunch at his parents' house tomorrow. It's Scott's birthday."

"A birthday brunch! How wonderful! What did you get him?"

"Nothing. His mother called and told me not to bring a gift."

"But you've got to bring a gift! Everyone always says No Gifts. And nobody ever means it. Trust me. Everyone will be bringing something. And you can't possibly be the only one at the party without a present."

For once, Lance was making sense.

And besides, it would be just like Ma Willis to tell me not to bring a gift when she knew full well that everybody, and by everybody I mean Chloe, would be bringing one. Anything to make me look bad in Scott's eyes.

Well, that wasn't about to happen.

"What on earth am I going to get him? The party's tomorrow and I haven't even begun to shop."

"Fear not! Uncle Lance to the rescue!"

With that, he grabbed his tweed jacket and raced out the door. Minutes later, he was back with a white oblong gift box.

"Voila!" he said, opening the lid. "A Christmas gift from my Aunt Celeste. A genuine Hugo Boss tie. I haven't had a chance to wear it."

I looked down at a lush black and gray diamond patterned silk tie.

"It's beautiful!" I cried. "Thanks so much, Lance!"

"A small price to pay for a wedding in the Cotswolds. Now I'm counting on you to make a good impression tomorrow. What are you going to wear? I know! How about a flirty little sundress?"

"Lance, the closest thing I have to 'flirty' are my jeans with the moth holes in the tush."

"Well, let's go buy you something!"

"Forget it. I don't have time to go shopping. I've got to walk off fifteen pounds by tomorrow morning. Don't worry. I'll think of something nice to wear. Now, please," I said, shoving him out the door. "Go. I've got to exercise!"

He left, chuckling at the thought of me exercising, and the minute he was gone I headed to the bedroom to slip into my sweats. Normally I wear them to veg out with my good friends Ben and Jerry. But today they were going to get a vigorous workout.

Before I started out on my walk, I decided to limber up with some leg lifts. So I got down on my Flokati rug and began. Right leg, lift. Left leg, lift. Right leg—Gosh, my Flokati was soft. And fluffy, too. I'd never realized it was so comfy before. Like a cloud of wool. Maybe I'd just close my eyes for a minute to gather my energy.

You know where this is going, right?

Three hours later, I woke up with drool on my chin and Flokati fuzz up my nose.

Thoroughly disgusted, I hoisted myself up and took my long-delayed walk—all the way to the phone to order Chinese food for dinner.

Okay, so I didn't go for a walk. And I ate Chinese food for dinner.

But don't have a hissy fit. All I had was two egg rolls and a bowl of wonton soup. Honest!

And I practically skipped breakfast the next morning. Just half a cinnamon raisin bagel. No butter. No jam. Which I ate standing up at the kitchen sink. And, as anybody who's ever studied physics in the *National Enquirer* knows, anything consumed while standing up has zero calories.

After breakfast, I spent a good hour showering, exfoliating, and wrestling my curls into an artfully tousled bed-head look.

Then I headed to my closet to choose an outfit. Deciding what to wear, however, was a bit tricky.

Ma Willis had told me to dress casually. But for all I knew, that was a trap. Maybe I'd show up in jeans only to find Chloe lounging about in a lavish designer dress. In the end I decided to compromise and go for the Elegant Casual look: My skinny jeans, a white silk blouse, and my one and only pair of Manolo Blahniks.

I was just about to get dressed when I heard Lance banging on my door.

"Jaine! Let me in!"

With a sigh, I shuffled into the living room and opened the door, prepared to hear another Ode to Gary.

"What is it?" I asked, a tad brusquely.

"The best news ever!"

"You got a riding crop to match your new tweed jacket?"

"No, but that's an interesting idea. Must Google 'riding crops' when I get back to my apartment. Anyhow, hon, I just got off the phone with my pilot buddy Frank. Frank does skywriting, and he's agreed to skywrite a love note from Cyril above Scott's parents' house today!"

"Cyril?"

"Cyril, your old boyfriend, the one who can't forget you. The one who sent you those gorgeous silk flowers, which, by the way, I'd like back."

Ah, yes. My mythical boyfriend, dreamed up by Lance to make Scott jealous.

"Here's what the message is going to say."

Lance whipped a piece of paper from his pocket and read:

Jaine Austen is Awfully Nice
Like Sugar and Spice
Love and kisses, Cyril

"Lance, that's way too long for a skywriter. The most they ever do is a word or two."

"That's what I thought at first. But thanks to

new skywriting technology, Frank assures me he can write out the entire message."

"You really think it can work?"

"Absolutely! When Scott sees it, he'll be positively oozing jealousy."

I liked the sound of that.

"Now all I need is the Willises' address."

I gave it to him, and I have to admit I was feeling quite pumped. It was fun having a skywriting ex-boyfriend who worshipped the ground I walked on.

"Wish me luck at the party," I said.

"Don't worry. You'll be fine. Just be yourself." Then, eyeing my ratty chenille robe with the jelly stains on the lapel, he added, "On second thought, be someone else. Try Gwyneth Paltrow. That should make a good impression."

"Thanks heaps," I snarled.

"No need to thank me, hon! That's what friends are for!"

And off he skipped, back to his apartment, to surf the Web for riding crops.

Chapter 28

I set out for Malibu, full of confidence. When I'd checked myself out in the mirror before leaving my apartment, I liked what I saw. My skinny jeans/white silk blouse/Manolo Blahniks ensemble looked quite fetching, especially when I added a pair of dangly silver earrings. So what if my earlier visits to Hell House had been a tad disastrous? There was no reason today couldn't be a perfectly lovely day.

After all, I reminded myself as I tooled along the Coast Highway, I was bright. Funny. Reasonably attractive. And I had a skywriting ex-boyfriend who worshipped the ground I walked on.—No, wait. I didn't have Cyril. He was just a figment of Lance's overactive imagination. But that didn't mean I wasn't attractive. Especially in my skinny jeans and white silk blouse ensemble.— Oh, no! Was that a big yellow mystery stain on the sleeve of my blouse? Why hadn't I noticed it at home? And why were my skinny jeans pinching me at my not-so-skinny waist? I'd hardly eaten a thing for breakfast. I peeked in my rearview mirror to check out my hair. What had seemed cute and bedhead-y at home now looked like a messy mop of frizz. Oh, who was I kidding? I could never compete with the spectacular Chloe.

Why on earth had I ever agreed to go back to Hell House?

I spent the rest of the ride reliving humiliating vignettes from my prior visits: Spilling wine on Ma Willis's heirloom tablecloth. Showing up reeking of Cat-Away. Sending Pa Willis to the hospital with an errant Frisbee. All of it in slo-mo and living color.

By the time I drove up to the Willises' driveway, I was ready to turn around and go home again. I'd call Scott and make up some excuse. A dental emergency. Or a flat tire. I'd think of something.

I was just about to make a break for it when the front door opened and Scott came out, looking great, as usual, in jeans and a T-shirt.

"Hi, Jaine!" he said, walking over to my Corolla, his brown curls glinting in the sun. "I saw your car pulling up."

I looked up at his Adam's apple and my heart (and other assorted body parts) melted.

Like a lamb trotting willingly to slaughter, I got out of the car.

"Happy birthday," I squeaked.

"It is, now that you're here."

With that, he wrapped me in his arms and kissed me. A hot, steamy one.

And just like that, I was filled with hope. Maybe this birthday brunch wouldn't be so awful after all.

His arm draped proprietarily over my shoulders, he led me inside the house and then out back to the patio, where the lynch mob—I mean, family— were gathered around the brunch table, sipping mimosas.

Sure enough, Chloe was there, too.

"Hey, everybody!" Scott called out. "Look who's here."

"Jaine, my dear, how lovely to see you," Ma Willis lied, wiggling her fingers hello beneath her gimlet glare.

I saw now that she hadn't misled me about dressing casually. Everyone except Grammy Willis (clad in an eye-popping hibiscus muumuu) seemed to be wearing jeans.

Chloe, a much better actress than Ma Willis, hopped up and pecked me on the cheek.

"So nice you could make it," she cooed. Her jeans were topped off with one of those flowy blouses with tiers of ruffles that only the truly skinny can get away with. On her feet she wore intricately tooled cowboy boots. Very Sundance Goes to Brunch.

I fought back a wave of jealousy and forced a smile.

Pa Willis, I gulped to see, was sporting a big black eye patch, his one good eye glued, as usual, to The Weather Channel.

"Omigod, what's she doing here?!" cried Grammy Willis, clutching a Bloody Mary in her gnarled fist. "Watch out, Brighton, or she'll poke your other eye out."

"Ignore her," Scott whispered in my ear. "The woman's a walking advertisement for euthanasia."

He led me over to the table, as far from Grammy Willis as possible, his arm still nestled over my shoulders.

I took a seat, and though I knew I was sitting in a viper's nest, I felt marvelously protected.

Throughout the meal, as Ma Willis rambled on about people I didn't know and places I'd never been, Scott murmured in my ear: about how pretty I looked. How sweet I smelled. How he wished it were just the two of us alone together.

He barely even glanced at Chloe.

Between the fantastic frittata I was eating, the mimosa I was drinking, and Scott's hand on my thigh, I was having a marvelous time.

I didn't even mind when Grammy Willis mistook me for Rosita and asked me for a refill on her Bloody Mary.

By the time the real Rosita wheeled out Scott's birthday cake, I was feeling foolish about ever having been worried about coming to the party.

Everyone sang *Happy Birthday* (except Grammy Willis, who was belting out the national anthem), and then Scott blew out the candles and made a wish.

I only hoped he was wishing for a gal in a white

silk blouse with a yellow mystery stain on the sleeve.

The birthday cake, you'll be happy to know, was divine: Chocolate with fudge frosting. I vowed to leave a ladylike portion of cake on my plate, a vow that flew right out the window as soon as I took my first bite.

Chloe picked at her cake, avoiding the frosting. (Don't you just hate her?) But who cared? I was the one sitting within kissing distance of Scott's Adam's apple, not her.

Just as I was scraping the last of the frosting from my plate, Ma Willis tinkled her champagne glass with a fork.

"Attention, everybody!" she said, with a side-long glance in my direction. "Time to open the birthday presents."

With that, Rosita wheeled out another trolley, this one piled with birthday gifts for Scott.

Aha! Ma Willis had been trying to make me look bad, after all, telling me not to bring a present. But thanks to Lance and his thoughtful Aunt Celeste, her dastardly plot was about to be foiled.

"Here's my gift!" I said, whipping the Hugo Boss tie from my purse.

I skipped over and put my gift box with the other presents, ignoring Ma Willis's withering glare.

Then we all looked on as Scott began opening

his gifts: From Ma Willis, a wallet that cost some endangered species its life. A book on meteorology from Pa Willis. A crisp five-dollar bill from Grammy Willis, who apparently thought it was still 1955. And a baby blue cashmere sweater from Chloe.

True, it was a gorgeous sweater, but Ma Willis was oohing and aahing like Chloe had just given him a Porsche. I wanted to wring her neck.

Scott saved my gift for last. Once again, I sent a silent prayer of thanks to Lance and Aunt Celeste. My Hugo Boss tie, while not a cashmere sweater, would make a respectable showing.

Scott shot me a heart-melting smile as he lifted it out of the box.

"Look, everybody!" he said, holding it up. "A Hugo Boss tie!"

And that's when I saw it. The price tag hanging from the tie. Not from Saks. Or Nordstrom. Or Neiman Marcus. But from Goodwill. For three whole dollars.

Damn Lance and his chintzy Aunt Celeste.

And I wasn't the only one who saw the tag.

"How clever of you, Jaine," Ma Willis said, malice oozing from every pore, "to have found something so lovely at the Goodwill. And such a bargain. Only three dollars. And once we get rid of that gravy stain, it'll be good as new."

Oh, hell. The tie had a stain right at the tip, which I hadn't noticed tucked away in the gift box.

I wanted to die. I wanted to fall through a hole in the patio and just die. But as that was not an option, I sat there staring into my empty mimosa glass.

"I love it!" Scott said, beaming me a big smile. "How did you know I shop at the Goodwill? I got these there last week," he said, patting his jeans.

What a sweet, thoughtful, wonderful lie. You can see why I was crazy about him, can't you?

But even under the warmth of his smile, I could sense the sharks circling in for the kill.

"So, Jaine," Chloe asked, toying with the fudge frosting on her cake. "How's your knee?"

"My knee?"

"The one you injured in that water-skiing accident."

So flustered was I by the Hugo Boss fiasco, that I answered without thinking.

"Oh, it's fine."

It was not until the words escaped my lips that I realized what she was talking about. Last time I was at Hell House, I'd faked a knee injury to get out of playing Frisbee.

"Wonderful!" Chloe cried. "Then you can join us horseback riding today."

Horseback riding? Was she nuts? The only horses I'd ever ridden were at a merry-go-round. And even then, I usually chose the ones that didn't go up and down.

"Yes," Ma Willis piped up. "Didn't I mention that we're all going for a ride?"

"No," I said between clenched teeth, resisting the urge to smash a slab of chocolate cake in her face. "You didn't."

"Well, we're all going."

"Won't it be fun!" Chloe said, clapping her hands like an irritating little tyke.

"You did say you've been riding all your life, didn't you?" Ma Willis asked.

I suddenly remembered my preposterous lie on that first dinner at Hell House, when I was so desperate to make a good impression.

"But I can't go!" I said. "I don't have the right shoes."

Thank heavens for my Manolos. They couldn't possibly expect me to go riding in them.

"Not a problem," Ma Willis said. "We've got lots of spare boots. What size are you? Ten?"

"Seven and a half!" I cried indignantly.

And sure enough, out from some closet, they dredged a pair of boots that fit me just fine.

"Are you sure you want to do this?" Scott asked. "You look a little uneasy. I don't have to go. You and I can stay here with Grammy Willis."

"But, Scott!" Ma Willis said. "You've been looking forward to this ride all week."

I could see from the look on Scott's face that he *had* been looking forward to this ride. And I was not about to be the one who rained on his parade. If I let him stay behind with me and Grammy Willis, he might realize how much he had in common with Chloe and how little he had in common with me.

Scott would go riding, all right. And so would I. No way was I going to let him go galloping off into the sunset with Chloe.

How hard could it be to ride a horse, anyway?

Poor Rosita was stuck with Grammy Willis while the rest of us piled into the family Mercedes and rode a mile up the Coast Highway to a stable where the Willises boarded a bunch of horses.

Ma Willis wanted me to ride a fire-breathing dragon named Rocky, but fortunately Scott intervened, and soon I was being led over to a geriatric nag named Mr. Muffin.

Thanks to a contraption called a mounting block, I was able to climb some stairs to the horse, and get in the saddle after only three mortifying tries.

"Are you sure you've ridden before?" Ma Willis asked with a sly smile.

"Of course," I said, refusing to back down. "It's been a few years, though," I added to Scott. "So I'm a little rusty."

"Well, we're off!" Ma Willis cried, leading the way out of the stable and across the coast highway to the beach.

All the horses started trotting after her—all of

them except Mr. Muffin, who was still as a statue.

"Okay, Mr. Muffin," I whispered in his ear. "Time to go. Giddyap! Hi ho, Silver, and all that."

But Mr. Muffin just stood there, no doubt dreaming of a nice relaxing nap.

"Squeeze him gently with your calves," said Scott, who'd hung back by my side.

I squeezed Mr. Muffin with my calves, and lo and behold, he started moving.

"Pull the left rein if you want him to go left, pull the right rein if you want him to go right, and pull both reins if you want him to stop."

"Right," I shouted. "Thanks. It's all coming back to me."

As if I'd actually done this before.

Crossing the coast highway was a tad terrifying, and I held my breath until Mr. Muffin and I made it onto the beach without a fender stuck to Mr. Muffin's tail.

I followed the others as they trotted along the shoreline. Somehow I managed to hang on to the reins and keep my tush in the saddle.

As Scott directed, I pulled left on the reins when I wanted Mr. Muffin to veer left and right when I want him to veer right. And believe it or not, the little angel actually did what I wanted. True, I'd seen geezers with walkers making better time, but I didn't care. By now, I was getting used to Mr. Muffin's easy rhythm and I actually liked it.

This horseback riding thing wasn't so bad, after all.

"Nice going, Jaine!" Scott waved to me.

I was feeling quite proud of myself when I looked over and saw a wedding party on the beach.

How romantic! Maybe one of these days I'd be exchanging vows with Scott at this very same spot.

The wedding in progress was one of those hippy-dippy affairs, the groom in cutoffs and flip-flops, the bride in sandals and vintage lace dress, her hair in Botticelli curls down her back. In her hands she was carrying what I would later learn was a "vegan" bouquet. Made of asparagus stalks, baby artichokes, and carrot sticks.

I don't know about you, but items from the produce section are not my idea of a fun wedding bouquet.

Mr. Muffin, however, seemed to be of an entirely different school of thought. He took one look at the carrots and woke from his geriatric stupor, in the mood for a snack. And suddenly, before my horrified eyes, my mild-mannered nag turned to greased lightning, thundering toward the bride.

I pulled the reins like Scott told me, but Mr. Muffin wasn't about to take orders. Not with those carrots within chomping distance. Frantically, I wrapped my arms around his neck, holding on for dear life.

The wedding party looked up, aghast, as Mr. Muffin came charging toward them.

"What's that horse doing here?" the bride shouted.

"I think he wants your bouquet," the groom shouted back. "Give it to him, Tracy!"

"But, Chad. I paid seventy five-dollars for this bouquet!"

"Just give it to him!" Chad said, snatching the bouquet from Tracy's hand and throwing it at Mr. Muffin. Then, pouting, he added, "I told you we should have had a church wedding."

"You think you know everything, don't you, Chad?"

Oh, dear. Why did I get the feeling this marriage wasn't going to make it past the reception?

But I couldn't worry about Chad and Tracy. Not now. I was still clinging to Mr. Muffin as he snatched up the vegan bouquet and galloped off down the beach. I just prayed he wouldn't dump me into the nearest sand dune.

At last Scott caught up to us and managed to get hold of Mr. Muffin, who had by now stopped to nosh on his vegan bouquet.

"Oh, Scott," I wailed. "I'm so sorry! I ruined their wedding! I should've never come along with you guys. I don't really know how to ride a horse."

"I sort of figured that out," he said with a wry smile. "C'mon. You better ride back with me."

I rode back to the stable with Scott on his horse, Mr. Muffin in tow. Nestled up against Scott, his arm circling my waist, I should have been in heaven. But all I felt was abject humiliation.

"That was quite a ride," Ma Willis said when we were all back in the Mercedes.

She was loving every minute of this.

"Your father had to cut the bride and groom a check for five grand to cover the cost of the wedding. Not that I believe for one instant that ragtag wedding cost five thousand dollars, but heaven knows we didn't want a lawsuit."

From the grin on her face, I figured five grand was a small price to pay to make me look bad in front of Scott.

"I feel terrible about this!" I said, shrinking into my seat.

"Don't," Scott said. "Accidents happen."

"Especially to Jaine!" Ma Willis chirped. "They seem to happen to her all the time, don't they?"

Why the hell couldn't Mr. Muffin have rammed into *her* instead of the bride?

No doubt about it. This had to be the absolute nadir of my life.

No, not quite.

The absolute nadir of my life came two second later when Chloe pointed out the window.

"Look, everybody!" she cried. "Up in the sky! Skywriting!"

Omigosh, in the all the sturm und drang of the

Runaway Mr. Muffin Affair, I'd forgotten all about Cyril and his skywriting love note. What was it supposed to say? *Jaine Austen is Awfully Nice. Like Sugar and Spice. Love, Cyril.*

Sure enough, I looked out the window and there in the sky were the words

Jaine Austen is Awful . . .

Where the hell was the rest of it? Damn it all. I knew Lance's friend would run out of smoke. And I was right.

"Jaine Austen is awful!" Ma Willis read aloud.

Things couldn't have worked out better if she'd paid for it herself.

It was less than a mile back to Hell House, but it felt like an eternity.

Everyone sat with their necks craned out the window of the Mercedes, watching *Jaine Austen is Awful* grow puffy in the sky.

"Do you have any idea who could have done this?" Scott asked me.

No way was I about to own up to Lance's plan to make Scott jealous with Cyril and his love note in the sky.

"None whatsoever," I said, doing my best to look perplexed. "It must be about some other Jaine Austen."

"Another Jaine Austen?" Chloe squeaked in disbelief.

"It's a very common name," I said.

"Where?" Ma Willis snorted. "In Northanger Abbey?"

Scott shot me the kind of look I give to people I see walking down the street shouting into nonexistent cell phones.

Clearly he was reassessing me as Significant Other material.

With nothing left to say, I tried my best to fade into the Mercedes leather, my heart and butt both sore from the wild rides they had just been on.

Chapter 29

Back home, I found Prozac napping on my computer keyboard, ignoring the comforts of her deluxe Kitty Condo less than five feet away.

Is that cat maddening, or what?

I stomped past the abandoned condo, now gathering dust at an alarming rate—a perfect candidate for Miss Havisham's rec room—and headed for the tub to strip off my sandy clothes and soak my blues away in a strawberry-scented bubble bath.

Soon I was up to my neck in bubbles, my muscles growing limp in the soothing heat of the water. With some deep breathing exercises (and the help of my good friend Mr. Chardonnay), I was able to forget the humiliations of the day and focus on a far more important priority: What to order for dinner.

I opted for Thai, and an hour later I was swan diving into a plate of pad Thai and spring rolls, with just a teensy bit more chardonnay to wash it all down.

Then I flopped into bed and lay there in a zombie state, Prozac snoring on my chest as I watched endless episodes of *House Hunters*.

Eventually, however, the effects of the chardonnay began to wear off, and once more my brain was flooded with images from my latest trip to Hell House.

No matter how hard I tried to concentrate on HGTV's endless procession of photogenic home buyers, all I could see was Mr. Muffin charging down that beach, the Goodwill price tag dangling from Scott's tie, and *Jaine Austen is Awful* blazing across the Malibu sky.

Worst of all was the expression on Scott's face in the Mercedes. No doubt about it. I'd lost him for good.

I needed something to make me forget. And chardonnay wouldn't cut it. This time I needed to go for the hard stuff.

And so fifteen minutes later, I was in the freezer aisle of my supermarket, loading up on Chunky Monkey.

Yes, there's nothing like a dose of pure butterfat coursing through your veins to make life seem worth living again.

I was heading up the front path to my apartment with a pint of Chunky Monkey in my grocery bag (okay, three pints), eagerly anticipating that first soothing spoonful sliding down my throat, when I heard a rustling noise from my neighbor's azalea bush.

Suddenly a lithe figure in a jog suit and ski mask came lunging out from behind the azaleas. Just like the assailant who'd gone after Candace.

Only this time the assailant had long black hair extensions.

Good heavens! It was Heather. She was the killer after all. A pageant mom who'd stop at nothing to see her daughter crowned Miss Teen Queen America!

My heart pounding, I raced off down the path.

But I hadn't gone three steps before Heather overtook me and clamped her arm around my neck in a suffocating chokehold.

As I stood there, pressed up against her body, her forearm squeezing my trachea, I suddenly became aware of a sweet citrusy scent in the air. I'd know that scent anywhere. It was the same cologne I'd smelled on Taylor's Vera Wang gown and in Dr. Fletcher's office.

And then I realized my attacker wasn't Heather—but Dr. Fletcher in drag!

Clearly he didn't trust me to keep my mouth shut about his penchant for ladies' underlovelies, and was here to silence me forever!

I gasped for air as his arm squeezed tighter around my neck. Was I going to die here in my flip-flops and *Cuckoo for Cocoa Puffs* T-shirt, never to see another sunset, never to smell another rose, never to eat another pint of Chunky Monkey—

Omigosh! The Chunky Monkey!

I remembered the frozen pints in the grocery bag still clutched in my hand.

Summoning my every last ounce of strength, I swung my bag of frozen ammo, hoping to make contact with Dr. Fletcher's head.

Bingo.

The next thing I knew, his arm slid from my neck and he'd dropped to his knees, clutching his forehead and moaning in pain.

"Hey, what's going on?"

I looked up and saw Lance skipping up the front path with that goofy look in his eyes he always gets when he's coming home from a hot date

"Quick, Lance!" I cried. "Call 911! This man is Amy Leighton's killer, and he just tried to kill me, too."

Lance looked down at Dr. Fletcher, gaping in disbelief.

"Are you sure it's a man? Isn't his hair awfully long for a guy?"

"Just call the cops!"

"Okay, okay," he said, whipping out his cell.

At which point, Dr. Fletcher staggered to his feet and began to make a run for it. I gave chase and, thanks to my amazing agility—and the fact that Dr. Fletcher had tripped over a loose brick in the pathway—I was able to catch him and shove him flat on his back.

Straddling his chest, I pulled off his ski mask, and sure enough, it was Dr. Fletcher, in a long black wig, hot pink lipstick, and turquoise eye shadow.

"We've caught a killer!" Lance cried, thrilled to the gills. "A heartless psycho murdering machine!" Then he turned to Dr. Fletcher and said, "I'd lose the eye shadow if I were you."

Lance helped me hold him down until the police showed up.

As soon as they did, I told them the whole story: how Candace had been blackmailing Dr. Fletcher about his cross-dressing and how he tried to kill us both to keep his secret safe.

"He tried to kill Candace at the pageant, but when that didn't work and he wound up killing Amy by mistake, he went after Candace with a knife outside her house. Dressed in a ski mask and jog suit. Just like tonight."

Dr. Fletcher insisted that he never tried to kill Candace, and that he was only trying to scare me. In fact, he even had the nerve to try to press charges against me for assault and battery! But the cops took one look at the bruises on my neck and hauled him off to jail.

After they left, I hugged Lance good night and headed into my apartment with my precious cargo—my three pints of Chunky Monkey. Without them, I might have been strangled to death.

So don't anybody ever tell me that ice cream is bad for my health. As far as I was concerned, Ben & Jerry had just saved my life.

YOU'VE GOT MAIL

To: Jausten
From: Shoptillyoudrop
Subject: Glorious Day!

Jaine, darling—
What a glorious day! Perfect weather for the poolside fashion show. I was afraid it might rain, but there's not a cloud in the sky. And best news of all: I just got off the scale and, in spite of the occasional Oreo I've been eating, I've managed to lose three pounds!
I can't wait to try on my dress!
XOXO,
Mom

To: Jausten
From: Shoptillyoudrop
Subject: Argggh!

I just took down my dress from where it was hanging on my closet door, and discovered the most godawful stain on the back. Daddy confessed he picked up the dress with greasy fingers (from eating fudge, no less!) and then painted over the stain with exterior latex house paint!

296

I may never speak to him again!
XOXO,
Mom
P.S. Off to the dry cleaners. I only hope they can get the stain out before the luncheon.

To: Jausten
From: DaddyO
Subject: Back in the Doghouse

Dearest Lambchop—Looks like I'm back in the doghouse with your mom. Remember that fudge stain I got on her dress? I thought the house paint had covered it up quite nicely, but unfortunately it dried stiff as a board.

I'm afraid your mom's in a bit of a snit. Something tells me I'll be sleeping with Nellybelle tonight.

Love 'n' snuggles from
Daddy

To: Jausten
From: Shoptillyoudrop
Subject: Thank Heavens!

Thank heavens for Tampa Vistas Dry Cleaners. Those angels promised to have the dress ready by noon. I'll be at the luncheon then, but the fashion show doesn't start until 1 PM, so if Daddy picks up the dress, he can bring it over to the clubhouse and I'll have it in time for the show.

I'm almost tempted to show up late for the luncheon and pick up the dress myself, but surely I can trust your father to pick up a dress and bring it to the clubhouse, can't I? I mean, how on earth can he possibly screw that up?

TAMPA TRIBUNE
GOLF CART RUNS AMOK, SINKS IN COMMUNITY SWIMMING POOL

In a freak accident, Tampa Vistas resident Hank Austen lost control of his golf cart and went plummeting down a hill of the Tampa Vistas Golf Course into the community swimming pool, interrupting a fashion show fundraiser for the local library.

Fortunately Mr. Austen sustained no injuries.

When asked to comment on the incident, Tampa Vistas Homeowners Association President Lydia Pinkus would only say: "Why am I not surprised? This is a man who chases raccoons in the middle of the night in his underwear."

To: Jausten
From: Shoptillyoudrop
Subject: So Much for Trusting Daddy

So much for trusting Daddy. I should have known something was wrong when one o'clock rolled around and there was no sign of him. The fashion show was well under way, and there I was, sitting at my table, wondering if I'd ever get a chance to model my gorgeous Pink Flamingo dress, when I looked up and saw a golf cart coming down the hill that faces the clubhouse pool. Then I noticed that the driver was wearing a hideous plaid cap with a pom-pom on top.

My heart sank when I realized it was Daddy! On Nellybelle!

By now his cart had picked up speed—and it wasn't stopping. Then, just as the fashion show announcer was saying, "Here's an outfit that's sure to make a splash on the social scene," Daddy came trampling over a bed of begonias, onto the pool deck, and into the pool!

Honestly, honey. I thought I'd die.

Apparently, after he picked up my dress from the cleaners, Daddy made the idiotic decision to drive Nellybelle to the clubhouse, taking a "shortcut" through the golf course. He wasted twenty minutes caught in a sand trap, and was pushing Nellybelle as fast as he could to make up for lost time, when he got to the top of the hill.

He started going downhill when he suddenly realized his brakes weren't working. Remember that leftover piece of metal from Nellybelle's engine that Daddy said couldn't be very important? Well, it was part of the emergency brake. Which meant he couldn't stop! Thank heavens there wasn't a wall separating the golf course from the pool, or he could have been seriously injured. As it was, the water kept him buoyant, and all he suffered were a few scrapes.

Nellybelle, I'm happy to report, wasn't nearly so lucky. The mechanics who came and towed her away said she'd broken an axle when she made contact with the bottom of the pool.

I know I should be angry with Daddy, but I'm not. I'm just happy he wasn't hurt. I shudder to think what could have happened if he'd rammed into a wall. Plus, he had the presence of mind to toss my Pink Flamingo dress from the golf cart before he plunged into the pool.

For all his flaws, he really does mean well.

What can I say? I love him to pieces. As I do you, honey—

XOXO,
Mom

To: Jausten
From DaddyO
Subject: Little Mishap

I suppose Mom told you about the little mishap at the fashion show. Poor Nellybelle. She was a fine old girl, and I'm going to miss her.

Luckily your mom has forgiven me.

I think the box of fudge I gave her helped.

Love 'n' snuggles from
Daddy

To: Jausten
From: DaddyO
Subject: Mom Was Right

I've been thinking it over, Lambchop, and I've come to the conclusion that your mom was right about Nellybelle. As much as I loved her, she was probably of inferior quality. I'll never make that mistake again.

Which is why I just ordered a top-of-the-line EZ Rider motor scooter from Big Al's Discount Scooter Warehouse—where every bike comes with a free harmonica! Can't wait to learn how to play it!

Love 'n' hugs from
Daddy

Chapter 30

I was jolted awake the next morning by a loud banging on my bedroom wall.

"Quick, Jaine!" Lance was shouting at me through our paper-thin walls. "Turn on the Channel Five news!"

Wiping sleep from my eyes and Prozac from my chest, I reached for the remote and clicked on the TV just in time to see a photo of Dr. Fletcher taken in happier days, smiling into the camera, the proud principal of Alta Loco High.

A perky newscaster with impossibly white teeth, perhaps a former Miss Teen Queen America, was talking about how Dr. Fletcher had been arrested for the assault of a Beverly Hills woman, June Austen—good heavens, could no one get my name right?—and was now a prime suspect in Amy Leighton's murder.

As I watched footage of Dr. Fletcher being escorted in handcuffs to a police van, I couldn't help noticing how frightened he looked. So weak and vulnerable. Not at all the image of a murderous psychopath.

Was it possible he wasn't the killer? I wondered, as I headed for the bathroom to brush my teeth.

But then I caught a glimpse of my neck in the bathroom mirror, blotched with ugly black and blue marks. Once again, I could feel Dr. Fletcher's arms choking the life out of me. And suddenly he didn't seem so innocent anymore.

Dr. Fletcher was the killer, all right, and I was glad he was behind bars.

It was with a sense of great relief that I tootled off to the kitchen to fix Prozac some Hearty Halibut Guts and nuke myself a cinnamon raisin bagel.

A sense of relief that came to a crashing halt, however, when I read the latest emails from my parents. I was sitting there, shuddering at the thought of Daddy behind the wheel of Nellybelle, plowing into the Tampa Vistas community pool, when Lance came knocking at my door.

"How're you feeling, hon?" he asked as he breezed in, decked out in cut-offs and a tank top.

"Okay, but my neck's a little sore."

"Acck!" he cried, eyeing my bruises. "You poor thing! You look like you've just done ten rounds with a Jersey Housewife. Stay right there, and Uncle Lance will fix you an ice pack."

He scooted off to my kitchen. Seconds later he came back out, chomping on a cinnamon raisin bagel.

"Hope you don't mind; I took your last bagel."

Of course I minded!

Then, tossing me a cold can of Diet Coke, he said, "Rub this on your neck. It's practically as good as an ice pack.

"I still can't get over it!" he said as he plopped down on my sofa. "I, Lance Venable, actually caught a killer!"

"You??"

"Yes, me! Don't you remember how I tackled that burly thug to the ground?"

"Burly thug? Dr. Fletcher can't weigh more than a hundred and forty pounds soaking wet. And you didn't tackle him. He tripped over a loose brick."

"Yes, but right after that, I tackled him and sat on his chest till the police came."

"Wait a minute. *I* was the one sitting on his chest."

"Technically, perhaps, but if it weren't for my arms of steel holding him down, he surely would have gotten away. That's the story I posted on Twitter, anyway, and I'm sticking to it."

Can you believe this guy? Talk about delusional.

"Well, gotta run," he said, getting up. "Must take a selfie of me on the front path to tweet to my followers. I've got three hundred twenty-two new ones ever since I tweeted about how I saved your life!"

Any minute now, he'd be awarding himself a Nobel Peace Prize.

"Mind if I take your Diet Coke?" he said as he grabbed it from my neck. "I'm thirsty from the bagel."

With that, he breezed out the door.

304

I was just about to dash after him and snatch back my Diet Coke when the phone rang. I picked it up to hear Heather's voice, bubbling with excitement.

"Jaine, dear. I just heard the news about Dr. Fletcher's arrest. I'm not the least bit surprised he turned out to be the killer. I knew there was something evil about him the first time I saw him!"

Was she kidding? The first time she saw him waiting for the elevator at the Amada Inn, she was practically kissing his fanny, hoping to get him to vote for Taylor.

"Anyhow," she was saying, "I've got terrific news. The teen queen crowning ceremony has been rescheduled for tomorrow, and Taylor is back in the contest!"

"That's wonderful. How did that happen?"

"My husband had a word with pageant head-quarters and everything got straightened out."

I remembered Nicky, her hit man of a husband. I just hoped there were no tire irons involved.

"Taylor really wants you to be at the crowning ceremony. She's so very fond of you."

The last thing I wanted was to sit around watching a teen queen get crowned with a clock-tiara, but Taylor was a sweet kid, so I agreed to go.

The minute I hung up, the phone rang again. It was Taylor.

You cynics out there who think she was calling because she wanted me to bring M&M's are all wrong.

This time she wanted Kit Kat bars.

Chapter 31

I showed up at the Amada Inn the next day, pitying the poor souls checking in, and took the hotel's one and only working elevator to the top floor. Over in the Rooftop Ballroom, rows of chairs had been set up for the crowning ceremony. Next door in the dressing room, nervous teens sat in makeup chairs as their moms fussed over them, applying blush, curling lashes, and adding wiglets to their already huge hair.

Making my way through a miasma of hairspray, I found Taylor decked out in her fifteen-hundred-dollar Vera Wang gown, having her hair done by a skinny guy in gold lamé jeans, who I could only assume was a professional stylist.

Heather hovered nearby, Elvis in her arms.

"Hey, guys!" I called out.

"Jaine, thank heavens you're here! Taylor's been asking about you all morning."

"Hi, Jaine." Taylor waved a manicured finger at me, and I surreptitiously pointed at my purse, to let her know her Kit Kats were close at hand.

Then I looked over and saw that, as bad luck would have it, Luanne and Gigi were at the very next makeup station.

Luanne was sipping coffee from a paper cup, shouting out unwanted directions as Gigi applied her own makeup. No designer duds for Gigi; her gown was a sequined special straight from a prom shop. But Gigi was a pretty girl, and she looked damn good in it.

"More blush!" Luanne screeched at her. "You need rosy cheeks."

Gigi rolled her eyes.

"Mom, I wanna be Teen Queen, not Ronald McDonald."

"I'm so glad Taylor had her makeup done by a trained professional," Heather bragged, loud enough for Luanne to hear.

"Some girls need all the help they can get," Luanne muttered.

Heather bristled. "Of all the nerve! Taylor, did you hear what she just said?"

Taylor shot her mom a warning look.

"Mom, if you make a scene, I swear I'm getting up and walking out right now."

Reluctantly, Heather clamped her lips shut and turned her attention to Taylor's hair.

"Here, Jaine. Watch Elvis, will you? I want to do Taylor's bangs. Nobody does bangs like I do."

She thrust the little beast in my arms, and he greeted me as he usually did—with a nasty growl and much baring of fangs.

"Here's his favorite chew toy," Heather said, handing me a bright chartreuse bone, covered liberally in dog spit. Elvis started gnawing on it as

Heather grabbed a comb from Mr. Gold Lamé and began working on Taylor's bangs.

Eventually Taylor was gussied up to Heather's exacting standards and twirled around for inspection.

"Gorgeous!" Heather proclaimed.

And I must admit, she was right. With her big brown eyes, tiny waist, and flawless complexion—all wrapped up in that Vera Wang gown—Taylor was quite a stunner.

"You look really nice," Gigi said, eyeing Taylor's dress with envy.

"Thanks," Taylor smiled. "So do you."

"That's the sportsmanlike way!" Mr. Gold Lamé exclaimed, waving his hair dryer in the spirit of peace. "May the best contestant win!"

"Don't worry," Heather said. "Taylor will."

"No way!" Luanne shot back. "My Gigi's going to walk away with that crown."

"Only if she rips it off my Taylor's head."

By now the two were glaring at each other in Dragon Mom mode.

"Wake up and smell the hairspray," Luanne sneered. "Gigi's going to win."

"Taylor!"

"Gigi!"

"Taylor!"

"Gigi!"

This fascinating battle of wits was in full swing when Candace's new assistant, a harried young slip of a thing, came hurrying by, her clipboard poking out from the crook of her arm. No doubt in a rush to obey Candace's latest command, she accidentally jostled Luanne.

And that's when things went from bad to World War III. I watched in dismay as Luanne's coffee went flying out of her paper cup—right down the front of Taylor's fifteen-hundred-dollar Vera Wang gown.

"I'm so sorry!" Candace's assistant cried.

But Heather was deaf to her apology. She whirled on Luanne, fire in her eyes.

"You did that on purpose!"

"I did not!" Luanne shot back. "It was an accident!"

But Heather wasn't buying it.

"Oh, please. You've been sniping at me ever since this pageant began. That was no accident. You spilled that coffee on purpose!" she shouted. "You spilled it on purpose!"

You spilled it on purpose!

And with those words everything clicked into place.

I knew who the killer was.

Not Dr. Fletcher, whose only crimes were assault and tacky taste in garter belts. The killer, I felt certain, was Candace.

Candace said she'd accidentally spilled Coke on Amy's red blazer the day of the murder. But what if it wasn't an accident? What if she'd spilled that Coke on purpose, so Amy would be forced to change into Candace's blue blazer?

All along I'd assumed that Candace was the intended victim and that the killer had killed Amy by mistake. But what if there was no mistake? What if Candace had been plotting to kill Amy?

Candace had been on the take, accepting bribes from desperate pageant moms. Maybe mousy little Amy hadn't been so mousy. Maybe she knew about Candace's cheating ways and had been threatening to expose her.

So Candace maneuvered her into a blue blazer and killed her to shut her up, careful to leave her body face down, to make it look like the killer had mistaken Amy for Candace.

Hadn't Bethenny been grousing about how her Tiphany clock-tiara had come without batteries? Then why was the tiara clock working the day it was used as a murder weapon? Because Candace had put batteries in the clock and then set the time to when she knew she'd be at the dance rehearsal. Then, smashing the tiara on Amy's skull, she'd stopped the clock, giving herself an airtight alibi.

Yes, I'd bet my bottom Pop-Tart Candace was the killer. I had to call Brunhilde and tell her what I knew. I just hoped she'd take me seriously, considering I didn't have a shred of evidence.

By now, Mr. Gold Lamé was dabbing club soda on Taylor's Vera Wang. Miraculously the coffee stain was coming out.

"See?" Heather said to Luanne. "Your nasty little trick has failed! Now nothing can stop my Taylor from winning the crown!"

"I'll be right back," I said to Heather, shoving Elvis in her arms. "I've got to make a call."

"Why? What's wrong?"

"I know who Amy's killer is."

With that I grabbed my cell phone from my purse and dashed out to the hallway.

"But I thought Dr. Fletcher was the killer," Heather said, hot on my heels, toting Elvis.

"Nope," I said, once we were alone in the corridor. "It's Candace."

"Candace? Isn't she was the one the killer was trying to knock off?"

"That's what she wanted everyone to think."

I told her my theory.

"What marvelous news!" she cried when I was finished. "I can't wait to see her royal snootiness rot in jail, after the way she treated my Taylor." Then her brow furrowed in doubt. "But wait a minute. What about that man who jumped out from her bushes and attacked her with a knife?"

"If you ask me, Candace probably staged that little scene herself. I wouldn't be at all surprised if she had Eddie stab her."

Suddenly from behind us we heard a mirthless laugh.

We whirled around to see Candace, with a sneer on her face and a gun in her hand.

A gun, which, I might add, was aimed most unnervingly at my gut.

"Eddie, stab me? Not bloody likely. He's such a wuss, I had to stab myself. But it was very convincing, don't you agree? It made everyone think I was being stalked by a killer!

"And I was careful not to go too deep," she added, quite pleased with herself. "Just a scratch, really. All better now!"

Indeed, all that remained on her arm was a tiny bandage.

"Well, enough about me," she said, getting down to business. "Time to get rid of you two. First things first. Hand over your cell phone, Sherlock."

Reluctantly I tossed my phone to her.

"Can't have you trying to dial 911 on the sly, can I?"

Damn. That's just what I'd been planning to do.

"Okay, girls. Time to take a little walk."

With her gun at our backs, Candace nudged us over to the elevators. I prayed that someone would walk by, but everyone was in the dressing room, getting ready for the grand crowning ceremony. If only Elvis would start barking and attract their attention. But, no. The little prince had apparently taken a vow of silence.

"Lucky for me," Candace was saying as she bonked my spine with the butt of her gun, "my new assistant overheard you saying you knew who the killer was. And I was afraid you might have figured out the truth."

By now my brain was spinning like a crazed hamster. If I could get Candace to confess to the murder, I'd have Heather as a witness. None of which would mean anything, of course, if she wound up using that gun on us. But it was worth a try. I had to keep her talking.

"You killed Amy to shut her up," I said, hoping to egg her on.

She took the bait.

"Silly little thing. She was going to report me to pageant headquarters for taking bribes. Very foolish of her. I wasn't about to give up the pageant. Not after all the work I put into it, not to mention all the money I siphoned out of it."

"So you spilled your Coke on her blazer so she'd be forced to wear one of yours. Then you knocked her off with the clock-tiara, setting the time for when you'd be at the dance rehearsal. And you were careful to leave her face down, so everyone would think the killer had mistaken her for you."

"Well, aren't you the smarty pants," Candace said, giving me a particularly sharp jab with her gun.

"Then you played the victim, pretending the killer was still out to get you, running around without makeup, looking your worst, very Woman in Jeopardy. You staged the phony stabbing, and claimed there was someone in a black van following you."

We came to a stop at the elevators and Candace stepped in front of us, her gun once more pointed straight at my gut.

"Congratulations, Ms. Austen. You win first prize in the amateur detective contest: An all-expenses-paid trip for two down a nice long elevator shaft."

Then she reached into her pocket and pulled out a walkie-talkie device. "Eddie!" she barked into it. "Get over here now!

"When he gets here," she informed us, "he's going to pry those elevator doors open, and you two are going to take an express ride straight to the bottom. A tragic accident. Some careless Amada Inn employee will have left the doors open by mistake. That's what Eddie and I will tell the police after we discover your bodies."

Then, in a moment of bravery that surprises me to this day, I said, "Let's get out of here, Heather."

Heather looked at me like I was nuts.

"But she's got a gun."

"She won't dare shoot it. Not without attracting a crowd. If she fires that gun, she'd be arrested on the spot."

"Not if I use Fluffy here as a pillow to silence my shots."

In a flash, Candace reached out and wrenched Elvis from Heather's arms.

Heather's eyes were wide with horror.

"You'd kill an innocent dog?"

"Whatever works."

"Bite her, Elvis!" Heather shrieked. "Attack!"

But Elvis, a graduate of the Prozac School of Heroic Action, just sat nestled in Candace's arms, sniffing her perfume.

"The party's over, girls," Candace said. "And if you want your sissy fleaball to be alive for your funeral, you'd better shut up and stay put."

"Sissy fleaball? How dare you speak that way about my Elvis?" Overcome with the fury of an outraged pet owner, she hissed, "Drop dead, bitch!"

"Sorry, sweetheart," Candace said, waving her gun. "You first. In fact, I'm not even going to wait for Eddie. I like Plan B better. Where I use the fleaball to silence my shots."

Oh, God. I couldn't let this happen. Why the hell did Heather have to antagonize Candace? Did she always have to be getting into a fight? I had to do something to stop the bloodshed.

If only I had my purse! I could try whacking her over the head with it. Or at least enjoy a final Kit Kat bar before going to meet my maker.

But I was totally defenseless.

And then, like a saliva-soaked miracle from heaven, I felt it in my pocket. Elvis's chew toy! Just where I'd shoved it before dashing out to call Brunhilde.

Now, as Candace put her gun up against poor Elvis's tummy, I grabbed the chartreuse bone and hurled it at her. Due to my expert aim—and the fact that she was standing less than three feet away—I managed to hit her smack in the face.

Startled, she dropped her gun—and Elvis.

As soon as the gun hit the ground, I kicked it away from her and raced over to get it.

Meanwhile, Heather, furious, had tackled Candace like an NFL linebacker.

"How dare you call my Elvis a sissy fleaball? I'll have you know he's a purebred Bichon stud!"

I'd kicked the gun a lot farther than I thought, and just as I was bending down to grab it, someone else snatched it out from under me.

I looked up and saw Eddie glaring down at me from underneath his bad toupee.

Oh, hell.

"Get up off my wife!" he instructed Heather, iron in his voice.

"What took you so damn long?" Candace hissed. "They know everything. Now hurry up and open those elevator doors, so we can throw them down the shaft."

Eddie stood there, pointing the gun back and forth between me and Heather.

I told myself what I'd told Heather earlier, that he wouldn't dare fire, not without attracting a crowd. I ordered myself to run for help. But all

I could see was Eddie squeezing the trigger and me being blown to smithereens.

So in a moment of cowardice that pretty much canceled out my earlier moment of bravery, I stayed put, frozen in fear.

"What are you waiting for?" Candace barked at Eddie. "Snap to it!"

But then something wonderful happened.

Eddie shook his head no.

"One murder was bad enough. I'm not going to stand by and let you get away with two more."

Now he was aiming the gun—not at me or Heather—but at Candace.

"Somebody call the police," he said with a weary sigh.

Not wasting a single second, that's just what I did.

Soon the cops showed up, and Eddie, after years of being bossed around and cheated on, was only too happy to tell the truth about Amy's murder.

Candace didn't even flinch as he sold her down the river.

The cops led her away, her spine ramrod straight, not a hair out of place, utterly composed in her moment of crisis.

The perfect role model for Miss Teen Queen America.

(Except for her handcuffs, of course.)

Chapter 32

Later that night, Prozac and I were sprawled out in bed, watching TV, the remains of a sausage and pepperoni pizza in a box between us.

We were watching *Shadow of a Doubt*, my favorite Alfred Hitchcock movie, but I wasn't really paying attention. All I could think about was my near brush with death.

"Oh, Prozac!" I moaned. "It was awful. I came *thisclose* to being hurled down an elevator shaft!"

Clearly moved by my plight, she scurried to my side.

Yeah, right, whatever. Scratch me behind my right ear, willya? Okay, now the left one. Now the right. Now the left—

I was in the middle of making her every wish come true when the phone rang.

My heart gave a little somersault when Scott's voice came on the line. I thought for sure I'd heard the last of him.

"Hey, Jaine," he said. "I was wondering if I could stop by to talk to you."

"Sure," I gulped.

"Great. I'm not far from your duplex. I should be there in about ten minutes."

Yikes! Only ten minutes for an extreme make-over!

I leaped out of bed, threw on jeans and an Eileen Fisher jersey knit top (half-off at Nordstrom's semi-annual sale), blew out my bangs, and slapped on some makeup.

At the last minute, I remembered my pizza breath, and dashed to the bathroom to brush my teeth vigorously, gargling twice with industrial-strength mouthwash.

Why the heck did I have to order a smelly pepperoni pizza?

I was just shoving an Altoid in my mouth when Scott showed up, looking yummy in slacks and a blazer.

"C'mon in," I said with an awkward smile. "Can I get you something to drink? Some wine, maybe?"

"No, thanks. I'm on duty. I can't stay long."

Then he launched into what was clearly a rehearsed speech.

"I just wanted to tell you how sorry I am for acting so standoffish the other day. I guess I was a bit overwhelmed. What with Mr. Muffin crashing the wedding, then seeing *Jaine Austen is Awful* in the sky . . ."

"It was supposed to say *Jaine Austen is Awfully Nice*, but the pilot ran out of smoke."

"So you knew about it?"

"Yes, it was my neighbor Lance's idea. He

wanted to make you jealous by pretending I had another boyfriend."

He smiled at that, a big beautiful smile that made my knees go mushy.

"You don't have to make me jealous, Jaine. I already like you. A lot."

Then he took my hand in his and led me to the sofa.

I liked where this was going.

"Look, Jaine," he said, once we were seated thigh by thigh. "I don't care if you don't ride horses or play Frisbee or drink fancy wines. I think you're terrific."

My heart swelled with joy. He thought I was terrific!

I swear I could hear angels belting out the hallelujah chorus.

Then he leaned in to kiss me, a sweet tender kiss that quickly turned rather steamy.

"Besides," he said, when we finally came up for air, "I can always teach you those things."

Huh?

Suddenly the angels stopped singing.

"Teach me?"

"Yes, so you can fit in with my family. I talked to Mom, and she wants to enroll you in a wine appreciation class. And take you shopping for a new wardrobe."

Whoa, Nelly.

"Let me get this straight," I said, sitting up

straight. "You think I'm terrific, but you want me to change. So I can fit in with your family."

"It'll be easier that way," he said with a sheepish shrug. "For all of us."

By now my blood was starting to simmer. We Austens have our pride, you know.

"Sorry, Scott. I want to be with someone who likes me the way I am. Not the way I could be if I took wine appreciation and horseback riding lessons."

With that, I sashayed over to the front door and held it open, very Bette Davis in high dudgeon.

"Now if you'll excuse me, I've got a box of wine to decant."

A look of annoyance flashed in his eyes. "If that's the way you want it . . ."

"That's the way I want it."

"We could've had fun, Jaine. You would've liked the Cotswolds."

Hell House with scones? I didn't think so.

Scott headed out the door, and as I watched him walk away, all I felt, strangely enough, was relief.

Thank heavens I'd never have to sit across a table from Ma Willis ever again!

And so it was with a bounce in my step and absolutely no regrets that I made my way back to my bedroom.

"Guess what?" I said, climbing into bed with Prozac. "I just broke up with Scott."

She trotted over to me, and began licking my cheek.

Just her loving way of saying:

Don't worry. I'll always be here for you, Jan.

Epilogue

Pageant fans will be happy to learn that Candace Burke is now directing the first ever beauty pageant at the Chowchilla Prison for Women, where she is awaiting trial for the murder of Amy Leighton.

And guess who's taking her place at Alta Loco's Teen Queen America? None other than Bethenny Martinez, whose self-help book, *Bethenny's Beauty Secrets*, has shot all the way up to 1,346,789 on Amazon's bestseller list.

Heather Van Sant has finally accepted the fact that Taylor has no interest in pageants. Instead, she's decided to enter Elvis in the Westminster Dog Show. She's already ordered him a beaded Elvis cape to wear to the event, and has hired me to write his official bio.

Taylor continues to be an honors student at Alta Loco High and has received early acceptance to Princeton. This summer she plans to visit Calw, Germany, to tour Hermann Hesse's birthplace.

And good news for all you Luanne fans. The feisty pageant mom and manicurist has found true love with a fireman who came to put out a blaze Gigi set while twirling her flaming batons.

Gigi, shaken by the Flaming Baton incident, has dropped out of the pageant world and is now studying to be a news anchor at the Kolumbia School of Broadcasting and Cosmetology.

Eddie Burke, out from under Candace's shadow, has polished up his old comedy act, ditched his toupee, and is now doing stand-up on the Florida retirement community circuit. My parents saw him at the Tampa Vistas clubhouse and thought he was very funny. (Well, Mom saw him. Daddy's been banned from the clubhouse ever since Nellybelle landed in the pool.)

With time off for good behavior, Dr. Fletcher wound up serving less than ninety days in prison for assaulting me. During which time, his secretary, the formidable Irma Comstock, visited him every weekend. They are now engaged to be married and are the proud owners of an online boutique called Peekaboo Lingerie.

And anyone who ever bought a lemon from Tex Turner will be happy to know that Tex is no longer selling BMWs—or any other car for that matter.

It turns out Tex wasn't the only one cheating in his marriage. Apparently Mrs. Tex had been having a hot and heavy affair with an opera aficionado she met on a trip to New York. She quickly divorced Tex, and without her funding, Turner BMW went belly-up. Saddled with debt and accusations of consumer fraud, Tex lost all his money and is now tending bar at the Strike It Rich Bowling Alley.

Lance's boyfriend, Gary, sold his script to

Twentieth Century Fox in a seven-figure deal and promptly dumped Lance for the cute waiter at Obika Mozzarella Bar. Lance moaned and groaned for a while, very Camille on her death-bed, but soon started dating Frank, the skywriter.

As for me, I finally broke down (as you knew I would) and let Prozac use my DVD armoire as a scratching post. She still refuses to go near her Kitty Condo. But that's okay. I'm using it to store my DVDs. They fit very nicely on all the little platforms. I keep my remotes in the condo pool. It's really quite handy.

Do I miss Scott? Sometimes on a lonely Saturday night. But then I think of going clothes shopping with Ma Willis, and I'm more than happy to be single.

Well, gotta go feed her royal highness.

Catch you next time.

P.S. Almost forgot. You won't believe this (I sure didn't!), but Grammy Willis ran off to Acapulco with one of her male nurses! It seems that the excitement of connubial bliss was just a bit too much, and the paramedics had to come and do CPR. But the male nurse recovered and is doing just fine now.

Center Point Large Print
600 Brooks Road / PO Box 1
Thorndike, ME 04986-0001 USA

(207) 568-3717

US & Canada:
1 800 929-9108
www.centerpointlargeprint.com